ALONE IN PARADISE
by
Patrick Stutzman

Alone in Paradise

©2012 by Patrick Stutzman
Cover Art © 2012 by Tomomi Ink
All rights reserved.

All characters in this book are fictitious. Any resemblance to actual persons, living or dead, is purely coincidental.

This book is protected under the copyright laws of the United States of America. Any reproduction or unauthorized use of the material contained herein is prohibited without express written permission of the author.

Dedication

For Michelle, Alexandrya, and Rebecca.

Acknowledgments

Special Thanks to Mindy Wilson for her superior editing skills,
Natasha Wicks for her continued inspiration,
and the Science Fiction Fantasy Saturday authors for their support.

Chapter 1

"Good morning, Anna."

No response.

"Good morning, Anna."

The clear, almost-monotone voice spoke, entering little by little into the lithe woman's consciousness. Different from the baritone voice she was used to hearing in the past, this one was a delicate, high alto and articulated her words a little slower than the previous one.

"Good morning, Anna."

The blonde's eyes snapped open and took in her immediate surroundings. Lying on a narrow cot within a cramped room while fully clothed in the same T-shirt and pants she had worn for the past 15 days, she took a few seconds to recognize the place as the only sleeping quarters aboard the ship she had used to escape from her former home's destruction. Her shirt, formerly bright white, now appeared to be slightly gray and showed various stains. The olive-colored cargo pants she wore no longer looked cleaned and pressed, as the press seam had softened and the corners of the pocket flaps now curled up slightly. Her bed sheets at the end of her cot lay bunched up from what appeared to be another restless night.

The bare walls, instead of giving Anna a little peace of mind, reminded her of the pictures of scantily-clad women that Ryan, the corporate enforcer that owned the ship before her, used to practically wallpaper the miniscule cabin. During her first night after being marooned on the moon, she ripped the pictures down, shredded them in her hands, and threw them out of the room in a fit of anger and frustration. She slept rather peacefully, but the feelings of rage returned when she awoke the next morning and found the bits of pornographic pictures scattered on the deck. Throwing the scraps into the power core, however, finally put the issue to rest.

Back in the present, Anna asked after a long yawn, "What time is it?"

"The time is 0600 hours, Earth – Greenwich Mean Time, Anna."

"That explains why I'm still tired," she sighed as she sat up and ran her fingers through her mussed hair. "Why do you insist on waking me up at this time every single day?"

"You have not specified a different time to wake up, Anna."

Running her tongue along the front of her teeth and not liking the aftertaste from last night's dinner of prepackaged spaghetti and crackers, she tapped the switch on the wall within easy reach from the cot. The cabin door slid open, and she stood and walked into the warm corridor. Feeling the cool surface of the wall as she made her way to the next door aft, she felt her initial surge of energy ebb as she opened the door to the ship's head and stepped through.

Anna gingerly picked up the sonic toothbrush that had formerly belonged to Ryan and proceeded to clean her teeth and tongue after applying the littlest bit of toothpaste to its bristles. Realizing too late that all of her toiletries had been left on the station when it exploded, she had no choice but to use the ones left behind on the craft. Unfortunately for her, most of them were designed for men: a sonic toothbrush, a tube of mostly-depleted toothpaste, a dull razor, a new bottle of spice-scented shampoo, a mostly empty bottle of after shave, and a half-used bar of white soap. Despite her gratitude for the supplies available, she was disgusted with the idea of having to put the dead enforcer's toothbrush in her own mouth and had taken the time to clean and sterilize it five times with hot water.

Half way through her dental cleaning, the computer asked, "When will Ryan be returning?"

Anna stopped brushing, withdrew it from her mouth, and replied with an annoyed tone, "He's not . . ."

"Why is that, Anna?"

She rolled her eyes and responded exasperatedly, "Because, he's dead. How many times do I have to tell you that?"

"You have not informed me that Ryan is deceased. How did he die?"

"I told you yesterday!" she exclaimed. "And the day before! And the day before that!"

Shaking her head, she mumbled, "The last thing I need right now is a computer with short-term memory loss."

Anna finished the last few strokes of the toothbrush and spat into the steel sink secured to the wall. She rinsed her mouth with a handful of water from the tap and washed the brush before returning it to its charge niche in the wall. As she dried her mouth with the one towel she found on the ship, she wrinkled her nose at the old, dirty smell it exuded and tossed it into the shower.

"You have not told me how Ryan died, Anna."

The blonde rolled her eyes toward the ceiling and asked as she unstrapped her wristcomp and set it on the back of the sink, "What is the last thing you remember, computer?"

A few seconds passed before the disembodied voice answered, "I have records dating back to 3 minutes and 16 seconds ago, but my records are blank until 15 days, 19 hours, and 53 minutes ago."

Anna removed her boots and set them under the sink, all the while reflecting back on the events of the last two weeks. Once she determined that she was not seriously injured from the crash, she set about locating an immediate food supply and verifying the hull integrity of the ship to work as a suitable shelter. Finding emergency rations proved to be fairly easy, all things considered, and took very little time. But, checking the status of the craft's superstructure and hull plating took the better part of 8 days, much longer than she anticipated.

During the inspection, she discovered the cause for the engine failure. A sizeable chunk of the station had slammed into the afterburners, crushing the outer manifolds and breaching the fuel tank in the process. After finishing the hull analysis, removing the debris took another 2 days and proved to be a mistake. With the debris gone, the remaining fuel leaked irretrievably into the ground below. Cursing her luck, Anna retreated into the ship, resigned to the idea that she would never leave the moon in her lifetime.

Giving way to self pity and depression, she spent the last 6 days sulking in her cabin or on the bridge in silence, wondering when she was going to die and if it would be painful. After she had gone several days without eating and could not stand the hunger pangs any longer, she decided that she would not let her situation get the best of her.

With a heavy sigh, Anna pulled her dingy socks and grimy shirt off and dropped them onto the floor at her feet, all the while mulling over the information the computer just gave her. Although she was stuck on this earthlike moon with only the ship's computer for company, she had not talked with it much. Since the crash, the extent of the computer's speech primarily consisted of asking . . .

"When will Ryan be returning?" the computer said, interrupting Anna's train of thought.

Growling from her throat, she unfastened her pants and let the garment drop to the floor, leaving her wearing her formerly white bra and matching panties. She planted her hands on her hips and shifted her weight onto her left leg, sporting a stern look on her face that betrayed her frustration at the lack of original conversation coming from her new partner.

"Computer," she commanded. "Do not talk to me, unless I ask you a question. Understand?"

"As you wish, Anna."

"Thank you."

Anna removed her bra and panties and dropped them to the floor on top of her pants. After sighing audibly, she grabbed the entire pile and stepped into the shower. She covered the drain with the towel, making it as flat as possible, and laid the rest of her clothes out around the shower. Once the clothes had been spread out, she reached in and turned the water on. Remembering that the water always started cold for the first few seconds, she waited until the water had warmed up sufficiently and stepped into the cascading water. After she finished washing herself a few minutes later, she shut off the water and dropped to her knees to clean her garments in the warm, soapy water before it drained away, making sure to leave the towel for last. A couple of minutes later, she pulled the soaked towel from the drain and scrubbed it as best she could in the limited time she had. She wrung out the clothes, draped them over her shoulders, and carefully proceeded to the ship's airlock, taking extra care with each step to not slip on the deck with her wet feet.

A minute later, the top hatch of the ship opened, and Anna's clothes and towel flew through the opening, one article at a time, to land with a wet smack on the vessel's white hull. Anna climbed out and stood naked next to the opening for a brief second before dancing lightly in place, realizing too late that the hull felt rather warm under her bare feet. After a few seconds, she became accustomed to the heat, thankful that the white plating reflected most of the heat away.

She looked up into the sky toward the distant sun, which looked significantly smaller than Sol in the sky. She turned her gaze to look aftward and looked past the long stretch of barren land created by the ship's forced landing. Dominating most of the sky was the gas giant around which her moon orbited, its red and orange bands of gas tainted blue by the atmosphere. White puffs of clouds floating in the distance partly obstructed her view.

Despite all of its natural majesty, Anna had grown discouraged over the past several days due to the fact that she had not heard any sounds other than her own voice, the voice of the computer, the hum of the ship's systems, and the occasional gust of wind blowing past her home. Not a single sound of any animal life reached her ears during her tenure planetside.

Anna breathed in the warm air deeply and basked in the sunlight for a few more seconds before picking up her clothes and laying them flat across the top of the spacecraft. She had opened the covers to the solar panels built into the dorsal side of the ship, giving her an unending supply of energy as long as the systems continued to operate, so she made sure to keep clear of the valuable, dark panels.

After she had set out her clothes, Anna looked down at her naked body and saw that her white skin appeared much too bright in the open, realizing that the six years she had spent aboard the station had gradually turned her pale. Taking advantage of the situation, she decided to recline on the hull to dry as well.

Finding an open space, she lied down on her back, stretched her arms behind her head, and rested her wet head on folded hands. She relaxed her body in the sunlight, taking in its warm rays. She smiled and laughed once through her lips as she reflected back on her life, not remembering one time in her life when she had sunbathed under the open sky. When she was last on Earth over six years ago, people resorted to tanning in beds that bombarded their skin with artificial UV rays. Nobody to her knowledge did it the old fashioned way anymore, like she did now.

While she lounged on the top of the ship, Anna's thoughts took her back to her years as a teenager growing up on an overpopulated Earth. Although she felt congested as she moved from place to place and even while she attended public school and her chosen university, she enjoyed her time spent with friends, ignorant to the issues plaguing society in regards to the ever increasing population despite almost constant flights to the half-dozen colonized worlds within the confines of human-occupied space.

Anna spent several minutes lying under the sun, rolling over after a while to help her backside dry off. Once she felt that she had dried off sufficiently, she returned to the upper hatch and reentered the ship, leaving the clothes to dry in the sunlight.

"Computer," asked Anna as she exited the airlock into the bridge lit by ambient light pouring in through the forward windows that she uncovered during her first day outside the ship. "Where is your computer core located?"

"Unable to comply."

Anna stopped in her tracks halfway to the pilot seat, stared at the inactive console, and exclaimed, "Oh, come on! I'm trying to repair you, and you won't even tell me where the problem is?!"

"You do not have proper clearance to access that portion of the ship."

"I've been on board for over two weeks! I . . ."

"I have no record of you being aboard this ship for that period of time."

Exasperated, Anna continued anxiously, "That's because your memory circuits are in need of repair, and I'm trying to fix it. Now, please tell me where your core is!"

"Unable to comply."

She stomped on the floor and screamed, "YOU'RE MORE FRUSTRATING THAN THAT DAMN COMPUTER BACK ON THE STATION! AT LEAST HE WOULD ANSWER THE MOST SIMPLE QUESTIONS!!!"

"When will Ryan be returning?" the computer asked again.

"SHUT UP! I FORBID YOU TO ASK ABOUT THAT FUCK RYAN ANYMORE! JUST TELL ME WHERE THE CORE IS!"

"Unable to comply."

Anna screamed angrily and stormed off the bridge. Retrieving her tool belt from the foot locker under her cot and throwing it over her shoulder, she marched into the engine room, searched for the first panel to her left, and flung it open.

From the overhead speaker, the computer asked, "What are you doing?"

Without looking away, she answered, "I am trying to locate your computer core, so I can fix you."

"You are not authorized to access that system."

"Tell me something I don't know!"

"If you do not stand away from the panel in 10 seconds, I will have no choice but to send a distress signal to the nearest ship requesting assistance."

Anna snorted, "Go right ahead! No one's going to hear you."

Several seconds later, the computer announced, "Very well, Anna. You leave me no choice but to send the distress signal."

"Good luck getting a response," she wished while rolling her eyes.

A few seconds of silence passed, while Anna moved from one panel to the next in her search for the computer core. Just as she thought she would accomplish her task in peace, the computer announced, "You are not authorized to access that system."

With a sigh, she snapped back, "Shut up."

"Unable to comply."

"What do you mean, 'Unable to comply'?"

"As long as you continue to access ship systems for which you are not authorized to access, I must continually warn you."

Anna turned away from the open cabinet and asked directly, "You mean to tell me that I have to put up with your blathering, even though you have already sent a request for help? What are you trying to do: annoy me to death?"

"I am warning you that . . ."

"That was a rhetorical question!" she sternly pointed out.

"In either case," the computer continued. "You are not authorized to access that system."

Slamming the door shut, Anna stated with frustration evident in her voice, "Fine! But if you'll just tell me where the computer core is, I will stop with the random searching and get to the root of the problem."

"Unable to comply."

"Unable to comply," she mocked back. "Can you say anything else besides 'unable to comply'?"

"I have a vocabulary consisting . . ."

"Shut up! Rhetorical . . ."

"Is there a question that I could answer?" the computer asked cheerfully.

"Where is your computer core?!" cried Anna.

"Unable to comply."

9

"FUCK YOU!"

"Unable to comply."

"FUCK YOU AND THE ASSHOLE WHO MADE YOU!!!"

"Unable to comply."

"IS THERE ANYTHING YOU **CAN** DO?!"

"I operate a large number of the ship's onboard systems . . ."

"OH, SHUT UP!" she screamed. "JUST SHUT UP!"

Anna ran from the engine room to her cabin, threw herself and her tool belt onto the cot, and started crying into her pillow. A few seconds passed, and she suddenly sat up, grasped her pillow with both hands and started beating the wall with it while screaming maniacally.

After senselessly assaulting the wall several times, Anna dropped the pillow back on the cot and collapsed into it, sobbing uncontrollably. But, her emotional outburst lasted for only a few seconds, as a thought crossed her mind. She sat up and contemplated the idea for a few seconds before slapping the door switch and leaping out the door.

Rushing across the bridge, Anna angled herself to move past the lenses that displayed the holographic control panels for the pilot and pivoted at the right point to change her trajectory. As she flew by the lenses, she waved her hand over each of them to activate the holograms. The orange displays came to life and appeared in front of the black upholstered chair secured to the floor at the nose of the craft. After a few seconds, the set of panels on the right side flickered but remained active.

With a broad smile as she tossed herself into the seat, Anna asked, "Computer, can you show me the deckplans for the ship?"

Barely a second later, the deckplans appeared before her. Leaning in to study the schematic, Anna quickly found the computer core, smiled broadly, and jumped from the chair through the holograms.

"Thank you!" she called as she retreated from the bridge.

She retrieved her tool belt from her bunk and ran back to the bridge, directly to an unmarked console on the port wall. Pulling a small prybar from the belt, she opened the panel effortlessly. Replacing the prybar in her hand with her flashlight, she searched through the densely-packed circuitry in the wall.

"Anna," the computer warned. "You are not authorized to access that system."

Anna gave the computer a rude gesture, not stopping her search as she did. Finding nothing wrong, she pried open the panel below it and continued her investigation. At last, she found that several boards had become jostled out of their sockets and were not active. She carefully pulled one of the boards out and looked it over but found nothing wrong with it. Likewise, all of the other boards appeared to have no defect or damage. Cautiously returning the boards to their appropriate sockets, Anna made sure that they were all securely in place.

"Computer," she asked calmly after a few seconds of silence. "What is the first thing you remember, and how long ago did that take place?"

"The first memory I have is emerging from the assembly plant in orbit around Earth . . ."

"Okay," chuckled Anna. "Not that far back. I mean within the last hour."

"I remember you crying in Ryan's cabin and hitting his pillow against the wall. That was 3 minutes and 47 seconds ago."

Anna nodded, "Okay, that's fine."

She waited for several seconds before asking, "What about now? What is the first thing you remember within the last hour?"

"I remember you crying in Ryan's cabin and hitting his pillow against the wall. That was 3 minutes and 59 seconds ago."

"And now?"

"I remember you crying in Ryan's cabin and hitting his pillow against the wall. That was 4 minutes and 5 seconds ago."

"YES!" cried Anna victoriously, throwing her head back and her hands into the air.

"When will Ryan be returning?"

Still overjoyed from her success, she cheerfully replied, "He's not. He's dead."

"You sound quite glad he's not coming back, Anna. Did you have something to do with his demise?"

The question immediately sobered the technician, and her gleeful expression dissipated into one of annoyance.

"He brought it on himself," Anna shot back. "He tried to kill me, and I defended myself. It was self-defense."

"That must be determined in a court of law, Anna. I demand that you confine yourself to your quarters, until the authorities arrive to escort you to Earth for trial."

"WHAT?!" she yelled. "I am doing no such thing!"

"If you do not comply, a charge of resisting arrest will be added to your listed charges."

"What charges?!"

"Murder in the second degree and theft of corporate property."

"Corporate property?!" questioned Anna. "What corporate property?"

"This ship belongs to NR Suppliers, Inc. and should be returned to them if Ryan has truly passed away."

"Run a diagnostic, computer!" she cried. "Is this ship going anywhere anytime soon?"

"Fuel levels are currently at 6%, insufficient to activate the jump drive."

"Right! Not enough fuel, combined with a ruptured fuel tank and damage to the sublight engines, pretty much states that we're staying here for a while."

"Your assessment appears to be correct, Anna."

"Thanks. Now, can you do us both a favor and increase my access level to your systems, so I can get this ship repaired?"

"Unable to comply."

Anna stared darkly at the open panel in front of her and flatly added, "That must be your favorite catch phrase."

"Actually, I do not . . ."

"Rhetorical!" Anna called out, interrupting the computer's reply.

She sighed aloud and looked down at her feet for several seconds, suddenly realizing that she had not eaten breakfast yet. Lightly rubbing her belly for a few seconds as she looked forward to her meal with a mixture of gratitude and dread, Anna finally turned on her heel and strode off the bridge, leaving her tool belt behind and the computer core open.

"Anna," the computer stated, disrupting her thoughts. "You left the panel open. Please replace the panel."

The woman stopped just outside the port door leading aft, turned back around with a sigh, and said as she returned, "At least you said please."

She walked back to the opening in the wall, almost dragging her feet as she moved, lifted the cover, and hammered it in place with the end of her fist. Giving a grim nod, she turned again and left the bridge without another word.

Chapter 2

Opening the door to the storage room next to her cabin, Anna opened the top box and stared at its contents: six brown, vacuum-sealed packages labeled "Meal, Ready-to-Eat". She scowled at the sight of the rations and sighed audibly as she debated whether consuming another one of the disgusting meals was worth the time. When she originally opened the crate, some of the entrées looked like they might be appealing, such as the beef ravioli and the chicken and dumplings. But, she threw out the two red glowfish filets, not wanting to take another chance at an allergic reaction like she had aboard the station about a month back. Now, she was down to two meatloaf meals, two spaghetti meals, a cheese & vegetable omelet, and a chicken fajita. Her heart sank as she weighed her options, knowing the back of her mind that she needed to find new sources for food soon or face starvation.

Anna gulped hard, quickly pulled out the omelet meal, and shut the box before she changed her mind. Strolling to the head, she prepared her breakfast and reluctantly took her first bite. The egg-based dish felt rubbery on her tongue, but it smelled like the real thing. After finding that she could tolerate the food, she consumed the rest of it along with the hash browns, peanut butter, crackers, and coffee that came with the MRE.

As she sipped the last of her coffee, Anna hummed through her lips as she recalled an idea. Pulling the cup away, she said enthusiastically, "Computer!"

"Yes, Anna."

"Change my morning alarm time to 0800 hours."

"Acknowledged."

With a smile, she mumbled, "Finally!"

Spying her wristcomp resting on the back of the sink, Anna retrieved it and returned it to her wrist. She rinsed out the beverage pouch and stuffed it back into the MRE bag, which she then dropped into another crate in the small storage closet that held over three dozen other empty bags still stocked with leftover supplies. Shaking her head and disbelieving that she used the number of rations she had, she vowed to take the time to forage through the forest around the ship.

Anna returned to the top of the ship, where she discovered a large shadow cast over the area. Looking to the sky, she found a thick cloud passing overhead that threatened in vain to give a short burst of rainfall. Deciding not to take any chances, she quickly checked her clothes and found them to still be a bit damp. She tossed the garments into the airlock and climbed back into the ship, sealing the hatch behind her.

Anna returned to the bridge and cracked open the pilot's right control panel and found the lens slightly out of alignment. With a final adjustment, securing the connections between the lens and its circuity, and recalibration of the system, the control panel ceased its incessant flickering and stabilized.

Breathing a sigh of relief, she planted herself into the pilot seat and looked over the displays floating in the air in front of her. Most of the readouts indicated no activity, especially the ones pertaining to the vessel being in flight. But, the sensors showing only white noise static bothered her. She remembered it working fine during the craft's descent through the atmosphere, so she surmised that the emission point was on the underside and was either touching the ground or was severely damaged or more than likely destroyed during the crash.

Anna returned to the airlock and tossed her clothes onto the deck of the bridge before opening the hatch leading to the ventral airlock and climbing down. She opened the lower hatch leading outside and found the opening cleared the ground by mere millimeters. Crouching down as far as she could, she could see along the belly of the ship for a good distance and noticed a sliver of sunlight reflecting off the hull. She determined that digging her way out should not be too difficult, provided that she could locate something to use as a shovel.

After climbing back onto the bridge, Anna requested, "Computer, show me the deckplans of the ship."

Once the diagram appeared for her again, she searched for the sensor array for several minutes. Despite her efforts to comb through every pixel of the plans, she could not locate it.

"Computer," she asked, finally giving up the hunt. "Where is the sensor array on this ship?"

"Unable to comply."

"Let me guess," she replied. "I am unauthorized to access that system."

"You are correct, Anna."

"Why is it not included with the deckplans?"

"The deckplans only show the areas available to the ship's occupants. Inaccessible areas do not appear in the deckplans."

"What document would I need to view to show the other areas of the ship?"

The computer stated, "You would need to access the official blueprints of the ship."

"Then, show me the blueprints of the ship."

"Unable to comply."

Anna sighed, "Because I don't have access?"

"You are correct, Anna."

"Remind me to wipe your systems at some point in the future."

"Unable to comply."

"That was a joke, computer."

A few seconds later, sunlight reappeared through the forward canopy. A bright smile lit up Anna's face upon catching sight of the light, and she raced to gather her clothes from the deck and return them topside. Once the clothes were laid out again, she paused to look around the vicinity again. This time, she peered away from the sun and into the trees surrounding the ship. She discerned a distinct break in the tree line about a hundred meters from the crash site. She had seen it before, but something was different as she noticed other breaks that seemed to create a winding path through the forest. Perhaps the shadows of some smaller clouds trailing behind the first one changed her perspective. Nevertheless, its presence incited a need to investigate this new discovery.

Anna grabbed her boots from her cabin and a couple of opened MRE pouches, hastily dumping their contents into the box before shutting the cabin door. After slipping on her footwear, she wrapped her tool belt around her bare waist and pulled the sidearm she took from Ryan's body out from the foot locker. Stuffing the weapon into the belt pouch she used as a makeshift holster, she climbed back to the top of the ship and studied the landscape again for a minute. Satisfied that nothing had changed or seemed threatening, she steadily walked down to the nose of the ship and onto the ground below.

Cautiously stepping past the tree line created by the ship's abrupt landing, Anna shifted her gaze from tree to tree, looking out for anything that could be considered dangerous but disregarding the dozens of small bushes and clumps of grass that littered the forest floor. Sunlight filtered through the leafy branches, creating bright spots in areas that showed a light amount of dust floating along, while the rest was cast in cool shadow that created an eerie but picturesque scene. As an afterthought, she drew her pistol and ventured into the woods, keeping the ship within sight as she explored.

Wandering through the forest did not bother her much. In fact, it was somewhat cathartic for her to finally get away from the vehicle that brought her here. The lack of any kind of animal life continued to disturb her. No birds could be heard. No bugs pestered her as she strolled. No trees or bushes rustled from small critters that she startled. Only the sound of the wind gently blowing through the trees reached her ears, and it sent chills up her spine. She expected something or someone to jump out at her from behind the closest tree and scream violently at her. But, the fear never came to fruition.

She remembered suddenly that her tool belt held a small hand scanner that she had mainly used for equipment analysis. Figuring that it might help alleviate any apprehensions she held, she withdrew the device from its specialized pouch and calibrated it for a long range biological scan. A few seconds passed, and the signal extending out to 100 meters brought back no signals of active life. Relieved at the result, she holstered the pistol back in her tool belt and went on foraging.

Anna's search garnered no results for the first half hour, as she found only trees and bushes that bore no apparent fruit. Half expecting to locate some form of vegetation rather quickly, disappointment quickly affected her mood. As she was about to give up the search and turn back, a new sound reached her ears. The noise of rushing water ahead renewed her interest in her search efforts, and she bolted further into the woods toward the source of the sound.

Running through the tree line, Anna nearly tumbled into the wide river that flowed by her feet. Appearing to be about ten meters across to the other tree-lined shore, the clear water that smoothly rushed by her bubbled around a set of rapids a short distance upstream. The beaten rocks, from what she could tell, traversed the winding ribbon of water and could possibly be used as a bridge.

Anna crouched at the edge of the stream and scooped some of the water up with the MRE pouch. She looked into the water she gathered, but the dark color of the container prevented her from seeing any further than the surface. Grasping the lip of the bag with one hand, she withdrew her flashlight and used it to look into the bagged water, but the intense light merely reflected off the surface and did not help her at all.

Dumping the water back into the river, Anna calibrated the sensor suite on the hand scanner for a biological scan after she pulled it from her tool belt. Once the system indicated it was ready, she scooped some more water into the plastic pouch and swept the scanner past it after initiating a new scan. Several seconds passed, and the results finally displayed a tiny level of soil and bacteria present in the water. But, it was mostly clean beyond that. Not totally satisfied with the results, Anna requested details on the bacteria, only to receive an "Unknown" result. Frowning, Anna dumped the water back into the river.

As Anna stood and turned to reenter the woods, one of the trees on the coast caught her eye, specifically the tree's fruit. Several globular pieces hung from the small tree's branches that glistened due to its yellowish skin, looking very much like golden apples. She stepped closer to the tree, eyeing the fruit with great interest. Once within reach, Anna plucked one of the pieces from the tree and examined it closer. Nothing seemed out of the ordinary, and she noted the hint of a scent that reminded her of pomegranates. Her mouth salivated as she stared longingly at the potential food, and she lifted the fruit to her lips.

Just as she was about to take a bite, Anna stopped short and mumbled to herself, "I really should check this first."

She swiped the fruit past her hand scanner and let the device analyze it for several seconds. The result came back with a list of vitamins and nutrients detected within, but she did notice traces of arsenic in the seeds.

With a shrug and a smile, Anna picked several more of the bulbous fruit from the tree and proceeded back to the ship. She raced up the nose of the vessel, nearly slipping as she climbed over the forward casement, and climbed through the airlock, pausing long enough to find that her clothes had almost completely dried. Spilling the fruit on the deck of the bridge, she sat on her legs on the floor, pulled her laser cutter from her tool belt, and sliced one of the bulbs open. Quickly picking out the few seeds embedded in the core, she scanned the fruit, discovering joyfully that the arsenic existed only within the seeds and did not affect the fruit around it.

Without wasting another second, Anna snatched up one of the slices and bit deeply into the fruit. As the juice trickled down her chin, she savored its sweetness and soft texture on her tongue. She moaned her acceptance and hastily took another bite, adding it to her first mouthful. She giggled like a school girl as she finished the food in only a few more bites. A few drops of the juice on her chin dripped into her lap, attracting her attention as another drop of the warm liquid splashed on her upper thigh. She wiped her chin with the back of her hand, gathered the rest of the fruit and harvested seeds, and stepped to the back part of the craft.

Anna dumped her armload into the sink and set the seeds on the floor. Looking at her reflection in the simple mirror positioned on the wall above the sink, she easily noticed the clear fluid staining her chin. She quickly washed her face and leg and scrubbed her harvest clean.

But, the question that appeared in her mind now dealt with where to store her newfound bounty. The only room that seemed the most appropriate at first was the head, but she turned her nose up to the idea of keeping food in the same room where she relieved and cleaned herself. Her cabin, just like all of the other rooms in the back part of the ship, had limited space, and the foot locker under the cot already held several pieces of equipment. She could use the MRE bags she kept in the small storage room to stuff the fruit into for the time being. Since she dug through that room multiple times each day, keeping track of the fresh food would not be very difficult. Gathering the food from the sink, Anna transferred it to the storage room and filled some of the bags after moving the remaining contents to other bags.

Satisfied with her solution for the time being, she retrieved her clothes from outside and got dressed again. Her garments felt a little stiff after setting in the morning sun, helping her realize that she actually missed the cleaning drone back on the station and all that it did for her. Anna vowed never to take another drone for granted again, should she ever see another one in her lifetime.

Chapter 3

Anna slowly awoke the next morning feeling quite rested despite all of the activity that took place the previous day. In addition to finding the fruit trees, she explored the surrounding woods a bit more to get a feel for the terrain and see about finding other sources of food. Although the fruit was indeed a welcome change from the ration packs, she could not live on it by itself after she exhausted the MREs. She found a few bushes that bore a dark red berry, but her analysis revealed that they contained a mild toxin that would not set well with her digestive system.

She stretched her arms and legs, helping her wake up, and rubbed the sleep from her eyes. Still fully clothed like every other time she went to sleep over the past several days, she sat up and pressed the switch to open the door.

The door did not respond.

Not giving it a second thought, Anna pressed the switch again, but the door still did not budge. Curiosity captured her senses as she stared at the stubborn door, and she wondered why it refused to open for her.

As she thought about it, she realized that the computer did not even wake her up. Did she wake up early for some reason? Anna glanced at her wristcomp and found the time showing 0917 hours. Why did the computer not wake her this morning?

"Computer?" she asked aloud.

"Yes, Anna."

"Why did you not wake me this morning?"

"No time is set for the morning alarm, Anna."

Anna cocked her head to one side, puzzled by its response. She could have sworn that she updated the alarm time to 0800 hours yesterday. Even if it was still having memory problems, it would have still awakened her at 0600 hours like it did every other time. She determined that she would have to look into the matter after getting some breakfast and moved to her next question.

"Computer, why won't the door open?"

"You are being held for the murder of Ryan McIlheny and are confined to quarters until the authorities arrive and take you into custody."

Anna's jaw dropped open. She couldn't believe that she forgot about the computer charging her with killing her assailer, even after her efforts to repair the ship.

"Are you serious?" she cried.

"Yes, Anna. You are to remain in your quarters, until the authorities arrive."

"Nobody is going to come, computer! We are the first forms of life to reach this moon, and its existence is not known by anyone other than us. We are out of range of any communication relay stations, and nobody comes out this way. We are marooned, unless I can get this ship repaired and get away from here!"

"You are to remain in your quarters, until the authorities arrive."

"I don't have any food in here! What if I have to use the head?"

"You are to remain in your quarters, until the authorities arrive."

Anna's frustration boiled within her, and she exclaimed, "BY THE TIME THE AUTHORITIES GET HERE, I WILL BE DEAD!"

"You are to remain in your quarters, until the authorities arrive."

"AREN'T YOU SUPPOSED TO HELP PRESERVE HUMAN LIFE?!"

"Your basic rights were waived after you admitted to killing Ryan McIlheny."

"WHAT?! YOU CAN'T WAIVE MY RIGHTS! I . . ."

"You are being held for the murder of Ryan McIlheny, which makes you a criminal in the eyes of the law. Criminals have no rights. You are to remain in your quarters, until the authorities arrive."

"THIS IS BULLSHIT!"

"You are to remain in your quarters, until the authorities arrive."

Anna kicked the door and screamed, "I HATE YOU!"

She flopped back down on the cot, nearly knocking it over, and dropped her chin into her hands as she planted her elbows on her knees, fuming the entire time over her twist of fate. Her sour mood did not last long, as the urge to empty her bladder slowly came to the forefront of her mind.

Anna slapped the door switch again to no avail. She slapped it again and again, each time more harsh than before, in the hope that something would trigger the hatch to open.

"Come on, damn it!" she muttered, frustration evident in her voice. "Open!"

Despite several more pushes of the switch, the door never moved aside. The anxiety within her built more and more with each passing second and with each attempt, finally climaxing into streams of tears cascading down her cheeks. With no other recourse coming to mind, Anna dropped and sat on the floor to cry against the door confining her to her room.

Seconds later as she could no longer hold back, she relaxed and let nature run its course. Instantly, she felt her pants grow warm and wet between her legs as her bladder emptied, driving her to cry harder and slam her fist against the door.

"ARE YOU SATISFIED NOW?!" screamed Anna amidst her sobbing, feelings of shame and humiliation consuming her. Her weeping continued for several minutes. All the while, the computer never responded.

After she calmed down and wiped the tears from her face, she stood and angrily peeled her pants and underwear off and dropped them on the floor in a heap next to the unresponsive door.

"I can't believe that I just washed them yesterday," she murmured disgustedly as she released her panties and let them fall and land on her pants.

Anna, hoping to clean herself as best she could under the circumstances, pulled her tool belt from the foot locker under the cot and withdrew the shop rag from its pouch. As she wiped her crotch and thighs, she looked at her tool belt, then at the switch on the wall, and at her belt again.

"Why am I so stupid?" she asked herself as she threw the rag to the floor, retrieved one of her tools, and began removing the bolts holding the door switch in place.

Immediately, the computer asked, "What are you doing?"

"Something I should have done 10 minutes ago," Anna replied sternly.

"You are not authorized to access that system. Cease your actions now."

Anna did not answer but focused on the task at hand. Within seconds, the last bolt dropped into her hand, and she pulled the switch from the wall. She quickly traced the wires for the door and the power to operate it and cut the computer's control wire after isolating it. Casting the wire cutters behind her onto the cot, she pressed the switch and smiled as the door slid open.

Grabbing her tool belt and loose tools, Anna walked briskly out of the cabin and to the bridge.

"You are in violation of the custody order issued against you," the computer ordered. "Return to your quarters immediately.

"Go to Hell!" Anna heatedly stated.

"Unable to comply."

Sarcastically, she jabbed as she hustled, "Why am I not surprised?"

Reaching the panel for the computer core, she ripped the panel from the wall within seconds and whipped her flashlight from its loop on her belt, as the panel hit the floor and tumbled away noisily. Shining the light inside, she searched frantically through the wires and circuitry.

"You are not authorized to access that system. Step away from the system now."

Ignoring the computer's remark, Anna located the large power cord connected directly to the computer core. Grabbing it with her free hand, she took a deep breath and commented, "Let's see how you like a little down time."

She pulled the power cord from its socket.

Instantly, all of the ship's systems powered down, plunging the interior into darkness, save for the bridge that remained illuminated by the ambient sunlight.

Anna looked over each shoulder to confirm that nothing was operating. While she did, she realized that the background hum of the ship's systems no longer filled her ears, dropping her shelter into an eerie silence that she had not heard since her childhood.

Concerned that nothing was working, she draped the power cord over the lip of the opening and jogged to the closest door leading to the back of the ship. She pressed the switch, but the door did not move. Sliding her flashlight back into its loop, she looked along the walls surrounding the entryway.

"There's got to be some sort of manual override," commented Anna as she searched around the door.

A brief moment later, she located a small, recessed panel next to the door as high as her waist. Pulling it open, she pulled the small lever behind it and watched the door slide open. Chuckling smugly, Anna walked through and to the head, where she opened the door the same way.

Stopping in front of the sink, she turned on the water and discovered to her dismay that nothing came out. With a sigh, she turned around and tested the shower and received the same result.

"Damn it," she cursed under her breath as she made a beeline for the engine room. "I'm going to get clean one way or another, and this fucking computer is not going to stop me."

Anna entered the dark engine room and activated her flashlight again. Through the darkness even without the help of her light source, she quickly found a flashing red button on a panel embedded into the wall on one side of the room. Walking cautiously while making sure her way was clear of obstacles, she read the label above the button that read "Auxiliary Power". She pressed the switch with her thumb and breathed a sigh of relief as the lights came back on.

She returned the flashlight to its place on her belt just as she felt her crotch start to itch from the urine drying on her skin. Without wasting another second, she rushed back to the head and tested the shower with positive results. Stripping down, she jumped in the shower and turned on the water. After drenching her hair, she remembered her fouled pants and undergarment in the other room. With a sigh, she shut off the water, dried off, and retrieved the clothes, laying them on the shower floor just like she did before.

Anna completed her shower and laundry, taking some extra time to relax under the hot water. She dried herself off and carried her wet pants and panties to the top of the ship to dry in the sun. As she stood on the ship, she decided to lie on the hull to dry off again. She relaxed next to her laundry and dozed off for a short while.

Anna woke up some time later and checked the status of her clothes. Finding them sufficiently dry, she slipped on her underwear and went back inside the ship to finish dressing.

As Anna slipped her pants on, she thought ahead to what life would be like without anyone to converse with, let alone a computer that would be at odds with her for the rest of the time they would be together. The personality exhibited by the electronic companion seemed basic at best, not willing to stray from its programming, and she wondered if Ryan had recently reset its personality matrix or if he did it on a regular basis to keep it under control. She remembered that the computer on the station where she lived previously awakened after she had lived there for four years, but it had been installed over forty years before that. Whether that computer had its personality matrix reset by the previous caretaker was never revealed to her, but Anna felt that she really did not want to wait around to find out. In either case, she had to negotiate some sort of arrangement to help get them both off of the moon and back to some semblance of civilization, for she was not sure if she could handle a pastoral existence for the rest of her life.

Feeling like she was ready to take on the computer again, she returned to the bridge. Lightly picking up the power cord, she nuzzled it back into its socket and waited for the verbal abuse to begin. However, the computer did not speak. She waited a few more seconds and looked inside the alcove to make sure the system was working. The computer seemed to be running fine, leaving her confused as to why it had not responded yet.

Anna started to wonder if she had damaged the system by shutting it down the way she had. The thought made little sense to her, as the computer has the capability to store vast amounts of information. But, she surmised that the sudden interruption in power could have damaged its operating system. As her mind wrapped around what else could have caused the problem, another idea entered her mind that brought up the possibility of her being truly alone. With no computer with whom to converse and no other companions, human or otherwise, she would be isolated. She remembered reading about cases while taking a psychology class in college that dealt with human isolation and how many of the subjects would exhibit signs of insanity after prolonged periods without any kind of interaction with others. Afraid of the same thing happening to her, she anxiously looked over the computer core's components, hoping to find something wrong to fix the problem. But, her search came up with nothing; everything seemed to be in proper working order.

Chapter 4

Anna looked around the bridge as she prayed for a solution. The hunt brought her to the control panels at the nose of the ship. Leaving the core behind, she dashed to the pilot's station and activated the holograms. The displays were blank, with the sole exception of a single switch in the middle of the central panel that consisted of a round, red button on a white, rectangular plate. The label above the button simply read, "Press to Initialize System".

Hesitantly, Anna nudged her hand into the red holographic button. The instant her fingertips contacted the image, the three panels dissipated. Fearing that the computer may be in need of reinstallation after it failed to respond after a few seconds, she took a step back and tumbled into the pilot's chair.

As she started to rise from the seat, the holographic panels appeared again. This time, they had the standard readouts like before. Anna smiled, glad to see that everything was returning to normal.

"Computer System XLT-014 online," the computer stated speaking with the same female voice as before.

Anna's gaze darted upward, surprised to hear the computer say that instead of ordering her to return to her quarters. The comment left her wondering if the computer was rebooting as a result of the power loss or if it stated that every time regardless. She waited for the computer's next statement with abated breath.

About half a minute later, the computer said, "Interfaced with *Arrow*-class personal transport, serial number AC019NX317. Please state the owner of the vessel with which I am connected."

Mildly shocked, Anna's realization that the computer had completely reset when she pulled the plug started inspiring ideas in her head on how to take advantage of the situation. Should she be honest and give ownership back to the company? If she did, she would be setting herself up for a mess of trouble again, and she did not really want the future headaches. If she claimed ownership and was later rescued, on the other hand, she could be accused of stealing the ship and face prosecution from her former employer. Then again, they sent a corporate enforcer to kill her, so they would probably not even take the chance and follow through with their original plan. At that point, they would just reclaim the ship and reprogram it any way they saw fit, regardless of what she had done to it. Then again, she . . .

"Please state the owner of the vessel with which I am connected," the computer repeated, interrupting Anna's thoughts.

What the hell.

"Annika Foster," she blurted out. "But, you may call me Anna."

"Thank you, Anna," it replied after a couple of seconds. "Are you affiliated with an organization?"

Without hesitation, she hastily stated, "No."

"Please provide the authorization code listed on your invoice."

Anna's expression dropped like a rock. Her eyes widened at the sudden realization that she had no clue on what to give to the computer. The code could be just about anything, and she knew enough about computer security systems to know that she would only have a limited number of attempts before being locked out. She could just unplug the computer and try it again, but doing so could wear down the system and possibly damage it if done too many times.

The computer requested again, "Please provide the authorization code listed on your invoice."

"Uh," hesitated Anna, wracking her brain for an answer and finding none.

Desperate for something to give her some time, she hastily asked a few seconds later, "Hold on for a minute."

She sprinted off the bridge and to the cabin where she had stashed Ryan's leftover clothes. Dropping to her knees in the open door and diving in with both hands, she swiftly rummaged through pockets in the hopes of finding some clue to what the authorization code would be. After finding nothing in the garment she checked, she cast it over her shoulder into the hallway behind her. While she searched, the thought of the code not even being on the ship crossed her mind and tried to push her further into despair, but she shoved the offending idea aside and focused on her hunt.

Exhausting all possibilities from the unused assortment of clothes without any results, Anna hopped up and bolted through the doorway toward her cabin, only to slip on a shirt she tossed to the floor only a few seconds before. She landed face down on the deck amidst the scattered clothes, sending a few garments away on a short burst of wind from the fall, but she regained her footing and shot across the corridor despite the pain throbbing in her arms and chin from the impact.

Impatiently squeezing her way through the door to her quarters, she scanned the wall for any indication of the authorization code but found only empty surfaces. The thought of the code scrawled on the back of one of his pictures of scantily-clad women flooded over her, and the feelings of despair rose up again. Shaking them away, she turned her room upside-down while she sought the password. The walls, the floor, the ceiling, bottom of the cot, and the outside of the foot locker had nothing written and gave no indication of what she needed.

As Anna threw open the foot locker and dumped its contents out, she spied a phrase carved into the bottom of the small trunk:

SOUTHERN BASEBALL. She furrowed her brow over the concept, not thinking that the sport even interested him while he was alive, but she decided to give it a shot.

Returning to the bridge, Anna cried as she screeched to a halt next to the pilot's chair, "Southern baseball!"

A few seconds dragged on for her, while the computer did not respond. Wondering if the computer was doing this intentionally to make her sweat, she believed it was doing a good job by waiting for what seemed like an eternity.

"Come on," she chanted repeatedly, anxious for some kind of response.

Finally, the computer flatly stated, "Authorization code accepted."

"YES!" bellowed Anna as she threw her fists above her head toward the ceiling, overjoyed that she passed the test.

Waiting only a few seconds, the computer continued, "Do you wish to choose an avatar?"

Anna dropped her gaze to the holographic control panels floating in front of her and asked, "I get to choose an avatar?"

"Correct. You may choose a holographic representation for the computer, with which you can interact. This feature is optional, and you may choose not to have an avatar."

"An avatar?" mused Anna with an expression of amused interest. "Hmmm."

She sat down in the chair and thought for a few seconds about what to choose.

"What options do I have?" she asked after realizing that she did not know what limitations she had on her decision.

"I have over 2,000 celebrities and historical figures from which to choose."

Anna's jaw dropped open in shock. Figuring that this could take a while, she decided to take an easy route for now.

"Am I limited in any other way?"

"My personality matrix is factory-specified as female, so you may not choose a male avatar."

Playing devil's advocate, Anna asked with a smirk, "What if I wanted to pick a gay man as my avatar?"

Without missing a beat, the computer replied, "He would be listed as a male avatar and is not an option."

Anna nodded, understanding her parameters. Despite that, she still was not sure who she wanted to represent the computer. With over two thousand to choose from, the task seemed overwhelming.

"Can I choose to create a custom avatar?"

"Yes."

"Well," she said, slapping her knees before standing and circling to stand behind the chair. "Let's see what you got. Pick a personality at random and display her for me."

A half-second passed before a short, middle-aged woman with brown hair tied into a bun on the back of her head displayed in full color in the middle of the bridge. She wore a long, black dress and, despite appearing old and plain, demonstrated some charm in her face.

The computer announced, "Marie Curie, Polish physicist. Born 7 November 1867. Died 4 July 1934. Achievements: Nobel Prize in Physics in 1903 and in Chemistry in 1911. Only person in the 20th century to win Nobel Prizes in two sciences."

Anna looked at Marie for a long moment, wondering if she would be comfortable with a scientist aboard her ship. At first, she thought it would be nice having an intelligent woman on board, but then remembered that she would only be accessing the information the ship's computer had available to it.

"May I hear her voice?" Anna inquired.

"Voice imprint is assumed, as no true voice imprint has been recorded for the personality."

A few seconds later, the image of Marie came to life and turned to face Anna."

"Good morning, Anna!" she greeted with a thick, Polish accent. "How are you today?"

"Uh, fine," Anna replied nervously, surprised by the accent and the difficulty she had understanding it without concentrating.

"Computer," she said after a few seconds of consideration. "I would like to choose another avatar. Somebody a little younger and American, please."

The image of Marie faded and was instantly replaced with a girl with straight, black hair and Asian features that looked like she was in her early teens. She wore a brightly-colored kimono with what appeared to be cherry blossoms decorating the outfit.

"Suki Yamato," the computer introduced. "Japanese-American musician. Born 14 January 2165. Died 3 February 2249. Achievements: Grammy award in 2177 for "Bells of Emperor Hiroto".

Anna chuckled and stated, "A little too young, computer. Maybe someone in her twenties or thirties?"

Suki faded and was replaced with a tall, attractive woman with long, brown hair and wearing a white halter top and blue denim jeans.

The computer stated, "Kate Mitchum, British model and actor. Born 16 July 2013. Died 16 May 2098. Achievements: London Critics Circle Film Awards' British Supporting Actress of the Year in 2039 for *The Desert Wind*, voted Sexiest Woman Alive by Esquire magazine in 2049, Academy Award for Best Actress in a Leading Role in 2054 for . . ."

"Okay," Anna interrupted while waving the information away with her hand at what she felt was going to be a lengthy list. "I don't need all of that. Let me hear her speak."

With a gentle, mezzo-soprano voice, the avatar said with a bit of a British accent, "People are always asking me what it was like to be in such a fantastic failure of a movie. I still can't believe how much hatred they have toward that."

Anna walked around the avatar, studying her from head to toe at every angle. After finishing her examination, she nodded and smiled, pleased with the result.

"I'll take her," she announced.

"Avatar selected," the computer confirmed. "Do you wish to name her?"

Without a second thought, she replied, "Her original name is fine."

A few seconds later, the computer said, "Avatar parameters established."

In the next instant, the avatar blinked, turned to face Anna, and said, "Hello. I'm Kate. How are you?"

Anna smiled in spite of herself, clearly amused upon seeing her new companion in action, and she attempted to hide her smile behind her hand. She looked at her hand, realizing that such a gesture did no good, and waved at Kate instead.

"Hi, I'm Anna."

"So, I will be representing your ship's computer from here on out. Do you need anything?"

Anna nodded, "Yes. I need the ship's blueprints. I am trying to locate the sensor array."

"All right," Kate sighed, surprising the human woman with the sound and motion that accompanied the breath. Kate walked a few steps toward Anna, clapped her hands together, and pulled them apart to bring the ship's blueprints into existence.

"The sensor array is located here," the avatar stated, pointing to a long mechanism attached just below the pilot's chair inside the outer hull.

Impressed, Anna nodded and observed, "That wasn't very hard. Now, I need to find something to act as a shovel, so I can dig my way to it."

"Actually," interrupted Kate. "That's not necessary. You will find a maintenance access hatch 3 meters behind the pilot seat."

Reacting to the good news she just received with raised eyebrows, Anna measured back from the seat to the deck plate in question. Not marked in any way, it appeared just like the rest of the floor on the bridge. She stepped up to it and knelt beside the deck plate, feeling along its edge for some clue on how to open it. Luck was not on her side for this search, as she came up empty-handed. Leaning forward with her hands on the plate to think about how to open it, she heard a click as her weight shifted. Curious of the unexpected sound, Anna leaned back and pulled her hands off the plate to watch the deck plate slowly swing open and reveal the hatch leading into the bowels of the ship. With flashlight in hand, she climbed through the portal.

The compartment provided little space for her to move, being filled with ship systems from one end to the other. But, she located a narrow crawlspace that traversed the area, which she reached using what she felt were contortionist techniques. She looked around her to find the sensor array but got lost in the myriad of systems in place.

"Kate!" she called out, her voice sounding hollow as it echoed against the metal parts around her. "Can you detect my wristcomp?"

The wristcomp's communicator turned on, and Kate answered, "Yes, I can."

Anna requested, "Please send me the blueprints of the ship."

The requested document appeared in her view, and she took a few minutes to locate her position and find the sensor array positioned behind a few other components directly above her.

"Whoever designed this ship clearly did not take maintenance into account," she grumbled as she began removing the first part in her path to the sensor suite.

Removing the three parts blocking her access to the sensors took only a few minutes for Anna to accomplish, and her test of the system in question confirmed that the sensors were fully operational.

With a sigh, Anna replaced the other parts back in place and commented as she did, "Time to find something to dig the ship out."

Chapter 5

"I am not sure if anything suitable is listed in the ship's inventory," Kate stated, taking Anna by surprise as she remembered that she left the wristcomp channel open. "But, you are welcome to review the manifest and see if you find anything."

"Ryan carried cargo?"

"It's mostly foodstuffs and personal effects, but something may be there that you could find suitable."

With a nod, the human replied, "Okay. Thank you."

While she climbed out of the maintenance crawlspace, Anna appreciated having a computer that she could finally get along with after all these years. As she reached the deck, Kate turned where she stood by the pilot chair and asked, "Do you want to look over the manifest now?"

Anna's nod confirmed the request, and the document appeared on the control panel. She reviewed the information and, with a grim smile, stated, "Doesn't look like I could use anything on here. Thanks anyway, Kate."

"What are you going to do?"

The human moved a few steps toward the airlock, stopped, and turned back to regard the hologram.

"I guess I'll have to use my hands," shrugged Anna before she completed the walk across the floor and into the airlock.

Kate called after her as the airlock closed, "Be careful out there!"

Climbing out of the upper hatch, the woman moved toward the front of the ship, slipping her work gloves onto her strong but slender hands. The tight-fitting neoprene gloves felt like a second skin, but the pleather pads on her palm and fingertips made her feel like a gecko or some other exotic creature. After securing them around her wrists, she sat above the forward viewport window and slid down to where the ship's nose lay buried in the soil.

Judging from the way the dirt and rocks had piled around the craft and up to the bottom edge of the windshield, Anna estimated that she would have to dig at least a couple of meters down to uncover the forward sensor emitter and another meter or two down and all the way around the nose to completely free the ship from being pinned to the moon. With a heavy sigh, she resigned herself to digging duty for the rest of the day.

After a few minutes, Kate appeared in the window and looked to be watching Anna work. At first, the human did not notice, but she glanced up and caught sight of the hologram standing on the bridge. The two stared at each other for a moment in what felt like an awkward silence. Finally, Anna slowly raised her hand and waved to her companion, prompting a return wave from the avatar.

Clicking her wristcomp on, Anna asked, "Is there something I can help you with?"

"No," replied Kate. "Just watching you work."

Unsure just how to respond, Anna remained silent for a few seconds. Her mouth hung open slightly as she searched for the words to say. She had never experienced anyone watching her like this, and it felt odd to say the least. The act of Kate observing her made her feel uncomfortable, especially knowing that it was really the computer that was driving the avatar to act that way. Why was the computer doing this? Was this a true reflection of the real Kate's personality while she lived? Perhaps this was just a learning process for the new personality matrix to get an idea of what the ship's owner was like. No matter what the reason, Anna felt that she had to do something to put her mind at ease.

Clicking on her wristcomp, she opened a channel and asked, "Uh, why don't you monitor the sensors and let me know if anything changes on it?"

"I am already doing that," Kate answered.

"How about run a diagnostic of the sensor systems to make sure they are in working order?"

"Diagnostic initiated. It should be done in about a minute."

"Checked the ship's power levels?"

"Currently at maximum."

"Run a self-diagnostic?"

"I did that when I was rebooting."

"Found some more food?"

"Have you checked the kitchen?"

Anna, originally hoping to throw the question in to test the computer's response, was stunned by her answer. She stared dumbfounded at the hologram for a few seconds trying to wrap her head around the question.

"Kitchen?"

"Yes, the kitchen," Kate stated.

"Oh, my god!" exclaimed Anna after a few seconds of thought. "I'm so stupid! I completely forgot. Where is it?"

"The kitchen is located directly behind the airlock."

The hologram's voice trailed off through the wristcomp, as Anna scrambled up the nose of the ship toward the airlock. Within seconds, she opened the airlock, slid down the ladder to the floor, and burst through the lower door into the bridge. Kate casually walked toward Anna, who ignored her and rushed into the back of the ship, and merely shook her head in disbelief upon seeing her actions.

As soon as Anna emerged in the small corridor that curved through the living area of the vessel, her eyes fell upon the one door in the ship that she had never opened: the unmarked hatch to the central room. For some reason, she believed it to contain some insignificant part of the ship and never bothered checking it out. With a shrug, she leaped to the entryway and pressed the switch. The door unsealed and slid into the wall like all of the others, revealing a dark, narrow room. Leaning in, Anna's jaw dropped as she gazed at the contents within. Against the forward wall sat what appeared to be a kitchenette, complete with a chest-sized refrigerator and freezer, counter space, cabinets, and a countertop oven. Three boxes clearly labeled as holding canned food that appeared to have been stacked in front of the refrigerator now rested in disarray on the floor.

"No way!" whispered Anna in disbelief.

She walked purposefully the couple of steps to the boxes and pulled open the nearest case to see several cans stacked inside. Pulling one of them out, she read the label marked "Whole Kernel Corn". She replaced the can and took out several others, finding more corn, green beans, and other vegetables. The other cases, much to her delight, contained enough canned goods to last her for at least another month without having to supplement it with any locally-grown food.

Pushing the boxes behind her, Anna threw open the refrigerator and gawked at the packages of chilled and frozen meat stored within. She chuckled at first, not believing her dumb luck, and followed it with full laughter as she rifled through the various meats to see what just became available to her.

"He must have stocked up before flying out to me!" she exclaimed merrily as she ripped open a package of sliced turkey and stuffed a slice in her mouth.

"Oh! That's so good!" cried Anna with her mouth full of food.

"I see you've found the kitchen," Kate dryly stated from the entrance.

Looking over her shoulder, Anna smiled when she looked upon the computer's representative. She finished chewing and gulped down the meat.

"Kate, I could kiss you!" she cheerfully stated and stood upright again.

The hologram smiled and answered, "Sorry, but I'm not that kind of girl."

Anna's grin shifted into a twisted smirk as she stared at Kate a few seconds for her response, but she quickly returned to beaming and ate another slice of turkey.

"You just made my week!" Anna confessed as she dropped her eyes to gaze at her newfound food again. "I can't believe that I never looked in here. I just walked by it, never suspecting what was in here. Thank you."

Kate smiled back and responded, "You're quite welcome. But, you should probably finish eating your lunch and get back to digging."

Looking up from the package, she asked with a serious expression, "What for? The ship's not going anywhere."

"No, but it is starting to get dark outside."

"What do you mean 'It's getting dark'?" Anna demanded, totally unexpecting Kate's statement.

"What don't you understand?" Kate said plainly. "It's getting dark outside."

After closing the package of meat and placing it back in the refrigerator, Anna ran through Kate and out the kitchen door. The act of passing through her set Kate off, forcing her to pause in shock for a second before marching after the blonde in a huff.

"Excuse you!" cried Kate. "Don't do that!"

"Do what?" Anna asked as she entered the airlock.

45

"Do what?! You ran right through me!"

Anna's voice echoed out of the airlock, "But, you're a hologram."

Stopping at the airlock door, Kate put her hands on her hips and scolded, "That doesn't make it right. I have feelings, you know. How do you think that makes me feel?"

With a smirk, Anna answered before shutting the door, "Like you're not really there?"

Kate stammered in disbelief at Anna's reaction, "Where are you going? Come back here!"

The airlock door suddenly opened again, showing Anna standing with a remorseful expression on her face.

"You're right, Kate," she apologized. "I'm sorry. I guess I'm just not used to a . . . pardon the expression, living hologram."

The avatar's face relaxed a bit and showed a hint of a smile. She glanced at the floor for a brief second and looked back at Anna.

"Well," Kate finally laughed. "Okay, but consider yourself lucky that I can't take a physical form. I'd have clobbered you by now."

Anna grinned at the response before turning and ascending the airlock's ladder while the door shut. She emerged through the top hatch and stood on the hull while she stared at the sky. The sunlight seemed to still be as bright as before, but she noticed that the gas giant loomed closer to g Lupi and threatened to eclipse it.

Anna toggled her wristcomp and asked, "Kate, are you sure it's getting dark out here?"

"The amount of sunlight being received by the solar cells has decreased by 8% since this time yesterday. Yes, it is getting darker."

She looked at the nose of the ship and back at the sky again. Cursing under her breath, Anna quickly returned to the nose of the ship and set to digging again. As the day progressed, she noticed the light slowly getting dimmer, but not enough to make it difficult to see without aid.

Finally, enough soil had been moved to give Anna clear access to the sensor emitter. She turned on her flashlight and found a few small cracks on the outside covering that she deduced occurred during the crash. In fact, most of the hull plating around it was crumpled and scarred from the impact. She took a deep breath, leaned back against the small ridge she created, and wiped her brow with the back of her wrist.

"Kate," Anna paged through her wristcomp.

"Yes, Anna."

"Are the sensors online?"

A second later, the computer's proxy replied, "No, not yet."

"Judging from the hull damage I see out here, I'll be surprised if it works again outside of having the emitter replaced."

"Anna, you haven't asked about the results of the diagnostic yet."

Mentally admitting the fault, she inquired, "Well, what've you got?"

"The circuit is not complete. According to the test results, the sensor array appears to have become separated at the point where the forward emitter and duplexer connect."

Anna mulled over her statement for a second and asked, "Kate, would the sensors normally be able to scan through a couple meters of soil?"

"Under normal circumstances, the sensor suite should be able to scan through about 20 meters of soil without any difficulty."

Anna paused and looked up at the forward window, just in time to see Kate walk into view and look back. Slightly frustrated, she ripped the gloves off her hands and stuffed them into her belt.

"Are you kidding me?!" she cried, standing up to stretch her back and legs.

"No, I'm not."

"You mean to tell me that I didn't have to sit out here for hours digging the ship out of the ground?!"

Kate hesitated, "Well, no. You didn't."

"Wha . . . why didn't you tell me?!"

"I'm sorry," she regretfully expressed. "I didn't know if you would be okay with me interrupting you."

Anna looked at the ground and then back at the hologram with a look of exasperation on her face.

"Interrupt me next time!"

"I'll remember that. Sorry, Anna."

"It's okay, Kate. We're both learning about each other." The smile from the hologram signaled her approval.

At that point, Anna climbed up to the top of the ship and into the airlock, meeting Kate at the inside door.

"I need you to send me a schematic of the sensor array, once I reach the system below the deck," Anna ordered as she marched to the access panel.

"On its way," assured Kate.

After climbing into the bowels of the ship, Anna crawled as far forward as she could and activated the holographic screen. The orange glow provided her enough light to remove the components between her and the sensor array and finally disconnect the sensors themselves from its mount against the hull. The system was heavier than she originally expected and almost smashed her hand against a brace as she maneuvered it out of place.

"Anna," Kate announced through the wristcomp. "The amount of sunlight being received by the solar cells has dropped another 25% over the past six hours."

Anna grunted as she slowly moved the system out to where she could bring her other hand up to help. She brought the sensor suite out to the crawlway from there in seconds and placed it on the grated deckplate.

"How is our energy consumption?" she asked after taking a breath.

"At our current rate, we have enough power to run current systems continuously for 11 days, 3 hours, and 48 minutes."

"Once we lose sunlight, how long will it last?"

After a few seconds, Kate answered, "At current consumption, 7 days, 12 hours, and 41 minutes."

"How long will we be without the sun?"

A few more seconds passed, and the computer answered, "According to the data you gathered on your survey, we will be without any sunlight for 23 hours and 47 minutes."

"Almost a whole day without sunlight?" Anna wondered aloud skeptically.

Surprised at the answer, Anna crawled to the access hatch and poked her head out. Kate was standing by the pilot's seat looking out at the landscape cast in twilight.

Curiously, she asked, "Really?"

Kate looked over her shoulder and replied, "Yes, it's true."

The technician thought for a few seconds before continuing, "But, it's just an eclipse. Right?"

The hologram answered with a serious nod.

With a quizzical expression, Anna asked rhetorically, "Why was I thinking that this was going to last for a long time?"

She shrugged and added with a smile, "Well, at least I don't have to worry about shutting anything down. Back to work!"

Chapter 6

Anna examined and repaired the sensor array while lying on the crawlspace floor for over an hour with only the light from her flashlight helping her see. She would have carried the array up to the bridge and fixed it under better lighting, but its sheer weight cast doubts in her mind as to whether she could safely move it without dropping it.

After she completed what she determined to be the problem as best she could, she carefully maneuvered and secured the heavy piece of equipment back into position. Once she attached the power feed to the unit, she returned to the bridge, sitting in the only seat available, and ran another diagnostic on the sensors. A few minutes later, the test results came back positive.

Breathing a sigh of relief, Anna tested the system by initiating a passive scan of the area. The dedicated display on the control interface floating in front of her replaced the white noise static with a 3D image of the landscape around her out to a range of approximately 10 kilometers.

"Not nearly far enough," commented Anna with a bit of disappointment in her voice. "I'll have to work on that."

As she looked over the display, she found that the large lake almost 5 kilometers away looked strangely familiar to her. She leaned in closer to the readout and studied it further for another minute.

"Kate," instructed Anna. "Cross-reference the sensor display with the survey results for the moon taken about a month ago."

"Okay," the avatar acknowledged.

Anna added, "Oh, hey! Once you are done, display the results on a separate . . . display, and orient the sensor readout to the moon's north."

"You got it, Anna."

Several seconds passed until the results appeared next to her. As she suspected, the ship crashed a few kilometers away from the spot where the flash was detected. Anna smiled, thankful for the twist of fate.

"You know what?" she quizzed cheerfully as she got to her feet. "I think I am in the mood to do a little hiking."

"Are you sure that's wise, Anna? Sunlight is rapidly fading. You may get lost."

"Where I am headed has a fairly easy route to follow," reassured Anna. "I will go to the lake at the far end of current sensor range. I plan to follow the river routes created between here and there. I shouldn't get lost. Besides, it might be a nice change of pace to see this place without the sun."

"Anna, I don't mean to interrupt you," Kate interjected. "But, I am picking up a telemetry signal."

"A . . . a what?" Anna asked, shocked at the news.

"A telemetry signal."

Taking the seat again, she requested, "Have they identified themselves?"

The computer paused for a couple of seconds and answered, "Mining probe NRS-MS14-17."

"A mining drone?!"

"Yes, Anna."

"Wow! I didn't think they'd still be floating around. Tell it to come here."

"Certainly."

She leaned back in the upholstered chair and thought aloud, "I had totally forgotten about the drones. I just assumed that they were lost when the station blew up. I wonder how many are left?

"Kate," cried Anna as she leapt from the seat and hustled to the airlock. "I'm going topside to wait for the drone. Let me know when it gets close."

"If you wish, Anna."

Emerging from the ship, Anna looked upon the darker scene around her. Cast entirely in shadow, the forest surrounding the crash site gave a haunting feeling that sent chills up her spine. The diminishing sunlight had also dropped the temperature just enough to be noticeable.

Looking to the sky, the gas giant lent the impression of a sinister, inky blob ready to swallow the star hugging the curve of its black mass. As Anna searched the skies for any sign of the drone, she noticed the pinpricks of starlight piercing the dark veil that had settled over the moon. Turning on her heel, she looked over the star patterns familiar to her from her tenure aboard the mining station that used to float just outside the planet's gravity well. As more stars rapidly appeared in the sky, she located one particular yellow star that she recognized as home.

Staring at the distant Sol, Anna sadly whispered, "What I wouldn't give to see my mom and dad right now."

She intently watched the star for several seconds, longing for some form of positive human contact. Reflecting on her current situation and the solitude it inflicted on her, she felt the sting of tears in her eyes. She tried in vain to blink and squeeze them away, but it only caused them to run down her cheeks even sooner. Unable to stop their flow, she flopped down on the hull. With her arms wrapped around her knees, she hung her head as she cried her lonely tears.

"Anna," the computer announced through the wristcomp, interrupting her grief. "The mining drone should be within visual range now."

After wiping away her tears, she replied, "Thank you."

Anna rose to her feet and turned, casting her gaze skyward. Far in the distance close to the treetops, she found a pair of red and blue blinking lights rapidly approaching. She could not help but smile, knowing that something familiar was coming her way. And, the idea of having a drone around to help her get things done thrilled her.

While she waited, a howl broke the silence from the woods. Anna gasped as she reflexively looked over her shoulder into the dark woods. The unexpected sound, one that sounded similar to a wolf from Earth but with a rough, raspy quality, reached Anna's ears and sent chills down her spine. She could tell that the wind did not create this outcry, and whatever it was seemed to be close by.

She looked back to the approaching lights, noticing that it gradually approached and was still a few minutes away. Growing impatient, she bounced on her toes a few times and looked over her shoulder again. Through the deepening dusk, she stared between the trees, hoping to catch a glimpse of whatever might be the cause of the howl she heard earlier. Her hand, trembling slightly, grasped her pistol and slowly pulled it out of its pocket. As she peered into the forest, she saw nothing to cause any alarm. All seemed at peace.

Anna sighed, relieved that nothing was there. Perhaps the wind did cause the howl that pierced the growing night. She tried to reassure herself that she was the only living being on the moon, and she was just jumping at shadows.

Then, she saw movement at the edge of the woods.

Anna gasped again. She scanned the tree line, keeping the weapon pointed shakily in the same direction of her stare. Noticing the unsteady grip on her pistol, she grabbed it with both hands and steadied her aim.

Off in the distance, she heard another howl that sounded like the first one, followed by another further away and another one behind her some distance. Finally, a howl that seemed to be right in front of her joined the chorus, completing the circle.

The fear consumed Anna's mind more with each successive cry she heard in the night. Unable to believe anymore that she was alone and unsure of what caused the hoarse wails, she looked at the approaching drone and fled back into the airlock.

Just as she moved next to the hatch, a dark form emerged from the trees. The shadowy twilight of the eclipse, combined with the shadows created by the ship from what was left of the trickling sunlight, masked the creature's true form. However, its bright yellow eyes seemed to glow in the darkness. Frozen in place at the sheer sight of the unknown beast, she stared at it, praying it would walk back into the woods. It sniffed the exposed dirt under its feet, looked around, and casually stepped toward the ship.

Slowly, Anna raised her pistol and pointed it at the beast. Even with both hands holding the gun, her fear overtook her strength, and it shuddered in her hands. She took a deep breath and gripped the sidearm again, steadying it once more. She directed it at the creature, her sights locked on it. Her heart raced, fueled by the horror the animal injected into her soul. Doubt dominated her thoughts: doubt in her abilities to fire the weapon with any sort of accuracy, doubt in her choice to lash out at it, doubt in the capability to live with herself by attacking a creature that is only trying to survive, doubt in whether it really was going to charge at her by seeing her as its next meal. Her trigger finger shivered, still exhibiting the terror she felt. Ready to prove herself the superior being and survive against a potential threat, she inhaled deeply once more, squeezed her eyes shut, and steadily pulled the trigger.

A split second before Anna fully pressed the trigger, the sounds of the drone's approach reached her ears. She opened her eyes and looked at the monster. The beast had stopped, and its shining eyes looked into the sky at the drone. Although Anna knew that the drone posed no threat, the creature turned and sprinted back into the woods.

Anna blinked, disbelieving her good fortune, and blinked again. After she confirmed that the animal was gone, she turned, holstered the pistol, and stepped toward the drone as it landed on the hull. She laughed slightly, recognizing the drone as one she maintained while living on the station, and placed her hand on the side of its shell. Through the blue light reflecting off its metal hull, she clearly read its embossed label, "*NR Suppliers, Mining Station 14. NRS-MS14-17*".

"You may not know this," she commented to the automaton. "But, you have impeccable timing."

She gave the machine a cursory examination and found it to be in excellent condition, considering that it had floated alone in space for over two weeks. The smile on her face grew wider while she assessed its condition, pleased that it had found its way to her after all this time.

Pointing a warning finger at it, Anna commanded, "Wait here. Don't move." Then, she returned to the hatch and entered the ship.

Walking onto the bridge, she stated, "Kate, can you establish a link with the drone outside and download its logs over the last 16 days."

"Of course."

"While you are at it, initiate an active scan of the area."

"Okay."

Instantly, the drone's logs appeared before her in a separate holographic window. She read the first few lines, confirming that it entered a sleep cycle, when it found that it had no place to dock upon its return for maintenance a few hours after the station detonated. Before it did, however, she noticed that it registered the presence of three other drones in its vicinity before going to sleep. When it awoke upon receiving a transmission . . .

"Transmission?" Anna wondered aloud. "What transmission?

"Kate, did we make a transmission within the last couple of days?"

"Transmission logs report the initiation of a distress signal yesterday at 0721 hours."

"Yesterday? What happened yesterday?" Anna pondered, lost in thought for a few seconds.

Finally, she cried, "Oh, yeah! Now, I remember! I was trying to fix the computer's memory circuits.

"Well, I'm glad that happened. Otherwise, you wouldn't have gotten this drone's attention."

"Thank you, Anna."

She continued reading the logs and learned that 16 other drones had assembled near the debris field created by the station's destruction. Since g Lupi's solar wind distorted the signal, it could not pinpoint the exact origin point of the plea and had four others go with it to search the planetary system.

"Sixteen others?!" said Anna with glee. "This is amazing!

"Kate, please have Drone 17 return to where the other drones are and tell them to follow it here."

"Will do."

"Also, keep in contact with the drone as long as you can and record how far it is when you lose contact."

"Okay."

Anna turned her attention to the sensors, where she found a number of life forms within range. She surmised that the blip appearing in the woods moving away from the ship was the creature she saw earlier. What astonished her was the dozens of others scattered around the area. Some were moving in groups, while others were only one or two individuals. As she watched, more signals came into being, as if the creatures were appearing out of thin air.

"My god!" she quietly wondered. "Where are they coming from?"

She continued to watch the movements on the sensor display for several minutes, completely enthralled with the mysterious beings.

Finally, Kate interrupted, "Anna?"

"Yeah," she answered distantly.

"Sunlight levels have dropped below the solar panels' ability to collect energy from it."

Absentmindedly, she said without taking her eyes off the readout, "Go ahead and close them."

As the sound of the hull plates sliding into place registered in her ears, Anna looked up and out the forward window into the darkness. With the lights on inside the bridge, she could not get a good look at the scene on the other side of the metal wall. She glanced at the sensors again. Upon seeing that the nearest organism was several hundred meters away, she stood and walked to the airlock, confident that the working sensor array would help protect her from the unknown.

"Kate," she ordered as she stepped along the inclined floor. "Return to a passive scan and inform me if any life forms come within 100 meters of our current location."

As she entered the airlock, Kate responded, "Certainly, Anna."

Poking her head out the open portal, she glanced around her to make sure that the coast was clear. Satisfied that she was in no immediate danger, she climbed outside and studied the woods, bathed in a deep dark shadow. The sounds of at least a dozen new species filled her ears. Some sounded like animals from her homeworld, such as the chirps and high-pitched cries from what she assumed were small, flying birds. Others did not sound at all familiar, but one of the ones she heard resembled the bleating of a goat. As she listened, the thought of her possibly being the first human to be exposed to this wildlife crossed her mind and brought a smile to her face. The wind picked up slightly and gently blew past her, whipping a lock of her hair into her eyes. Brushing back her hair, she caught a glimpse of a small animal in flight near the tree line.

Suddenly, her wristcomp signaled a message. Opening the channel, Anna heard Kate warn her of a fast-moving anomaly that just entered her chosen perimeter.

"I saw it, Kate," she responded through the wristcomp. "I think it's just a bird or something."

She turned in place and looked skyward. The diamond pinpoints of hundreds of stars filled the night sky, accented with hints of a nebula and other nearby celestial formations. The only area devoid of stars was directly overhead, where the gas giant blotted out g Lupi. The sunlight created a bright halo around the planet that seemed to crown her moon.

Anna, while keeping her eyes glued to the planetary exhibit, stretched out on the hull, and stared at the stars for several minutes. With the breeze softly caressing her face and the sounds of nature surrounding her, she felt calm and at peace for the first time in years.

Chapter 7

"Anna?"

No response.

"Anna?"

Still, no response.

"Anna!"

The woman awoke with a start, sitting up suddenly and looking around. She was still on top of the ship, and the eclipse had not passed yet. In fact, nothing appeared to have changed.

Slightly embarrassed after realizing that she had dozed off, Anna looked at her wristcomp, just as Kate called her name again a little more anxious than before.

"Sorry, Kate. I must have fallen asleep. What's up?"

Her artificial companion proclaimed, "I have been tracking the first creature you encountered, and it is approaching our current position from the northwest."

Anna looked over her shoulder, but the ambient light from the eclipse barely allowed her to see anything in clear detail. Vowing to eat more carrots, she squinted and stared into the darkness more intently.

A few minutes later, a pair of glowing yellow eyes emerged from the trees. From what she could make out, the beast stepped ever so slowly toward the ship, sniffing at the bare ground every few steps.

Cautiously, Anna lowered herself against the deck and stretched her hand toward the dorsal hatch's keypad, all the while keeping her eyes fixed on the native creature that seemed to be paying no attention to her. Her fingertips brushed the keys but could not reach them enough to enter the passcode. She dragged herself along the smooth hull, looking away only long enough to make sure she went the right direction, and touched the first key. The resulting beep pierced the relative silence of the night, sounding like a deafening chime in her ears. Her gaze flashed instantly back to the creature, whose eyes now focused on the source of the sound.

Fear emerged inside her once again. Anna hastily keyed in the remaining digits of the code and opened the airlock. The swish of the portal's opening practically drowned out all other sounds around her. She watched the creature stare back at her as she re-entered the ship.

Reaching the floor, she placed a hand on her chest and breathed a sigh of relief, feeling safe within the confines of the ship. Waiting until her heartbeat calmed down, she stepped onto the bridge, where she found Kate staring out at the dark trees.

"Kate," Anna addressed. "I'm going to grab something to eat. Do you have any kind of recreational software on file?"

The avatar appeared to think for a second and answered, "I have several game titles on file from which you may choose."

"Such as?"

"I have adventure games, board games, card games, and strategy games available for your entertainment."

Anna weighed her options and requested, "What do you have in card games?"

"I have Blackjack, Bridge, Cribbage, Draw Poker, Freecell, Gin, Golf, Hearts, Klondike, Phase 10, Rummy, Spider, Strip Poker, Texas Hold 'em . . ."

"Hold up!" interrupted Anna skeptically. "You have Strip Poker?!"

"Yes."

Shaking her head in disbelief, she mumbled, "Why am I not surprised?"

"Surprised at what?" Kate asked genuinely.

"Never mind," Anna quickly replied, ignoring the question.

"Okay. I also have Texas Hold 'em Poker, Tri-Peaks, and War."

Anna sighed and stated after a moment of contemplation, "Okay, queue up Cribbage. I haven't played that since middle school. Time I familiarize myself with it again."

"Excellent!"

After making a ham sandwich and picking up one of the fruits she had harvested, she returned to the bridge and found Kate sitting on the floor just behind the pilot seat with a holographic version of cribbage waiting for her. Anna smiled, took a bite of her sandwich, and sat across from her companion.

An hour passed, and the two ladies had played through several games, punctuated with idle conversation and playful banter throughout.

"Fifteen!" cried Anna as she dragged the 6 of Hearts to the pile atop the 9 of Spades.

"No way!" Kate replied with a smile on her face. "You're cheating!"

The blonde shrugged, "How can I be cheating? I'm playing against a computer."

"You," the hologram began, pointing her finger accusingly at her human counterpart. "Actually, you have a point."

The pair giggled, and Kate looked at her hand of cards floating before her face. As she reached for her next play . . .

THUMP!

Anna flinched from the unexpected sound, and the two ladies looked at the forward viewscreen, where they saw a large, muscular, canine-like creature with thick, dark blue fur standing on the other side of the window. From her angle, the thing looked as if it stood about a meter high at the shoulder. Two of its front paws pressed against the bottom of the window, while the third arced over its head and pushed against the reinforced glass near the top. Its bright yellow eyes, reflecting the ship's light or glowing of its own accord, stared hungrily at the two humanoids inside. The lips on the beast's long, triple-jawed snout peeled back, baring a row of sharp, yellowed fangs. As a thin stream of drool spilled out of its maw, its guttural growl sent chills up her spine.

Acting on instinct, Anna backed away from the front of the ship on her hands and feet, watching the creature as she moved. The animal growled again and barked loudly as it slashed two of its sharp claws against the window. It raked the transparent barrier again and again but appeared to make no progress. Suddenly, the canine stopped and howled into the night, the sheer volume of its cry forcing Anna to cover her ears.

Kate stood and walked up to stand opposite the beast, enticing it to scratch against the viewscreen at a more furious pace. She watched it react to her proximity, growling and scraping the window.

Anna, seated on the floor against the airlock door, watched the scene unfold. Her heartbeat pounded within her chest, and her breathing came in short, quick pants. Frozen in place, she could not tear herself away from the wolf-like monster.

"I don't think it can get in," Kate commented with a smile, turning back to regard Anna in the back of the room. "You have nothing to worry about."

"Really?" Anna asked, fear dominating her voice. "Tell that to him!"

Kate looked back at the creature and walked away from the pilot station, leaving the beast snarling and gnashing its teeth at her.

As the hologram crossed the floor, she added, "The hull seems to be strong enough to keep it out. You should relax."

Anna watched the creature for another moment. It finally calmed down but continued to stare right at her. It licked its chops and dipped its head for a brief second. As it did, something flickered under its jaw near its neck, too quickly for her to make out what it was.

"I don't know if I can," whispered Anna meekly.

Stopping in front of the frightened woman, Kate looked down and stated, "Well, I don't expect that creature to break in here anytime soon. I suggest that you find a way to face your fear and conquer it."

Anna looked up at the computer's representative and leaned to the side to look upon their intruder. As she observed the wild animal standing on the nose of her ship, Anna noticed its lean frame. For a fearsome predator, it seemed like it was on the brink of starvation. That certainly explained its behavior in her mind. If it was that hungry, she deduced that it would compete against her for any food in the area, and she could not allow that.

With her eyes glued to the beast, she stood and slapped the door switch, letting her enter the airlock unhindered.

"Anna, where are you going?" Kate asked as she picked up her pace toward the airlock.

Responding in a low voice, Anna said, "I have to take care of this."

"Are you sure that's wise? That creature is waiting outside, ready to attack anything that moves."

Anna blinked and looked at the holographic woman.

"That's why I have to take care of this."

"Anna, don't!"

But, Kate's demand was met with the closing door.

The upper hatch opened with its sliding metal sound, and Anna leaped through the opening with her pistol in hand. She wheeled about to face the front of the ship but almost lost her balance from spinning too fast. As she steadied herself with her free hand, the creature's head lifted and looked over the edge of the ship at her. With a single bound, it leaped onto the top of the ship, landing lightly on the hull. Though the darkness surrounding them did not help her see exactly what the beast was doing, she could tell that it lowered its head and stared at her, growling with bared teeth. In response to its threat, she raised her weapon and aimed at its dark mass.

Several seconds passed, which felt like an eternity to Anna. She had never faced down a wild animal before, let alone one that considered her its next meal. She knew it held the same desire to survive as her, and it would use every scrap of strength at its disposal to make it happen. Remnants of her fear that she had thought cast aside emerged bit by bit in her mind, reminding her of the peril she had put herself in. She wanted to run. She wanted to run and hide far away from this place, this animal, and any others like it.

Suddenly, it charged at her. Anna's fear surged within her. She channeled it into her hand and fired at the rapidly approaching predator, but the shot flew past harmlessly into the forest beyond. She fired again with the same result. The sound of its approach, its solid footfalls against the metal hull, filled her ears and pushed her fear to the forefront again. Anna screamed as her hand shifted, and she fired a third shot as the creature leaped at her.

Anna raised her arms in front of her just as it hit her. The force of the impact shoved Anna to the hull, pinning her underneath the animal. She slammed her forearms into the beast's jaw and neck to keep its sharp fangs from her throat, shrieking with each blow she threw at it. Several seconds passed before she realized through her adrenaline-induced frenzy that the canine did not move.

Hesitantly, she stopped thrashing and looked at the body above her, staring dumbfounded for a few seconds at its lower jaw and the yellow eye that seemed to stare at her near its neck. The being did not move at all, as if it had died on top of her. Its weight pressed against her, making breathing that much harder.

Anna pushed against its head and one of its lower legs. After quite a bit of effort, she finally rolled the beast off of her a few seconds later. It tumbled for about a meter and came to a stop on its side. Still, it did not move. She jumped to her feet, pulled the flashlight from her belt, and aimed it at the animal while keeping her sidearm trained on it. Despite her best efforts to keep her hand steady while working to calm her breathing, the beam of light danced over the body.

The large canine was a hexapod, but unlike the other hexapods she had seen depicted in various fictional programs. While those of fiction showed them having three legs on each side of their bodies, this one had two sets of legs at its front and rear ends. The two lower legs at each end appeared to be like normal, but the third was on top of its body between what she figured to be its shoulder blades and atop its tailbone. As the animal completely relaxed as the last of its life force dissipated, the lower legs shifted and seemed to straighten in an angle that pointed it directly away from a central axis.

Stepping around to stand in front of the creature, Anna discovered that her third shot burned through its head just above its left eye, whose light faded as she watched. She felt bad about shooting it, even though she knew it was self-defense.

She shoved her pistol back into her pouch. As she did, she felt tears welling up in her eyes over what she had done, accompanying the feelings of guilt and shame. Her knees buckled, dropping her to kneel in front of the alien maw that now hung open. The tears flowed down her cheeks and onto the hull.

"I'm sorry," she whispered between sobs.

She sucked in her breath after a few seconds and screamed, "I'M SORRY!"

Off in the distance, scattered howls erupted from the forest in all directions, alerting Anna to a potential situation. Despite the fact that she wanted to study the body further, she did not want the carcass on the ship, thinking that it would attract other predators. At the same time, it was too heavy to effectively carry away fast enough to avoid any unwanted attention.

"Kate," she asked after toggling her wristcomp. "How close is the closest life form?"

A second later, Kate replied, "The closest signal is about 600 meters due south and moving southeast. Is everything okay up there?"

"I'm fine. Thanks." Anna nodded before closing the channel. "I'll come back inside in a minute."

Maneuvering next to the animal, she pushed the body over the side of the ship and winced as it hit the ground with a dull thud. She sighed and made her way to the ground, where she grabbed two of the beast's legs and dragged it toward the woods.

Several minutes later, Anna finally reached the tree line and stopped to catch her breath. As she did, she received a call on her wristcomp.

"Anna," Kate began. "I am receiving multiple signals closing on our location from the east about 40 degrees above the horizon."

Her eyes darted skyward, but she could not locate the incoming anomalies. Thinking the eclipse played a big part in obstructing her view, she stepped back into the forest for cover.

"How many signals?" she asked.

"Thirteen."

Anna furrowed her brow for a second, trying to contemplate what they could possibly be. Then, it dawned on her.

"The drones!" she cried. "Great! Send . . ."

Pausing to calculate, she continued a few seconds later, ". . . four of them to my current location."

"Are you certain?"

"Yes, I have a job for them.

"Oh! While you're at it, how far away is the nearest life form?"

"The closest life form is about 700 meters to the south east and moving in that direction."

With a smile, Anna concluded, "Okay. Thanks!"

A few minutes later, the drones descended from the sky, four of which broke away from the group and moved straight to Anna, who rose to her feet and stood next to her kill with a huge grin on her face.

As they softly landed a few meters in front of her, she called back to the ship through her wristcomp, "Kate, tell them to pick up the creature in front of me, drop it off in the river nearby, and return back to the ship."

"Understood, Anna."

"While they do that," she added as the drones extended their grasper arms and lifted the body from the ground by four of its legs. "I am coming back to work on a program that will allow me to talk to the drones directly through my wristcomp."

Chapter 8

Anna stirred in her cot as she slowly woke up. Opening her eyes, she looked upon the ceiling of her tiny room and sighed deeply. She stretched under her covers, her hands bumping the walls on either side of her. After running her fingers through her hair and brushing back any stray locks clinging to her face, she pulled the covers off her naked body and opened the door, leaving her clothes behind.

Before going to sleep several hours before, she deduced that wearing her clothes to bed would only serve to increase the frequency of her laundry. Since she only had one set of clothing, fewer washes would help them last longer, and not wearing them while she slept would mean longer spans of time between washes. Although she hated the idea of wearing dirty clothes for an extended period of time, she really had no choice, at least until she found a way to return to civilization.

Stepping into the hall, Anna's eyes shot directly at Kate rounding the corner toward her.

"Good morning, Anna," she said with a hint of cheer in her voice. She stopped in her tracks and regarded the flesh-and-blood woman standing before her.

"Is there a reason why you're naked?" asked the avatar.

Groggily, Anna replied, "I just woke up, and I'm going to take a shower. No point in putting anything on just to walk 3 meters."

Silently, Kate nodded with a look of humored disbelief and walked past the blonde toward the bridge, while Anna finished her stroll to the head.

After her shower, Anna returned to the curved corridor, feeling refreshed and ready for the day though her hair was still slightly damp. She stopped outside the door to the head and looked at the door across the way where Ryan's unused clothes lay in a heap on the other side. She seriously entertained the idea of rummaging through the articles to see if she could salvage anything to wear in addition to her scant wardrobe, but a loud groan from her stomach broke her train of thought. With a slight shrug, she changed her plans and walked to the kitchen to make her breakfast.

Fifteen minutes later, Anna strode onto the bridge, eating a plate of turkey mixed with corn and rice and still not wearing a stitch of clothing. She looked up after stuffing a forkful of food into her mouth and saw that light had not returned to the landscape yet.

"Still dark outside?" she asked after swallowing her bite.

Kate, standing by the pilot's chair, looked over her shoulder and commented, "Still naked?"

Anna shrugged defensively and shot back, "You got a problem with it?"

"I'm just curious," the hologram replied. "I am not bothered by nudity. I am a computer, after all."

Smiling as she chewed and swallowed her food, Anna added, "I'm glad to hear that. If something should happen to my clothing for whatever reason, I may have to walk around like this for a short time while I make replacements.

"Besides," she continued. "It's not as if you could do the same thing."

"Actually . . ."

Anna looked up from her plate just in time to see the hologram's image instantly shed all of her clothing. The human's eyes grew wide at the sight.

"Is this better?" asked Kate with a sultry voice.

Without a change in her expression, Anna answered, "Not really."

As Kate's clothes digitally returned, she affirmed, "I can change my clothing to suit your tastes at will. I have over 500 different outfits on file that I can choose to wear at any given time."

"Five hundred?! That's quite an impressive wardrobe. Too bad I can't borrow some of those."

"Perhaps you can."

Raising an eyebrow, Anna queried curiously, "Come again?"

"I have information about a device that was recently released to the general public: a belt that generates holographic clothing."

"Holographic . . .clothing?" Anna replied skeptically.

"Yes. Originally marketed as a novelty item, a large number of celebrities and wealthy people began wearing them to make a statement against the continual harvesting of cotton, wool, and other plant fibers for making clothing. The movement increased in popularity, eventually lowering the price to where the middle class could afford to purchase hologarments of their own."

"So, do you have one of these belts here that I can look at?"

"Inventory does not have one listed, but I do have schematics for one."

Anna paused again, ate another bite of food, and asked while chewing, "Why do you have that on file?"

"I am not sure why, but I suspect that Ryan accidentally downloaded it while he was on a previous assignment."

"Maybe he had something else in mind," Anna mumbled darkly.

Kate paused and leaned closer before asking, "What was that?"

"Never mind. Let's take a look at this schematic."

A split second later, the technical readout of the belt appeared in the air between the two women. Anna furrowed her brow as she read it, pointed to a few spots, and silently mouthed several terms as she lingered on certain areas.

"This is an interesting concept," she announced a couple of minutes later. "Do you know if any issues have been reported about the hologram getting around body parts?"

"What do you mean?"

"I'm referring to the physics of beaming the light from the hologram to areas of the body that do not have line-of-sight with the projectors on the belt. I'm surprised that they would be able to get to areas like the tops of shoulders and outer sides of arms."

Kate answered after a second, "I have no such issues listed on record. Then again, I am not connected with any customer service databases that would deal with such issues."

With a nod, Anna conceded the point and looked back at the schematic, finishing her breakfast while she studied.

"If I am to build something like this," she observed while chewing her last bite of ham. "I am going to need two lenses shaped for holographic projection. I count a total of five in the ship."

"That's right, Anna."

"The three that are currently in use for the control panels at the front would be too bulky for the belt. The other two are being used by you. Although the idea of not having to worry about clothing is appealing, I don't want to lose my only friend over this.

"So, I'm going to have to rely on the clothes I have for the time being."

"I understand."

Pointing over her shoulder as the schematic dissipated, Anna said, "I'm going to take care of these dishes and then dig through Ryan's clothes. Wish me luck!"

"Good luck!" Kate called as the technician retreated from the bridge.

About twenty minutes later, Anna returned wearing dark gray sweat pants and a wrinkled white T-shirt cinched around her waist by her tool belt.

"It's not the most fashionable outfit, but it covers the important parts," resigned Anna with a shrug.

She clapped her hands and continued, "Okay, so how much longer until the eclipse ends?"

Kate looked outside for a second and answered, "About 10 hours, and then we'll have sun again for the next 29 days."

Slumping her shoulders, Anna interjected, "Yeah. Maybe that's why I haven't been sleeping very well."

"What do you mean?"

"Well," shrugged Anna. "Whenever I have tried to go to sleep before the eclipse, I'd go back to my bunk and lay down. But, I'd have a hard time going to sleep. Perhaps my mind knows that it's still daylight outside and is playing with my sleep schedule.

"But, I fell asleep a lot easier a few hours ago, and I took a nap while I was lying on top of the ship stargazing."

Kate appeared to think over her statements and answered a few seconds later, "You may be right about that. Perhaps I can find something to help you with that."

"That would be great!" beamed Anna. "Thank you.

"Now," she continued as she stepped past the avatar and sat down in the seat. "Have any of the local wildlife come any closer to us over the last several hours?"

"A couple of creatures came to the tree line directly ahead about three hours ago, but they stayed only for a few minutes before retreating back into the forest."

Anna nodded as she watched the sensor display.

"How are the drones doing?"

"While you slept, the other four that 17 sent out to locate you found us and joined with the rest."

"So, now we have 17 drones altogether?"

"Yes."

"Good!" Anna cheered. "They could really help us out around here. I have some ideas on what they can do."

"Like what?"

"First, the drones will need fuel to stay running. They run on hydrogen, just like the engines of this ship. I could recalibrate some of them to seek out hydrogen instead of what they had been mining up to this point and start collecting fuel. The only problem is that the tanks they have now are filled with the gas they collected about three weeks ago, and we have nowhere to store the hydrogen that they would collect.

"Looks like I'll need to patch up the fuel tank. But before I can do that, I will need to find a way to get underneath it to seal it all the way. I don't want to get trapped in there. So, I can either dig a trench underneath it or somehow get the ship off the ground."

Anna disappeared in her thoughts, leaving Kate to stand idly behind her. Half a minute had hardly passed, when the hologram interrupted her thoughts.

"Anna, why did you have the drones carry the creature you killed to the river?"

"Hmm?" she asked, slowly acknowledging her question. "Oh, the one that attacked me? I had to do something with it, and I didn't want it attracting any others over here."

"If anything, I would think that your shooting at it would attract more attention."

Anna shrugged and admitted, "You're probably right."

"Was it bleeding when it died?"

"No!" the blonde exclaimed. "Of course not."

"Why do you think it would have attracted other predators?"

Turning in her seat, Anna replied, "The body would surely attract other predators after it begins decomposing."

With a nod, Kate said, "True, but the body is not going to do that for a while."

Anna nodded again and asked, "What should I have done?"

Kate crossed her hands behind her back and answered, "You have been concerned about food and clothing lately. Have you not?"

"Well, yeah."

"It would seem to me that the animal you had recently slain would help you solve those problems for the immediate future. Although I can't be sure without scanning it, I would think that the meat it would provide, along with some local vegetation, would help supplement your diet. And, the animal's skin could be used for clothing after your current garments are no longer wearable."

Anna paused and considered the suggestion for a brief moment.

"That's certainly a good idea about the food. I'm sure that I could forage for plants after the eclipse has passed and check the meat to see if it is edible. But, I see a couple of problems."

Placing her hands on her hips, Kate asked with a curious look, "And, what would those be?"

"One," she noted while holding up a finger for emphasis. "I don't know how to skin an animal, let alone create leather from its carcass. And two, the river would have surely taken the body further downstream by now."

"I have basic leatherworking knowledge in my database, so I can help you with the skinning."

"YOU have leatherworking information?!" cried Anna skeptically. "Why on earth would you have that on file?"

"Survival skills," Kate flatly answered. "One never knows when it will be useful.

"As for your second point, why don't . . ."

"I could send a couple of drones out to search the river and retrieve the remains!" Anna blurted with a snap of her fingers.

"Drones 4 and 6," she ordered through her wristcomp without waiting for a response from the hologram. "Fly to the point where the body was dropped earlier and search for it along the river downstream. Return it here, once it is found."

Anna sat back and smiled to herself, relieved that she did not have to hunt down the dead predator on her own. She glanced at the sensor display and watched the drones fly away.

After a few seconds, she turned back to Kate and inquired inquisitively, "So, what other survival skills do you have on file? Hmmm?"

"Well," the avatar began, crossing her arms as she spoke. "I have basic knowledge in firecraft, first aid, fishing, foraging, hunting, leatherworking, navigation, ropes and knots, shelter building, swimming, tool making, and tracking."

"Really?" Anna responded, sounding impressed.

"Yes. The files are rarely accessed, since most humans tend to stay in or near urban environs."

"I'll be honest, Kate. I don't think I will need some of those, such as tool making. But, some of the others will come in pretty handy here, especially foraging and hunting."

"Let me know when you want to learn," the holographic woman stated. "And, I'll be happy to help you."

"Okay," Anna grinned. "Does now work for you?"

"I suppose. Where would you like to start?"

"Well," Anna remarked with mock contemplation. "Since I'll be needing it really soon, how about leatherworking?"

A little over an hour later, Anna's lesson continued inside the ship.

"WHAT?!" she cried in surprise. "What do you mean I have to pee on it?"

Kate looked up from where she knelt next to a holographic skin projected on the floor of the bridge and replied, "Since you lack the modern curing chemicals that were created centuries ago, you will need to cure the hide the old-fashioned way by applying urine to the skin."

"I am NOT dropping my pants and squatting over an animal skin!"

"What's the big deal? You don't seem to have a problem taking your pants off any other time?"

"I . . ." Anna started, pausing after taking in the other's comment. "What did you say?"

"Just a joke, Anna."

Anna visibly relaxed, smiled, and stated after a second, "Funny."

"Anyway, the problem is that I really don't want to relieve myself on the animal skin. It'll get messy and . . ."

"No!" Kate interrupted with a hint of a laugh. "You don't have to do it that way! You could collect your urine over time in a container and apply it that way."

"Really?"

After seeing Kate's nod, Anna continued, "Well, why didn't you say so? That's fine."

As the hologram shook her head in apparent amusement, Anna's wristcomp signaled an incoming message.

"Yes?"

A clipped, artificial voice responded through the channel, "Body . . . found . . . and . . . returned."

Anna cheered, "Excellent! Set it on the top of the ship."

"Acknowledged," the voice answered before she closed the link.

Turning back to Kate, she announced before rushing to the airlock, "I'm going to look at our little bounty and see how it looks now."

Chapter 9

"Okay," Anna said as she poked her head out the upper airlock. "Let's take a look at this . . . SHIT!"

Dropping back into the airlock and slapping the switch just as another living predator snapped its triple-jawed maw at her after its short charge, Anna slid down the ladder to the floor, panicking from her near-death experience. She punched the door leading to the bridge and nearly collapsed onto the floor at Kate's feet.

"Oh, Anna," Kate off-handedly stated. "I meant to tell you that I'm detecting a new life form on top of the ship."

Anna slowly lifted her gaze, her stare shooting daggers into the hologram's computer-generated heart.

"A little late on the warning, Kate!" she cried in response. "It nearly bit my head off!"

"Sorry about that. You rushed out so fast, that I didn't get a chance to warn you."

Brushing herself off after stepping out of the airlock, Anna replied as the door slid shut, "Well, feel free to stop me next time. Otherwise, I might end up being a midnight snack."

"I'll remember that. What do you propose we do, now that you have another one up there?"

Anna pondered the situation for a moment in silence. As she did, she mumbled, "How did they get a live one up there in the first place?"

"According to the video footage, the drones managed to track one down, seized it, and carried it here," Kate interjected, interrupting Anna's thoughts.

Anna answered, "Well, I really don't want to kill another, if I don't have to. I had enough trauma the first time."

Activating her wristcomp, she ordered, "Drones, let the creature go. This time, go find a DEAD body and bring it back."

"Acknowledged," the drone answered.

"Belay that, drone! Go find a dead predator like the one you are taking back and return with the dead one."

"Acknowledged."

Anna closed the channel and sighed heavily.

"Kate, I'll be right back," she said as she moved toward the door leading aft.

"Where are you going?"

As the door opened, she replied over her shoulder with a wink, "I'm going to collect some hide-curing solution."

Two hours passed before the drones returned again, during which time Anna finished her lesson on leatherworking.

"Finally!" exclaimed Anna as she ended the communication with the drone. "At least I won't have to deal with the living one that was up there a while ago. I'm glad it finally got bored and left on its own."

"And," Kate interjected. "Its current location has been tracked to 3 kilometers southwest of here. I don't think it will be returning anytime soon."

"Good," Anna nodded.

She turned toward the airlock but stopped after a step. Turning back to the hologram, she asked, "Are you sure that no living creatures are outside the ship?"

Kate answered, "I confirm. The closest living creature is 1.5 kilometers to the northwest and moving north. You should be safe."

"Okay. Where did you say that survival knife was?"

Casually pointing to a removable panel on the starboard wall, Kate said, "In there."

Anna stepped up to the panel and quickly removed it with her pry bar. Within the embedded alcove rested a shiny survival knife sheathed in black leather along with an all-weather camouflage poncho, a set of computer-enhanced binoculars, a filtering canteen, and a couple of extra power packs designed for her pistol.

"Well, well!" she remarked with a smile. "Remind me to hug a boy scout the next time I see one."

Lifting the knife out of the alcove, Anna slid it from its sheath and examined the silver blade, serrated on the back side near the handle. The grip, covered in soft, black leather, felt comfortable in her hand, making her feel as if she could hold it for hours. Replacing the knife in its holder, she placed it into one of her belt pouches and grabbed the poncho. As she did, she noticed a brown, leather knapsack hanging in the back of the locker. She regarded the container with raised eyebrows for a second before turning back to the article in hand.

The typical, green camouflage pattern that dominated the outer layer of the garment did not surprise Anna in the least, but the touch plate that blended in with the colored patch on the neckline piqued her curiosity. Pressing her thumb on the plate, she quickly drew her hand back as the color scheme shifted to various shades of tan and brown. Embarrassed by her initial reaction, she took a deep breath and touched it again, changing the coloration to white and grays. Twice more brought it through a scheme with white, gray, and black patches and then back to the green motif.

After returning the poncho to the alcove, Anna replaced the panel on the wall, silently climbed outside, and tended to her prey.

Standing over the body, she looked over the dead creature and found that she did not look forward to the task at hand. Even though the lessons Kate gave her seemed pretty easy to accomplish, the idea of plunging her hands into the remains of a creature that lived mere hours ago made her feel a bit squeamish. She glanced at the knife in her hand, clean and shiny as if it had never touched another living thing before. Looking back at the beast, she knew deep inside that its death was her fault, but the act could not be reversed. She agreed with her holographic friend that the creature needed to be slaughtered and skinned to help ensure her survival, despite her misgivings about it. And, nobody was going to do it for her. With a deep breath, Anna returned the knife to its sheath and called a couple of drones over.

"Pick up the body," she ordered while pointing at the carcass. "And, take it over to the tree line."

As she watched the drones lift the lifeless body and deliver it across the clearing, Anna sighed aloud and glanced around the dark clearing, reaffirming that no living creatures were within range. Satisfied that the coast was clear, she climbed to the ground and hustled to where the drones held the dead creature.

Within a few minutes, Anna had the body suspended in the air by the drones while they rested on the ground and proceeded to bleed the beast. The fluids drained from one of its three hind legs and spattered onto the dirt. Its stench smelled of decay and quickly assaulted her nostrils, almost driving her to the point of vomiting. She fought to resist the urge, but the scent made matters worse. Positive that the odor would attract other predators to her location, she returned to the ship to wait for the bleeding to finish.

Anna moved through the clearing at her normal pace at first. With each step, she became more nauseated with the scent of the dead blood still in her nostrils. She picked up her pace to a jog, afraid that she would retch at any second. A short moment later, she ran to the nose of the ship and knocked on the window. Inside, Kate appeared and looked at her with an expression of curiosity.

"Open the airlock!" screamed Anna.

Kate merely nodded as the sound of the airlock opening reached the human's ears. Anna bolted for the opening and climbed inside. As she reached the floor, the inside door opened for her, and she sprinted for the head.

Following Anna into the back of the ship, Kate called out, "What happened?"

Anna said nothing as she dropped to her knees in front of the toilet, all the while moaning her disgust over the situation. A split second later, her stomach gave way, and she vomited into the bowl. The avatar reached the door and watched Anna empty her guts into the toilet. After the episode subsided, Anna slowly stood, washed her face, and brushed her teeth.

"What happened out there?" asked Kate while Anna brushed.

Pausing mid-stroke, Anna glanced at the hologram out of the corner of her eye and replied, "I'm not sure if I can use the carcass. Its blood smelled so bad, that it made me sick."

Kate frowned and nodded slightly, "Perhaps the creatures here break down faster after death."

"That doesn't make sense to me," Anna interrupted. "Doesn't that depend on bacteria and other things?"

"Yes," agreed Kate. "Maybe there are more bacteria here than we realize."

Anna paused again and added before spitting, "That can't be good."

"We don't know if that is the case. We would have to take samples and study them."

"Okay," Anna nodded. "We can do that. Meanwhile, I'm going to move the body over to the river and skin it. It shouldn't take too long."

"Very good, Anna."

"That's my only towel," she thought aloud. "I'm not using that!"

She stepped toward the door and stopped in front of the computer's representative.

"Excuse me, Kate. I need to get by you."

With a smile, the hologram stepped aside and allowed Anna to pass by.

After grabbing a scrap of clothing from Ryan's old clothes, Anna returned to the airlock, climbed out, and hastily moved to the nose of the ship. Kneeling in front of the window, she hailed Kate through the wristcomp.

"Are there any creatures in the area? I'm going to move the body now."

With a nod, Kate answered, "The area's clear. Good luck!"

Several minutes later after she confirmed that the blood had drained out, she instructed the drones to move the body to the shore of the river. After Anna watched them set it down, she took a deep breath, drew the knife from its sheath, and stepped toward the carcass.

With the lessons she received from Kate based on the quadrupeds from Earth, Anna hesitated at first. The six-legged creature hanging in front of her brought the question of its alien physiology to mind, and she pondered about where to begin. After a few seconds, she decided to start like she would with a creature from her homeworld and ignore the extra set of legs. She put the blade in place and completed her first incision, when her wristcomp signaled an incoming message.

"Yes, Kate. What is it?"

"Anna," she stated. "I am detecting multiple signals approaching from the west. They are moving faster than the other creatures in the area. Sensors indicate to me that they are airborne."

With a shrug, Anna casually asked, "So, what's the big deal?"

"Every life form they come across disappears from sensors."

The statement hit Anna like a rock.

"How long until they get here?" she questioned in a serious tone.

"Their current vector takes them just south of the clearing in about 30 seconds."

Figuring that they were going to fly on the opposite side of the ship from her, Anna started to dismiss them as no possible threat. She glanced at the dead body next to her and remembered the predator's blood on the ground at the edge of the clearing. Visions of large birds of prey swarming all around the ship filled her mind.

"Oh, no!" she muttered just before sprinting into the woods, leaving the skin and sweater behind.

"What's wrong?"

"Check . . . the birds' . . . flight path!" Anna panted as she ran at full speed.

Kate responded, "Nothing has . . . correction. Their path is veering toward us now. ETA is 12 seconds."

"Tell the drones . . . to drop . . . the carcass . . . and get away!"

Suddenly, Anna tripped on something hard, hit the ground, and slid into a large root. At that second, multiple screeches filled the air ahead. Looking toward the ship, she could see the faint gleam of light off the white hull through the trees and dozens of small, dark shapes swirling around the place where the drones earlier held the creature. The percussive sounds of numerous impacts against solid wood and the ground reached her ears, telling her that they blindly attacked the source of the scent they craved by ramming into it.

Anna judged the distance between her and safety inside the ship and, despite the distance being over 20 meters, knew that she would be ripped to shreds before she even reached the vehicle. She felt that she was too close to the swarm to safely avoid them but did not want to move for fear of attracting their attention.

Or, maybe that's what she should do.

Glancing around her, Anna spotted a dead branch lying on the ground a few meters from her. She cautiously inched her way along the ground to it and pulled it in once she grabbed it. Slipping her hand into her tool belt, she retrieved her laser cutter and, using her body to obscure her actions, used it to ignite one end of the branch. She fanned the flames, coaxing them to grow a little more, returned her cutter to her belt, and slowly stood. Her stomach churned as second thoughts questioned the sanity of her current course of action. But, she felt that she could wait no longer and, after taking a deep breath, walked toward the ship.

Within seconds, the swarm turned its attention to her approach. Anna drew her pistol and fired a warning shot into the flock, hitting one of the creatures in flight and forcing the rest to scatter for a moment. They regrouped and flew straight toward her. She waved her makeshift torch back and forth in a wide arc as they converged on her. The rush of air threatened to extinguish the flames, but they continued to burn for her. She fired another shot at them, briefly dispersing them again.

The flying predators, from what she could tell as they flew around her, were about twice as big as her hand and looked very similar to the bats she remembered from Earth. Their rapid movements, combined with the darkness surrounding them, made garnering any reliable details next to impossible.

Anna waved her torch all around her as she stepped onto the front of the ship and gradually backed up over the front viewscreen to the top. The fire kept the avians at bay, but the flames appeared to be dying out. Their defiant screeches pounded at her resolve. As the torch moved away from one side of the cloud of airborne beasts, it surged closer to her, forcing her to swing back at them.

"Kate!" cried Anna at the top of her lungs. "Open the airlock!"

As she heard the telltale sound of the opening hatch, Anna stepped quicker. She fired another shot and pegged another one that dropped onto the hull and died. The group scattered for a second, giving her enough time to turn and leap into the airlock.

"Close it!" Anna bellowed as she slid down the ladder and tumbled to the floor. The hatch shut above her and, before she could get to her feet, screamed again as a sharp pain pierced her shoulder. The predator that slipped inside screeched as it tasted its first human.

Chapter 10

Anna dropped her torch and pistol and desperately grabbed for the little animal clamped to her shoulder. It flapped its wings as it tried to defend itself while feeding on its new prey, buffeting her hand as she reached for it. Unable to get a good hold on it, she rolled over and bore all her weight onto the tiny body, causing it to squeal in pain while it remained pinned under her. It bit harder into her, and she screamed again in agony. She pressed into it again and again, until it finally released its hold on her. Instantly, she leaped away from it, drew her survival knife, and plunged it into the heart of the beast before it could take flight. The creature screeched intensely, as Anna stabbed it a second and third time, until it finally ceased moving.

Dropping the knife in her hand, Anna slumped to the floor of the airlock in a fit of sobbing from the pain and stress. The airlock door slid open, and Kate looked down at her.

"Oh, my god!" the hologram cried. "Are you all right?"

The blonde woman bawled for a few seconds without a response. Finally, she asked, "Can you scan my shoulder?"

Kate nodded as she knelt at the doorway and stared at the injury.

A few seconds later, she said, "You've taken some muscle and tissue damage in your right shoulder, but nothing too serious. I do not detect any toxins or poisons in your system.

"Is there anything else I can do, Anna?"

Anna calmed down, took a deep breath, and sat up, wincing in pain as she moved.

"No," she answered. "You've done all you can do right now."

She rose to her feet in stages and eventually walked to the head, where she cleaned and dressed the wound. As she did, Kate watched her from the doorway and offered words of encouragement and support.

Cleaning the blood away from her shoulder revealed that the three puncture marks were not that big, which did not surprise her considering the size of her assailant. She continued to apply pressure to the injury, until she had properly bandaged it.

"How much longer until the eclipse ends?" Anna asked after finishing her first aid.

"Five hours and 21 minutes," replied Kate emotionlessly.

Nodding to acknowledge hearing the answer, Anna returned the first aid kit to its niche under the sink and stepped out of the head. She moved cautiously and purposefully, making sure to move her arm at the shoulder as little as possible.

Kate watched the blonde woman walk by her toward the bridge, forcing her to rush to catch up after Anna passed through the door without saying a word.

"Are you all right?" asked the hologram with concern.

Anna, after traversing the bridge and flopping down into the pilot's seat, finally answered, "I don't want to go outside again. At least not until the sun has come out again."

Nodding, Kate commented, "I can understand why."

Peering at the sensors display, Anna watched the cloud of airborne predators move eastward away from the clearing and eliminate two more unknown creatures.

"Is it just me?" she wondered aloud gloomily. "Or, does it seem like every creature on this moon wants to kill me?"

Kate circled around the chair and crouched down in front of Anna. With a sincere look of compassion on her face, she stated, "It sure seems like it right now. But, we can't be too sure, given the little knowledge we have of the wildlife of this world. If it's anything like

Earth, I'm sure that it has its share of herbivorous creatures that don't want to eat you."

A sideways smile broke through Anna's pouting face as she said, "Yeah. You're probably right."

"I know I'm right," Kate reassured. "Come on! We need to get your mind off all of this for a while. Want to continue that cribbage game we started? I saved it at where we left off."

With a nod, the ladies moved to the middle of the floor and continued their game without any further disturbances. As their diversion progressed, Anna's mood gradually lightened to where the only reminder of her incident was the dull pain in her shoulder and the bandage that masked the small wound.

* * * * *

"Anna," Kate said, breaking the silence that ensued while the blonde studied the backgammon board floating in front of her. Anna, sitting cross-legged on the floor and resting her chin in her hand, shifted her eyes from the board to the hologram's face.

"Sunlight levels outside have increased by 5% over the last 2 minutes."

Anna's face lit up with the news, the first scrap of news about the outside she heard in the last several hours. Without saying a word, she scrambled to her feet and dashed to the forward window. Leaning on the unadorned console, she looked outside at the landscape, still mostly dark but a shade lighter than before. Her face gave a look of giddy anticipation as if she had never seen a sunrise. Affording a glance at the sensor display, she noticed that no life signs appeared within range anymore.

"Where did they go?" Anna reflected softly.

Kate stepped forward and asked, "What?"

Pointing at the holographic panel, Anna answered, "The wildlife. They're gone."

"Hmmm," the avatar remarked. "They probably returned to where they were before the eclipse began."

"Well, yeah. But, where specifically do you think they went? Do they retreat into caves? Do they do something that makes them undetectable to our sensors? What?"

Kate shrugged, "I don't know."

"Neither do I," added Anna. "Maybe that's something I'll have to look into sometime in the future."

Stepping away from the front of the ship, she continued, "I know that I want to get out there and look around a bit more."

Anna stopped halfway toward the airlock, turned back to face her artificial friend, and amended while casually extending her hand, "At least to get an idea of what's out there."

"Sure. These sensors can only show so much."

"While I'm exploring, I can check out that area I discovered before I crashed here and see what's over there."

Kate cocked her head to the side and stepped toward her with a look of worry.

"Are you sure that's wise, Anna? That area is over 5 kilometers away through thick woods. If anything should happen to you . . ."

"If anything should happen to me," Anna interrupted, waving away the comment. "Then, I can be picked up by the drone that I take along and be brought back here."

Kate leaned back on her leg and crossed her arms, skeptical of the plan.

"Besides," coaxed the mechanic. "I'm not leaving immediately. I am not going to go until after the pain in my shoulder subsides somewhat. And, I want to plot my course and pack supplies before I even think of setting foot away from the ship."

"Well," the hologram hesitantly uttered. "Okay."

Anna smiled.

"But, you call me at the first sign of trouble!"

"Kate," warned the blonde woman. "You are starting to sound like my mother."

Balking at the comment, Kate replied defensively, "I just want to make sure nothing happens to you. Rule number 1, you know."

Anna sighed, "Yeah, I know. Part of me wishes I could take you with me."

Pointing to Anna's wristcomp, Kate answered, "You will."

Several minutes later as the area grew brighter, Anna emerged through the top airlock and surveyed the top of the ship. Several skeletons that appeared to be from the swarm of small predators littered the hull around the hatch, picked clean of any flesh and giving a gruesome appearance to the ship. Now visible in the daylight, she saw that their mouths appeared to be quite similar to the one attached to the larger creature that stalked the ship several hours before. The three appendages that used to be wings looked like nothing more than long-fingered hands on short, stubby arms. Small pools of blood around the skeletons had dried over the last few hours and now clung to the white hull plating like spilled wine.

As Anna placed her hands on the hull to lift herself out of the airlock, she heard a light peck against the ship not far from her. She instantly turned in that direction but saw nothing there. A couple of seconds later as she wondered about the source of the sound, something cool and wet tapped her cheek. Wiping off the liquid, she looked at her finger and realized that it was merely water. Glancing skyward, she realized that the dark clouds rolling in finally brought rain, which grew stronger by the second. With a slight frown, she climbed back down and closed the airlock again.

Walking back into the bridge, Anna heard the rate of the raindrops pelting against the hull rapidly increase, and the sound sent her mind back to her childhood for a moment, summoning visions of her living in the high-rise apartment with her parents in Seattle. Rain was not uncommon, but she spent many afternoons staring out the window at the gray skies, watching the raindrops smack against the window before her face and fall to the streets below.

"Anna," Kate said a moment later, interrupting her daydream.

Snapping back to reality, the blonde shook her head slightly and apologized, "Sorry. I was just reminiscing."

Without another word, Anna crossed the bridge and sat down in front of the control panels. She made a few adjustments to the sensor display, shifting the view to include the cloud bank passing overhead.

"Well," she sighed as she watched the large, gray mass slowly advance across the area. "Looks like it may last a while."

Kate stepped behind the chair and asked, "Are you going to stay in during the storm?"

Shaking her head, Anna replied while she stood, "No. I don't want to waste anymore time. I'm going to go retrieve the skin and sweater I left by the river."

Returning to the storage locker, she pulled the camouflage poncho out and slipped it over her head while she walked to the airlock again.

Emerging outside, Anna looked around to see if anything was lurking nearby, despite the fact that the sensors already told her that she was by herself again. Satisfied that the coast was clear, she climbed out and hiked to where she had left the animal skin.

Shock and disappointment hit Anna when she returned to the rapids. Shreds of the sweater lay strewn along the muddy bank, and only small chunks of the hide remained, scattered about around the tree where she left it. Crouching down and picking up one of the leftover pieces of the furry leather, she looked it over, observing the holes and gouges all over the lump of flesh. Feelings of anger and frustration welled up within her, anger at the flying creatures she suspected were responsible for the damage and anger at herself for leaving it behind. She hurled the useless piece into the woods and, after hearing it hit against a tree several meters away, winced as the pain in her shoulder reminded her that she was still injured. She waited a few seconds for the pain to subside before returning to the ship.

"The skin is gone," Anna informed Kate as she walked onto the bridge, leaving the poncho to dry in the airlock. "It appears that those pests ravaged it during the last part of the eclipse."

"Oh, no!" the hologram exclaimed. "I didn't think that . . ."

"Neither did I. I guess they will go after any kind of animal matter they find. The sweater I used to mop up the blood was ripped apart, too."

Kate's face appeared sad as she consoled, "I'm so sorry, Anna."

Anna shrugged and stated, "Nothing I can do about it now. If I want another one, I would have to hunt another of the creatures during the next eclipse."

She stopped and thought for a second before asking, "Kate, when is the next eclipse expected to happen?"

"According to your survey," Kate answered. "The next eclipse, and every one after that, will occur every 29.79 days."

Anna raised an eyebrow while she considered the data for a moment.

"And, how long will the eclipse last each time?"

"The eclipse will last for 0.99 days."

"So, we have 28.8 days of sunlight to do whatever we want. Right?"

"Yes. That's correct."

"Just like clockwork," Anna thought aloud before adding, "Okay. I'm going to start gathering supplies for my little hike after the rain stops."

The storm passed a few hours later, reducing the heavy rain to little more than a light mist wafting through the region. Venturing out wearing the poncho again and armed with her pistol and survival knife, Anna wandered into the forest to forage for food.

Several hours later, various leaves and berries filled the used MRE pouches carried in Anna's belt. Feeling more and more confident with each successive find, she figured that she could procure enough food in the area surrounding the crash site to sustain her for months, if not years.

As she knelt next to another bush bearing dark blue berries, Anna swept her hand scanner past the closest clump. A few seconds into the scan, a glint of light caught her eye a short distance away. She ceased the scan prematurely, stood, and cautiously approached the source of the sparkle, her hand resting on the handle of her pistol. Despite her careful moves and soft footfalls, she cringed with each of her first few steps, as she heard the grass rustle beneath her feet.

Stopping a few meters away from where she saw the reflection, she stopped and stared at the long, metal shaft lying in the grass. Following its length, her eyes found other components that she recognized as . . .

"A landing strut!" she exclaimed under her breath as she rushed forward to it. Dropping to her knees next to the object, she lightly rubbed her hands along the metal rod. Cool to the touch, feeling the metal under her fingertips sent shivers down her spine. Her gaze panned up and down its length, assessing the damage it received on impact, and confirmed that the only damage it received was at the top where it was ripped from the ship during its descent.

Grinning from ear to ear, Anna called through her wristcomp, "Kate, dispatch a drone to my current position. I have something for it to pick up."

A few minutes later, one of the mining drones glided through the trees, barely able to fit between them, and engaged its vertical thrusters a few meters away to float in place and wait for instructions.

"Drone," Anna commanded via the wristcomp. "Pick up the landing strut and return it to the ship."

"Acknowledged," it replied through the channel in a monotone, metallic voice.

The drone maneuvered above the strut, extended its grasper arm, and grabbed the landing support. When it attempted to lift its cargo, the strut did not budge. As the drone increased its thrust, Anna immediately recognized the strain being exerted on the arm.

"Stop!" she cried at it, relief flooding through her as the thrust decreased dramatically a split second later.

Returning to the wristcomp, Anna paged Kate again and stated, "Kate, send three more drones out here. I overestimated the drone's strength outside a zero-g environment."

"Understood," the avatar replied. "Three more are on their way."

After waiting a few more minutes, the other drones arrived and, together with the first one, lifted the heavy landing gear from the ground and slowly carried it back to the ship.

"I might have some issues with the drones, if I am going to use them to help repair the ship," she commented to herself while she followed them. "Not sure if I can do anything about it, either."

Anna shrugged the idea away, vowing to look into it later as time permits. She looked at the food she had gathered, smiled, and knew that she was ready to make her final preparations before trekking into the woods on her personal mission.

Chapter 11

"Are you sure this is a good idea?" Kate asked, while Anna stuffed a couple of used MRE bags into the knapsack she pulled from the storage locker.

Anna remarked with a smile, amused a little by the computer's concern, "This spot that I'm going to has been nagging at me ever since I discovered it. If I don't do this, I will always wonder."

"What if you get hurt or killed?"

"If I get killed, then you don't have to worry about me anymore. If I get hurt, I'll just call a drone to come get me. Honestly, Kate. It's no big deal."

Crossing her arms, Kate tapped her foot silently against the floor and sternly added, "I really must insist this is not a good idea. You should be making sure you have enough food supplies to last until you are rescued."

Anna, not appreciating being treated like a baby sister, turned around and faced the hologram with a slightly annoyed look on her face.

"Your concern has been noted," she chided and continued after a heavy sigh. "Look, I appreciate what you are trying to do. But, I have to do this. No, I need to do this. I need to get out and find out more about what's out there, if I can increase my chances of survival here. The trip there and back will allow me to learn more about the land, the plants, and maybe find out where the animals went. Staying cooped up here will not do that. With all of the survival knowledge in your database, one would think that you would know that.

"So, I'm going," Anna concluded. "And honestly Kate, there's really nothing you can do to stop me."

Silence fell between the two ladies for a long moment, during which time Anna stood firm and refused to back down. Finally, Kate dropped her head and stared at the other's feet.

"You're right. I'm sorry," Kate apologized.

Anna took a deep breath and, as her face relaxed, replied, "It's okay. I understand. But, I . . ."

"You have to do this," interrupted the hologram. "I know. Go, good luck, and God speed."

A smile formed on Anna's lips, relieved to finally have the computer's understanding.

"I really feel as if we should hug or something," the blonde said, prompting Kate to smile in return.

Without another word, Anna stepped into the airlock, waved goodbye to the hologram, and closed the hatch behind her.

Reaching the river several minutes later, she consulted the map saved on her wristcomp, confirmed her course, and looked at the rapids foaming in front of her.

The water level had risen a little from the recent rainstorm, covering the rocks that served as her bridge to the other side. Although she could still see them through the clear water, the faster current made the once simple crossing more treacherous than before, and she knew it would not be smart to cross without some form of support. She turned and scanned the tree line with her eyes, hoping to find a branch or some other object she could use to steady herself against the rushing water. Nothing was in immediate sight.

Anna stepped back into the woods and searched for anything that might help her. Eventually finding a dead branch on the ground and finding it pretty sturdy, she returned to the rapids. Back at the bank, she removed her tool belt, folded it, and stuffed it into her knapsack, taking care that nothing could fall out after sealing the belt inside.

Bracing herself with the stick, she stepped carefully onto the rocks, testing her weight on each rock before taking another step forward. She felt the tug of the flow at her feet but fought hard to keep her footing. The stick seemed to help her and gave her more confidence with each move she made.

Halfway across, she heard a sharp crack, barely audible over the roar of the rapids. Looking down to find the source and squinting against the mist spraying in her face, she tried to find what snapped for only a second, before the branch in her hands broke near the bottom. With her support gone, Anna dropped like a stone into the river.

A second later, Anna bumped against the rocks just before breaking the surface of the river, gasping for air. The rush of the water flow threatened to push her over the rocks, making her grab for something to anchor herself. The river, deeper than she expected, forced her to tread water to stay afloat. Steady against the rocks, she got her bearings and walked hand-over-hand to the opposite shore.

After climbing onto the bank, Anna flopped down on her back for a moment to catch her breath. Dripping wet from head to toe, she fought the temptation to return to the ship, dry her clothes, and try again. But, she realized that she might end up in the same situation as before and saw no point in taking the risk.

A few seconds later, one of the drones appeared above the trees and coasted down to float a few meters away from her over the river. For a moment, it appeared to be staring at her. Sheepishly, Anna smiled and waved at the drone, but it merely remained in place.

Touched that Kate would send a drone to check up on her, Anna got to her feet. After staring at it for a few more seconds, she gently shooed it away with both hands. Yet, it still did not move. Growing impatient, she stamped her foot and stiffly pointed back at the ship. A few more seconds passed, and the drone finally flew away.

Determined more than ever, Anna vowed to push onward, despite the perils she might face ahead. Before continuing, she removed her clothes, one garment at a time, and wrung them out. They still clung to her body after putting them back on, but she felt confident that they would dry faster because of it and hoped they would be dry by the time she reached her destination. Her boots proved to be the hardest to dry and resorted to trudging forward in them.

About half an hour later after reaching the fork in the river and following the smaller river feeding into it, Anna stopped to test the water in the tributary. Finding that it was safe to filter, she withdrew her canteen from the knapsack to fill it. As she dipped it into the water, she thanked the powers that be for the knapsack being waterproof and protecting her precious tools. Upon seeing movement out of the corner of her eye, she froze.

On the other side of the river several dozen meters upstream, Anna caught sight of a dark green animal stepping up to the bank and lowering its long-necked head to the water. As its triple-split snout opened to drink, its head shifted slightly as if adjusting to the weight of its thick, curled horns framing its head. Although it sported six legs like the original predator she fought, the two legs on top of its body seemed smaller than the ones on which it stood. Its long, thin tail whipped through a tuft of grass behind it. The three eyes circling its muzzle seemed to be a little further back on its head and faced outward instead of forward.

Anna stared at the strange beast for a long moment, observing its every move. It lapped the water from the running stream with a long, tapered tongue that shot in and out of its mouth, paying no mind to the intruder that knelt downstream. For this moment, the world seemed at peace.

While she remained still, Anna finally noticed the chirping sounds that filled the air. Although she did not see them, the idea that some form of bird living in the open brought a gentle smile to her face. She found the small reminder of home comforting.

Suddenly, the animal raised its head but did not move from its spot. One of its eyes, from Anna's perspective, was trained on her, watching her in return, waiting for any threatening move. For several seconds, the two studied each other in silence, half expecting the other to take some sudden action. Finally, the untamed beast bolted away into the woods, bounding on four of its six legs as it retreated to the safety of the forest.

Anna sighed, satisfied with the tranquil moment, and finished filling her canteen. After capping the container and replacing it back on her tool belt, she wondered why Kate had not called her to inform her of the life sign in her vicinity. She toggled the switch on her wristcomp to activate the holographic screen, but it did not respond. She pressed it again, her face starting to show her worry, but the screen still did not activate.

"Oh, god!" she cried softly as she unstrapped it from her wrist, held it in front of her, and then lifted it to her ear. She listened for a second but heard nothing coming from the device. As she worried that it had perhaps been dashed against the rocks when she fell in the river, her hand began to feel a warm wetness on it. Pulling her hand away, she saw the water dripping out of her wristcomp into her palm.

"I thought these things were watertight," she said to herself, just before shaking the rest of the water out of it. Cursing herself for not putting it in her knapsack with her tool belt, she studied the outer casing but found no evidence of any damage.

"Perhaps some water seeped through the seam," mumbled Anna while continuing to stare at it. "Makes sense, considering that's how it came out."

Mentally noting that she needed to examine it further after returning to the ship, she looped it securely around her belt and set off on her hike again.

After a few steps, she stated with a smile, "Bet Kate's freaking out right now."

Almost an hour later, Anna climbed up a small hill alongside a narrow, cascading waterfall and stopped at the bank overlooking a lake that appeared to be several kilometers across. The surface of the water appeared to be calm and a clear blue that reflected the white clouds floating overhead. More trees lined the opposite shore, giving the appearance that the lake had been dropped into the middle of the forest. With the view of the blue-tinted gas giant looming in the sky ahead of her, she felt the view was truly breathtaking.

After enjoying the vista for a few minutes, Anna wondered how she missed her destination. According to her calculations, the site should have been about half a kilometer downstream from the lake. She gently lifted the wristcomp up with a couple of fingers and thumbed the switch to activate the screen, but it still did not turn on. Figuring that it probably still needed to dry a little more, she decided to take a break.

Spying a stretch of grass along the coast not far from the river, she leisurely strolled to the bank. Setting the knapsack on the ground, she stripped her damp clothes off, laid them flat on the grass, and stretched out next to them. The warm rays of the sun felt good on her skin, and she smiled as she closed her eyes and laid her head back.

Anna's mind wandered while she reclined in the soft grass, thinking about the creature she discovered earlier and how its actions reminded her of a deer that she had seen in a movie as a child. Events surrounding that image returned to her, helping her recollect the Saturday afternoon she spent with her parents visiting a local theater and playing in the park after the movie.

Anna stirred from her unexpected slumber a while later. She sat up on her elbows and looked around, taking a few seconds to remember where she was. Spying the wristcomp looped around her tool belt, she leaned over and pressed the button to activate the screen. To her disappointment, the holographic display still did not appear. Scratching her head as she unfastened the wrist device from the belt, she lifted it to eye level and gave it a scrutinizing look. She shook it slightly and heard no water inside. Thinking for a second, Anna pulled a thin bolt from one of her pouches and pressed the inset Reset button on the wristcomp's underside. A split second later, it signaled an incoming message.

"Yes?" she answered as she pressed the button.

"Anna!" cried Kate. "Where have you been?!"

Rubbing the rest of the sleep from her eyes, the nude woman replied, "Sorry. I dozed off. How long have you been calling me?"

"I've been trying to contact you for three hours now, when I lost your signal! Are you okay?"

"Yeah, I'm fine," Anna stated as she checked her clothes, finding them drier but not completely done. "The wristcomp went out after I fell into the river. It must have recently finished drying, because it worked after a reset."

"I'm glad to hear that. Did you encounter a life form earlier?"

"Yep! It posed no threat and reminded me of a deer from back home, except it was green and had the extra legs like the first animal we met."

"I see," Kate commented.

While Anna slipped her slightly wet sports bra over her head, she said, "Can you locate me on sensors?"

"Yes, I have your location at the shore of the lake to the west. Is that correct?"

"That's where I am! I overshot the site. But now that the wristcomp is back online, I should be able to backtrack and find it without any problems. Go ahead and link the ship's sensor readout to my wristcomp. I'm going to start heading that way."

A while later after Anna had finished dressing and walked downstream, she found a narrow stretch of the river that she crossed with little difficulty. Referencing the map again, she figured that she stood about 300 meters upstream from the locale she sought. Drawing her sidearm, she stepped into the woods toward her goal.

With each step closer to her destination, Anna felt more nervous with anticipation, not knowing what to expect when she got there. Part of her believed that she would not find anything at all, confirming the station's computer's suspicion that the imager on her old utility skiff merely recorded a reflection off of the river. But, perhaps she would find something else, like some piece of space junk that fell into the moon's gravity well. In either case, she confirmed that the very spot would be over the long hill that she approached.

Anna climbed up the steep surface and stopped cold as she gazed in astonishment at the area before her.

Chapter 12

Barely visible through the trees, Anna stared in awe at the stone pyramid erected in the middle of the forest. Constructed in sized layers that reminded her of those built by the Aztecs, the dark gray structure stood several stories high with vines clinging all over the outside. Located around the roofed structure at the top were four thin obelisks, one at each point of the top floor, which rose defiantly into the forest canopy. The peaks of the obelisks appeared to be made of a bright silver metal.

"That's it!" she whispered in reverence while staring at the pyramid's summit.

Anna looked at the ground and found that what she thought to be a long hill was in fact a stone wall that, despite being partially buried under the sod, framed the plaza that surrounded the large pyramid in the center. Stalks of grass grew tall between the large, flat stones that paved the ground leading to the pyramid and the smaller buildings encircling it. Judging from the amount of growth around the structure, the area appeared to have been unoccupied for quite some time.

Anna studied her immediate surroundings again before moving cautiously toward the pyramid. The sounds from the native birds seemed more distant, almost as if they stayed clear of the ancient buildings. Deciding not to take the apparent peaceful situation for granted, she gripped her pistol tightly, keeping it ready.

The uneventful move to the closest structure, a small, one-story stone building lacking a roof, set Anna's mind at ease for a few seconds before she stopped to examine the ancient construction. The architecture was simple and reminded her of ruins she had seen in school holoprograms. Something about this structure was different, but she could not put her finger on it.

Anna passed a couple more of the small buildings on her way to the middle of the compound, both of which were built much like the first one she had passed. Finding nothing inside the first, she mostly ignored them and focused on the stairs leading up the side of the central building.

Finally reaching the bottom of the stairs, Anna looked up the length of the flight leading to the top of the pyramid. The stonework, appearing crisp and new from the wall where she first saw it, betrayed its age to her, its edges becoming smooth over time from erosion. The steps were cracked, creating pockmarks and small holes in some places. The glyphs carved into the banisters on each side of the stairs mirrored the rest of the structure, blurred as a result of wind erosion. Anna glanced at the carvings again, deciding to study them later, and began her ascent.

Several minutes later, Anna reached the top. Sitting down on the top step to catch her breath, she surveyed the area again while she rested. Through the trees, she could hardly make out the river that flowed by. She looked over her shoulder at the top of the pyramid again for a second and then back at the surrounding forest. Pondering the scenery, she thought it odd that the trees in this area seemed so much taller than the ones around her ship, almost as if some outside force influenced their growth rate.

Catching her second wind, Anna stood and strode to the entrance leading inside. After looking through the open doorway leading inside for a few seconds, she turned on her flashlight and entered the pyramid. The darkness within descended upon her almost immediately when she set foot through the doorway as if it was a living entity, so much so that it blocked out all ambient sunlight after the first few meters. Only the beam from her flashlight cutting through the oppressive darkness allowed her to see ahead, causing her to feel a bit uneasy as she delved deeper inside.

From her limited observations, the room was vacant with the sole exception of a stone outcropping on the wall opposite the entrance. The item, extending only a quarter of a meter from the wall, appeared to be nothing more than an unadorned stone beam that tapered to a flat edge.

Anna walked to the odd beam and studied it for a brief moment, surmising that, if whoever created the pyramid conducted rituals like the Aztecs did many years ago, the purpose of this particular item must have served some mysterious purpose that eluded her. With her flashlight guiding her eyes, she examined its entire length, until she found a seam in the wall around the shaft. Deciding to test the beam, she gently pulled down and found that it did move rather easily. Moving it further toward the floor, she heard an audible click and witnessed a portion of the floor drop and slide open, revealing a stone staircase leading down into the pyramid.

With a broad smile on her face, Anna walked down the stairs into a small room directly below the house at the peak of the building. Using the light she carried, she quickly surveyed the room. Finding it to be roughly the same size as the previous chamber, this one was at least decorated a little more. A few tall pottery urns stood in the corners of the room, but many more appeared to have been present but are now shattered remains all over the floor.

The wall, decorated with murals of various plants and animals, intrigued Anna more than the pottery. Many of the plants depicted pictures of familiar-looking grains and bizarre vegetables in woven baskets. Despite the hairline cracks in some of the murals, the images remained mostly intact but had faded badly over the span of time since they were initially created.

In the middle of the side wall, the doorway leading into the darkness beyond beckoned her to continue. Passing through took her to a corridor that established the perimeter of the level and eventually took her around to another set of stairs leading further down. According to her estimates, these steps were directly below the outer staircase. Seeing nothing barring her way, she took a deep breath and pushed onward.

The chamber she entered at the bottom of the stairs was much larger than the one before, almost big enough to house the initial room she had first entered at the top of the ziggurat. The walls that lined this room were adorned much in the same manner as the one above, but the murals here depicted different scenes. Although the pictures here were as badly faded as the previous ones, one particular scenario captured her attention almost immediately.

On the far side of the room near the doorway, glittering in the light from her flashlight appeared to be a metallic object embedded in the wall that appeared to be gold. Her eyes locked on the artifact, Anna crossed the room and examined it. The item at first inspection seemed to be nothing more than a gold spearhead attached to a thin wooden pole extending into the tiny alcove in the wall from behind the stones. Curious as to why such a thing would have been placed here, she stepped back a few paces and surveyed the wall around it. Within seconds, her eyes widened at her newest discovery. The spearhead aligned with an illustration of a spear being held by a creature she had never seen before.

The individual in the picture appeared to be a lifesize being with three arms and three legs arranged in much the same fashion as the animals she had so far encountered. It had light brown skin and appeared rather muscular under the dark blue leather it wore. Its head, or its close approximation infused into the top of its body, sported a mouth at the very top locked in a tight-lipped grimace and two eyes below its orifice, spread out in such a way that Anna deduced the existence of a third eye facing the other direction.

Anna stared at the image for a long moment, until the impact of the flashlight against the stone floor broke her trance. Glancing numbly at her only light source on the floor for a second, she cursed herself as she retrieved it. Returning her gaze to the mural, she studied it for a moment longer before activating her wristcomp.

"Kate," Anna called through the device. A second later, she heard the avatar's voice, barely understandable as the message came through garbled and riddled with static.

"Kate, can you hear me?"

The sounds of static filled the chamber for a couple of seconds before the signal finally cut off.

"Damn!" she whispered as she shut down the holographic screen. Turning on her heel, Anna marched back up the stairs, retracing her path until she received a clear signal again at the base of the pyramid.

"Kate," she said as she attempted to call her ship again. "Do you read me?"

Behind minimal static, Kate replied, "I can read you now. What did you find?"

"You wouldn't believe me if I told you. I am standing at the base of a pyramid."

"A pyramid?" asked the hologram skeptically. "Are you sure?"

Anna snapped back, "Yeah, pretty sure…"

After a second's pause, Kate said, "Sorry. What kind is it?"

Turning to look at it as she talked, Anna related, "It's a kind of step pyramid. It reminds me of what the Aztecs built in ancient Central America."

"Intriguing. Do you have any idea who might have built it?"

"That's the thing," Anna stated with a smile. "I'm not sure, but I don't think it was human."

Hesitantly, Kate asked, "How do you know that?"

With excitement in her voice, Anna said as she hopped in place, "I found these pictures on the wall inside, and they . . ."

"You went inside?!" cried Kate. "That was dangerous, Anna!"

"Well . . ."

"You could have fallen into a trap or gotten hurt inside . . ."

"Yes, but . . ."

"How would you get assistance from a drone, if you are stuck somewhere . . ."

"WOULD YOU SHUT UP AND LISTEN TO ME?!"

The following silence calmed the irritated expression on Anna's face.

"Thank you," she finally stated. "Inside the pyramid is a picture on the wall that depicts a 3-armed, 3-legged alien holding a spear."

Kate interrupted, "Technically speaking if this is their world, then you are the alien."

"Semantics!" Anna scolded.

"But, don't you see the significance of this?! This is the first piece of solid evidence of a sentient species not originating from Earth!"

"Anna . . ."

Rambling on, Anna continued animatedly, "Sure, we've got humans, dolphins, and whales. Some people joke about white mice, but I don't buy that crap."

"Anna . . ."

"But up until now, we thought it was just us out here. This is amazing!"

"Anna, have you taken a moment to consider that they might have died out?"

Kate's quandary hit her like a rock smashing through plate glass, and the resulting silence sobered her up instantly.

"Wh . . . what do you mean?"

"The pyramid that you have been recklessly exploring, even though it is positive proof of non-human intelligent life, may be all that is left of a species that has long been extinct."

As Kate continued, Anna's elation dissipated almost as quickly as it had filled her moments earlier.

"Besides, your scouting mission around the gas giant revealed no evidence of an existing civilization on the surface of the moon to indicate that an intelligent life form currently lives here. With that information, a logical conclusion would be that the only form of intelligence living on this moon right now would be you."

Looking at the ground at her feet, Anna replied with obvious disappointment, "I suppose you're right."

"I am sorry, Anna. But now that you know what is at that location, you should head back and continue working on the ship."

"No."

Kate paused for a second before asking over the channel, "No?"

"I want to check out the rest of the pyramid first," Anna answered, glancing over her shoulder as she spoke.

"Anna . . ."

"It shouldn't take too long. Besides, I've already gone through half of it, and it's not that big. Really, how long could it take?"

"Anna, you shouldn't . . ."

Kate's objections were cut off mid-sentence, due to Anna closing the channel and shutting down the holographic screen.

"I'll be okay," she whispered just before turning and climbing the stone steps again, all the while ignoring the chime coming from her wristcomp.

A few minutes later, Anna returned to the spot where she found the gold spearhead in the wall. As expected, nothing had changed, so she decided to move onward.

Stepping through the doorway and following the corridor around, she passed through a long, narrow room that seemed to hold no purpose in her mind. The only objects within were metal shafts extending from floor to ceiling that she deduced were from the obelisks on top. The hall on the other end took her to a set of steps leading to the next floor down. As she descended, she deliberated over the purpose of the metal beams penetrating deep into the building.

The landing below opened to a room much smaller than all of the others she had previously entered. Barely able to stand fully on the floor without brushing her shoulders against the walls, she looked at the door blocking her path merely half a meter in front of her. Although similar in appearance to the other doorways she passed through before, this one appeared to be sealed shut. Unlike the other doors, this one had half a dozen stones protruding out from the wall on each side.

Sitting on the steps, Anna puzzled over the door for several minutes. She believed the doorway to be rigged to require the stones to be manipulated in some way to open. How and in what order evaded her, and nothing around her provided any form of clue. She remembered hearing stories back on Earth of tomb robbers being killed by such doors trapped with falling stone slabs or poison needles, and she feared that the same might be true here. Not wanting to fall prey to an ancient security system, she made her way back upstairs and returned to the room with the golden spearhead.

Anna pored over the faded pictures, checking every detail for some indication on how to proceed. For several minutes, nothing came to the forefront of her mind to tell her she found her answer, and she was ready to give up and search elsewhere. But, her eyes fell upon the spearhead again, and she noticed the detailing engraved in the metallic weapon. On the surface was a doorway with three asymmetrically-placed circles around it. With a smile, she memorized their positions and hurried back to the door at the foot of the stairs.

Standing before the stone portal, she grabbed the stone at the first location and pushed it into the wall with some effort, followed quickly by the second and third stones. She stepped back and waited for the door to open. Several seconds passed, and nothing happened. Finally, she heard a click. The smile on her face quickly changed to horror, and a scream tore from her mouth as she fell through the trap door that opened beneath her feet.

Chapter 13

Anna slowly awoke and opened her eyes. At least, she thought she opened her eyes. She felt her eyelids slide up. She blinked a few times, but the only thing that changed in her vision was the appearance of the faint blue dots glowing from her left shoulder.

"Great!" she snarled as she realized that she was immersed in total darkness.

With a heavy sigh, Anna moved to get up, when the searing pain shot through her leg, driving her back to the dirt on which she laid. Screaming in agony, she grasped her lower leg and felt the fractured bone under her muscles. Fortunately, she did not feel any blood as she attempted to pull her pants leg up to her knee. But, the pain was almost unbearable after the first tug, forcing her to abandon the effort.

Fighting back the tears, Anna willed the pain away with little success, but it was enough to help her concentrate on assessing the rest of her situation. She activated her wristcomp's screen and, using the low amount of light it generated, looked around her. Several of her tools laid scattered in the dirt around her, including her flashlight that sat just an arm's-length away. She stretched out, doing her best to ignore the pain surging in her calf, and grabbed the end of the metal handle. Grimacing through the pain at her small victory, she dragged the flashlight to her and turned it on.

Sweeping the bright beam of light around her, Anna quickly determined that she now sat in a large cavern somewhere under the pyramid. Looking up revealed nothing but a gray, rocky ceiling. However, she found the opening in the side wall through which she entered and fell a distance of what she estimated to be over 10 meters.

Anna gathered her tools, dusted them off, and returned them to the pouches on her belt. While she did, she could not help but think about her broken leg. The idea of the condition in which her leg may be sickened her, and she knew that she would have to do something about it if she was to find a way out of the cave.

The thought of getting out reminded Anna of the promise she had made with Kate about calling for help if she needed it. She turned on the communicator and called the ship, only to receive static as her response. Glumly, she shut down the wristcomp and returned her attention to her leg.

Gingerly, Anna checked over her leg to find the point of fracture, wincing each time she pressed too hard. Finally locating the source of her pain, she realized that she would need medical attention to mend her leg. If she was back on the mining station, she would be carted off to the infirmary and have the bones stitched together and be back on her feet within a day. The way she looked at it now, she figured that she would be bedridden for several weeks. Even then, she could not be sure that she would walk normally again.

Remembering her first aid training from many years back, Anna looked around for something that could act as a splint. Her initial scan of the area revealed only small rocks and dirt, none of which proved to be of any use to her. But, she searched out a little farther to find what appeared in the dimmer light as a skeleton piled against the far wall of the cavern. Seeing several bones that would work for her purposes, she decided to find a way over there.

After a few deep breaths, she looked down her leg, untied her boot, and slowly pushed it off her foot, screaming when the pain intensified until the footwear had cleared her heel. Anna removed the knapsack from her back, stuffed the unused boot inside, and rested her injured leg on it, doing everything in her power to keep the leg as still as possible while she did. She looped the shoulder straps around her leg to secure it in place, returned her flashlight to its slot on her tool belt while making sure that it stayed on, and pulled the survival knife from its sheath. Taking a deep breath, she stabbed the knife into the ground toward the distant skeleton and pulled herself through the dirt, grunting from pain and the effort the entire way.

Several minutes later after hauling herself over rocks and mud, Anna collapsed next to the bones that she desperately sought to reach. With her muscles sore from pulling her weight across a couple dozen meters of rough terrain, the thought of moving again anytime within the next few minutes repulsed her.

Catching her breath at last, Anna mustered the strength to roll over and examine the skeletal remains next to her. Most of the bones were too small or too thin, but she did salvage a couple of long, thick bones that resembled human femurs. Lopping the bulbous ends off with her laser cutter, she set them next to her leg on the knapsack. Lacking something to tie them against her leg, she dialed down the power of the laser cutter and carefully cut her pants leg off just below the knee of her broken leg, doing her best to not look at the apparent swelling. Slicing the material lengthwise into several strips, she created her splint, fighting against the pain as much as possible by biting down on the handle of her survival knife. Despite her effort to resist, she screamed as she worked.

Anna's painful shriek, despite being muffled by the knife handle, echoed throughout the cavern for several seconds after she attempted to set the bone back in place and splint her leg. The agony had diminished enough where she could bear it with only a little effort, but she knew that she had to get back to Kate as quickly as she could move to give herself the best possible treatment.

After returning her knife to its proper place, Anna carefully rose to her feet, using the rock wall behind her to help support her weight. Although she could stand on her feet, the pain returned if she bore too much weight on the splinted leg. Promising to find something to work as a cane or crutch at her first opportunity, she pushed the thought aside and examined the cavern, attempting to find a way out and up to the surface. The underground chamber proved to be longer than she expected, but she did notice that it sloped gradually upwards. Following the wall and using it for support, she hobbled toward the higher end of the room and, much to her delight, found an exit big enough to walk through comfortably.

* * * * *

Hours later, Anna still wandered the tunnels underground searching for the path leading to the surface. She searched every tunnel she found, only to discover that they just penetrated deeper.

Through all of her walking, her improvised splint still held. The pain flared every so often, reminding her that she was still wounded and needed to take better care to keep the bones from separating again.

Exhausted from her exploring, Anna found a large, flat rock on one side of the cave and sat down to take a breather. Her feet were sore, but she dared not take her other boot off for fear of doing something that could injure her good leg. The jagged, uneven floor did not help matters much.

The thought of trying to contact Kate again crossed her mind, and she turned on her wristcomp, only to get a burst of static when she opened the channel. Quicker than she could think about it, she closed the projected screen and listened for several seconds. The sound of the burst echoed away in both directions, but she heard nothing in the silence that followed.

So far, Anna had not encountered any other living creatures in the underground channels, but she felt that luck was on her side. If she speculated correctly in assuming that caves may be all over the area, it would explain where all of the animals went after the eclipse ended. If that was the case, why had she not seen any of them beyond the one creature by the river?

Pushing the thought aside to contemplate later, Anna slowly and begrudgingly rose to her feet to continue her quest to find the exit. After taking a couple of steps, she heard something behind her that sounded like whispering. She turned as fast as she could without losing her balance and directed her flashlight back down the tunnel, only to see the few rocks scattered about on the ground that she had already passed. Dismissing it as the remnant of an echo she created earlier, she turned back and continued on her way.

* * * * *

Sometime later, Anna stopped again at the abrupt end of the natural corridor. She looked all about for any way to keep going, but all she found was a small opening in the ceiling from which water slowly dripped to the rocky floor. About a big as her hand, she immediately knew that she could not possibly hope to fit through it.

"No!" she lamented in despair. "There's got to be a way out!"

She turned and leaned against the cavern wall, looking back the way she came. She looked up at the opening again and aimed her light inside. After a couple of minutes investigating the hole, she concluded that she would have to cut a lot of rock away to widen the hole, and her cutter would not hold enough power to complete the task. Sighing from frustration, she backtracked down the tunnel, hoping to find a branch she missed.

As she began the trip back, Anna reflected on the wandering she had done over the past few hours and started to think that she might be lost. Without any kind of point of reference except for the cave in which she woke, she really had no idea as to which direction she was going or how far she had walked. As far as she knew, she could be standing right under her ship and would never know it. She had not anticipated staying away for this long and, if she had, would have brought more food.

Food! Through all of her troubles, she had not even thought about eating and did not realize just how hungry she really was. She reached into one of her large pouches, opened the container with her rations, and plucked one of the small fruits out. She hungrily ravaged the fruit, but it was not enough. She fished a couple of crackers out and wolfed them down. She had to stop herself after that to make sure her stores lasted for a while longer, trying hard to ignore the hunger pangs in her belly. The continuous pain from her fractured leg helped tremendously.

Several minutes later, Anna stepped to the middle of an intersection. The smaller side tunnel stretched down into the inky black depths, while the main channel curved to the side at a more gradual incline. She stopped and took a deep breath, hoping to regain a little strength back to continue her journey. Examining the features of the cragged walls around her, she concluded that all of the intersections looked more or less the same to her even after hours of wandering.

As she prepared to move on, she heard what sounded like breathing coming from the side passage. Reflexively, she redirected her light down the shaft into the face of a blue-furred predator not more than half a dozen meters away, its six legs gripping the wall all around it. The bright light, reflected back at her from its three concentric eyes like a cat, forced it to squint and turn away for only a couple of seconds before it slowly turned back, a feral growl emanating from its throat.

"Oh, god," Anna whispered as she slowly moved the flashlight to her other hand and reached for her pistol. The beast charged her just as she pulled the weapon from its pouch. The creature slammed into her, throwing both of them against the stone wall behind her and knocking her sidearm and flashlight from her grip. The impact stunned Anna for a second. Acting on sheer instinct, she grabbed her assailant's snout with both hands, closing its triple jaws. It ripped its maw away from her hands and lunged for her throat. She blocked the attack instinctively by throwing her forearm in its way. As it clamped down, she felt its teeth sink into her flesh and a gush of blood splashed onto her face.

Anna screamed as the pain from her new wound flooded through her arm and into her torso. Fighting the urge to pull her arm free, she created a fist with her free hand and punched it in its face, but the blow did not seem to faze it. She punched it again and again, meeting its furry skin each time until her fist sank deep into something soft.

The beast yelped in pain from the final blow and released its grip on her arm. Quickly pulling her arm away, Anna managed to muster the strength to push the monster off of her with her uninjured arm and roll down the tunnel away from it. Stopping after a few meters, she clamored to her feet and drew her knife. Her opponent was a fair distance up the cave, looking around for its prey with its two remaining eyes. Only a few seconds passed before it located her, growled again, and charged at her once more.

Dropping to a low stance, she stared at the creature as it approached, gripping her knife tightly and anticipating its next move. She did not think about what she was doing nor allow her fear to inhibit her actions. At this moment, Anna acted solely on instinct.

Running to a few meters from its prey, the predator sprang forward, diving at Anna with its three jaws bared. The woman sidestepped her attacker and, while it sailed by, stabbed her knife into it. She felt the steel blade sink into its flesh and slice down the length of its body.

The creature shrieked in pain before it hit the ground and rolled away. With the advantage of her surprise attack, Anna dashed forward and pinned its snout to the ground with one foot while standing over it. In the dim light provided by her distant flashlight, she could tell that her blow had cut the beast down through its abdominal cavity. Its breathing now sounded raspy, labored, and wet. Without another thought, Anna crouched down and plunged her knife into its torso, hoping to kill it quickly despite having little knowledge of its anatomy.

When she finally saw it no longer breathing, she stood and numbly returned to where she was first attacked. At she stepped next to her laser pistol, her surge of adrenaline ebbed, releasing her. The pain encompassing her entire body hit her like a train. Her face contorted as she collapsed to the ground and sank into unconsciousness, the cry of pain never escaping her throat.

Chapter 14

Anna slowly awoke and opened her eyes to see a ceiling built from dark gray stones. Sitting up with a start when it suddenly hit her that her surroundings were much brighter than before, she looked around at the small room she recognized as the chamber at the top of the pyramid.

Confusion quickly set in, and she frantically looked around the room from her position on the floor. The room and everything outside looked exactly the same as it did when she first entered. Her clothes were clean and in decent repair, and all of her tools were properly stowed away in her belt pouches.

Looking at her arm, Anna stared dumbfounded at the unbroken and unscarred skin. She felt no pain from her forearm. Driven by curiosity, she pulled the leg of her pants up and saw no bruising on her skin. In fact, her calf felt fine. She ran her fingers up and down her leg, feeling the bone for any sign of a fracture, but the bone was smooth and in one piece.

Had she dreamed the last several hours? All of the evidence would indicate that she had. Her clothes were undamaged. Her wounds were gone, as if they had never happened. None of her tools were out of place. Despite feeling incredibly hungry, everything seemed fine.

She reached into her pouch and pulled one of the small fruits out and took a bite, savoring its flavor as the juices tickled her taste buds. She did not know why, but her mood elevated every time she ate one of the native fruits.

Rising to her feet, Anna eyed the lever protruding from the back wall. She stepped up to stand beside it and, keeping her feet next to the wall, pulled down on the handle. But, it did not move. Raising an eyebrow, she pulled down on it again, but it still did not budge.

Perhaps she did dream the whole thing.

Scratching her head, Anna stepped outside and looked skyward at the scattered gray clouds passing overhead and then to the ground, where the underbrush still poked out between the large stones paving the area around the pyramid. Glancing at the obelisks at the corners of the top platform, she decided to take a scan of them before heading back to the ship.

Withdrawing her hand scanner from its pouch, she swiped it by one of the spires for several seconds and watched the screen for the results. The handheld device performed erratically, telling Anna that it might have a high amount of electromagnetic energy emanating from it. Thinking that it might explain why she had such an elaborate dream, she returned the scanner to her belt and descended the stairs.

Seconds after she stepped onto the ground, her wristcomp signaled an incoming message. Activating the screen, Anna answered the page.

"Hi, Kate! How has . . ."

"WHERE THE HELL HAVE YOU BEEN?!"

Anna paused for a second and softly responded, "Wh . . . what? I don't understand."

Kate yelled over the channel, "YOU'VE BEEN GONE FOR OVER A MONTH!"

Anna fell silent as confusion set in again. It didn't feel like a month had passed.

"Are you sure?" she asked skeptically. "I haven't been . . ."

"Look at the time on your wristcomp."

Glancing at the time displayed at the bottom of the screen, Anna skimmed it and replied, "It shows that it's been only a few hours."

Kate stated flatly, "Synchronizing now."

Anna waited for the update to complete and, after its completion, stopped cold. According to what she read, over 32 days had passed since she left the ship.

"What the hell?!" she muttered under her breath as her eyes grew wide.

"See?" Kate gloated.

Anna looked over her shoulder at the top of the pyramid for a long moment, believing now that it was not a dream. Wondering what had happened while she was out, Anna said distantly, "Let me get back to you."

"Anna, what are . . ." Kate began before Anna closed the channel.

Marching back up the steps, Anna entered the upper chamber again and moved straight to the lever on the wall. She pulled her hand scanner out again and turned it on, but its performance remained unstable with its display showing distortions and static. Replacing it in its pouch, she knelt next to the tapered beam where it joined with the wall and examined the spot where the two met. The seam, still present from what she remembered before, did not appear any different. She attempted to move it again in different directions, but it remained frozen in place. Half tempted to cut into the lever to try to gain access to the suspected mechanism, she took her laser cutter in hand and held it for several seconds, running her thumb along its smooth casing while she calculated the consequences of either choice she could make to deface the device to learn how it worked or leave it unscathed as a significant archaeological and anthropological find. Unsure as to how the race that built the pyramid, if they still existed, would react if she cut into it and not wanting to go down in history as the one person to ruin any possible relations between their races before they have a chance to begin, she decided to leave it alone and put her laser cutter away.

Anna rushed back outside and circled the building, looking for any kind of entrance or opening other than the one she had already used. Although her initial search gave her nothing, a second walk around helped her locate a small window on the second tier. The opening provided little help for her quest to regain entrance, for it was only about as big around as her arm and seemed to only allow air and light to pass through.

Frustrated, she finally gave up and called Kate back.

"Okay," she yielded. "I can do nothing more here, Kate. I'm coming back to the ship."

"Good. Maybe we can finally get back to the business of your extended survival," Kate retorted.

Defensively, Anna stated, "Hey! I told you that this was something I needed to do."

"You also said that it wouldn't take too long, which reminds me. Where have you been for the past month?"

As she stepped into the woods toward the river, Anna replied, "Honestly, I don't know. I walked into the pyramid, and I thought that I had fallen through a trap door to a cavern somewhere underground and got lost. But, I woke up later and found myself inside the pyramid again. I don't know what happened or how I got there, but I have no knowledge of what happened to me during most of that month since I last spoke with you.

"I couldn't have fallen into a coma," she mused aloud. "I would have atrophied from starvation and died. I don't recall encountering anyone else, so abducted is out."

Could the energy from the obelisks have dropped her into a hypnotic state? It seemed plausible at first, but she would have succumbed to starvation that way as well. Something was amiss, and the knowledge of that much of her life missing without an explanation fiercely gnawed at her. She had to find out what happened to her and why.

While she walked downstream toward the crash site, Anna discussed various matters with Kate, including the task she placed as top priority: restoring the engines on the ship. The hologram indicated that she took the initiative of sending half a dozen of the drones to the gas giant to harvest hydrogen and return once the canisters were full. Using the drones as her access to the physical world, Kate had filled 14 canisters with hydrogen gas during Anna's hiatus, leaving 54 more to be filled before reaching maximum capacity. The avatar also mentioned that she had the drones begin searching the local area for possible food sources and start patching the breach in the fuel tank.

"How does the tank look?" Anna inquired, genuinely interested in the response.

"At this point," Kate answered. "The fuel tank is mostly patched, but a few small holes are still present. It appears that some fragments were lost, when the station debris hit it. If we can find some metal plating to seal the hole, then we should have a repaired fuel tank."

Anna smiled and said gleefully, "That's good news! What about the engines themselves?"

"I haven't even looked at them," Kate confessed. "A lot of the damage to the engines, according to the visual feed I received from the drones, tells me that more than the manifold may be in need of repair. If my assessment is correct, the fuel injection system may be damaged."

Slouching her shoulders, Anna sighed, "I guess I will have to look into that when I get back."

The rest of her walk back to the ship was largely uneventful. The ship was a welcome sight to her as she entered the clearing, thankful that she made it back to familiar surroundings without incident. She was quite surprised to see the level of activity in the clearing, though.

All of the drones appeared to be performing some sort of task. Some were gathering and storing food in the storage containers they normally used for the gas they had previously mined. Some were using their manipulator arms to till soil in square plots near the ship for what she assumed to be crops. A couple of drones were flying around the perimeter of the clearing, appearing as if they were on patrol. She counted them and, coming up four short, assumed the rest were away on some sort of mission.

Wasting no time, Anna jogged up the nose of the ship and climbed into the airlock. As the internal door opened, Kate faded into view by the pilot seat with a smile on her face.

"Welcome home, Anna," she greeted happily.

Anna smiled back and replied, "Thank you. It's good to see you again."

"Likewise. I assume that you will want to rest a while. Right?"

"Yeah," said Anna as she set her knapsack on the floor next to its wall locker and traipsed to the lone chair on the bridge. Flopping into the comfortable seat, Anna pulled her boots and socks off and propped her bare feet up on the control panel, wiggling her toes.

"I feel like I haven't taken those boots off in weeks!"

"If what you said is correct, you haven't," Kate drolly added.

Anna chuckled, "Yeah, guess that's right."

Stretching in her chair, she suddenly realized that the pain in her shoulder was gone, too. She sat up and pulled her shirt sleeve up over her shoulder. The bite marks from the attack in the airlock were gone without even a scar remaining.

"Kate," Anna asked with concern in her voice. "Could you scan my shoulder?"

The hologram shifted to give her a clear view of the shoulder and stared at it for a few seconds.

"That's odd," Kate remarked. "There's no sign of your previous injury. No muscle scarring, nothing."

"I know! Why is that?"

"I don't know, Anna. I can't explain it."

Turning around in her chair, Anna quizzed, "Do you think an ample amount of EM exposure over an extended period of time could cause this?"

"According to what we know about the electromagnetic spectrum, no," Kate answered. "If anything, you should have some sort of radiation exposure, maybe some cells exhibiting early signs of cancer, depending on the form of energy to which you were exposed. But, you shouldn't have healed like this."

Grimly, Anna nodded, "That's what I thought. Something happened. I don't know what, but I want answers."

Leaning back on one leg, Kate crossed her arms, looked at Anna sternly, and inquired, "And just how do you propose to get those?"

Sitting forward and putting her socks back on, Anna stated, "I'm going back to the pyramid."

"Hold on! You're not going back there. You just got back!"

Looking at the hologram squarely, Anna said, "I'm not walking this time. I'm taking a drone with me."

"Wh . . . a drone? What do you hope to accomplish with a drone that you didn't do before?"

"Conduct a deeper scan of the pyramid. My hand scanner has to be within one meter of anything it scans for it to be truly effective. I can attempt extended scans with it, but it cannot produce detailed results out further than a meter. Drones are capable of scanning planetary distances on their own, so one should be able to focus a scan through a building less than a kilometer away."

"But," Kate protested. "You said that you aren't walking back. Do you intend for the drone to carry you?"

"Nope," smiled Anna. "I'm going to ride it."

* * * * *

Hours later, Anna finished making her adjustments to Drone 17, the one she had picked as her favorite since it was the first one she found. Sacrificing one of the internal compartment panels from inside the bridge, she sliced four chunks off of one side and gave the rest to another drone to use as material to patch the rest of the fuel tank. With the pieces she acquired, she fashioned handles and footrests for herself and welded them to the drone's upper body.

"Okay, Seventeen," she said through her wristcomp. "Let's take you for a test flight."

Anna climbed onto the drone's back and, lying on her belly, settled into place. Although the drone was not originally built to accommodate a rider, its relatively smooth dorsal hull plate allowed her to rest fairly comfortably on top of it.

Resting her head against the drone, she ordered, "Go up about 5 meters and hold position."

In a split second, the drone's thrusters engaged, pushing it into the air. Anna felt the rush of air against her entire body as it moved, and it gave her a little thrill. After a few seconds, the drone stopped moving and remained in place while its thrusters continued to fire.

"Kate," Anna called out. "How's Seventeen's fuel output?"

"The drone's fuel consumption has increased by 3% to accommodate for your added weight."

"Not too bad," remarked the blonde. "Seventeen, fly around the clearing at 5 kph."

The drone moved forward and, as it approached the edge of the trees, curved to the left in a wide arc, until it matched the clearing's boundary. Anna raised her head and felt the soft breeze against her face. She looked at the ground below and watched as they drifted past the other drones hard at work around the ship.

Wanting to test the drone's performance as well as the strength of her new emplacements, Anna cried, "Seventeen, increase speed to 40 kph."

Seventeen surged forward, almost catching Anna off-guard. Gripping the handles tighter, she pressed against the foot plates and grinned when they held against the added pressure. She pulled on the handles with the same result. Happy with the results, she pushed herself up on her knees and watched them fly around the ship a few more times before ordering them to land.

"How did it go?" Kate inquired over the wristcomp.

"Excellent!" Anna exclaimed proudly. "I feel safe aboard it.

"Now," she continued. "Off to the pyramid!"

Chapter 15

The wind rushed through Anna's hair as she and Seventeen soared over the treetops toward the pyramid. Although she knew the flight would only last a couple of minutes, the freedom she felt exhilarated her, and she mentally resolved that she would do this again while the drones still had fuel.

As expected, the flight ended about a minute later when the drone gently touched down several meters away from the base of the staircase leading to the top of the ancient structure that dominated the plaza. Anna slid from the top of the drone and gazed at the pyramid for a long moment, contemplating how she was going to attempt to crack the mysteries within. She thought about taking the drone to the top of the building but dismissed the idea, thinking that the same energy field that disrupted her hand scanner would probably do the same to her robotic companion. In fact, she was not sure how far the field's effects reached.

"Seventeen," she stated. "Conduct a scan of the general area, concentrating on EM emissions. Route your results to my wristcomp."

Without a response, the drone rose a few meters up and slowly rotated around, taking a full minute to complete the turn. As it began, Anna activated the screen of her wristcomp and created the link to the drone's systems. The scan results appeared on the screen as they were being received by the drone and showed a little less than half of its sweep when she first connected. Everything seemed fine, until the data from around the pyramid appeared. A high concentration of EM energy appeared in a dome around the structure that extended only a few meters out from the base.

"Okay," ordered Anna after studying the results for a few minutes. "Concentrate a scan on the building due west from our location."

Seventeen turned and faced the pyramid, and Anna turned her gaze back to the holographic screen floating above her arm. The readout confirmed that the drone was sending the signal out, but nothing was coming back.

After letting Seventeen try to break through the EM bubble for a minute or so, Anna stopped the attempt and contemplated another method. Thinking that the shaft in the side of the pyramid that she discovered earlier may provide a way for whatever may be inside to access something beyond the bubble, she instructed the drone to maneuver itself to that side and direct its scan toward the opening. Seventeen positioned itself and commenced its scan but yielded nothing new.

"Damn!" exclaimed Anna after checking the new results, frustration evident in her voice.

She thought for a few seconds more and decided to try something else. After instructing the drone to focus its scan on her and store the results until she downloaded them, Anna walked halfway up the stairs and climbed over the side rail to land on the top of the second tier. She walked around to the opening, flailed her arms about for several seconds as if she was trying to get the drone's attention, and retraced her steps back to the ground. Once she stood next to Seventeen again, she downloaded the sensor information and replayed the feed that showed her infrared signature follow the path on the pyramid. Her wristcomp signal, however, disappeared as soon as she passed through the EM barrier.

With a frown, Anna remarked dourly, "Well, that was helpful."

Wracking her brain to find a way to penetrate the field, Anna rejected idea after idea, certain that they would not work. Finally, she snapped her fingers as a thought hit her mind.

"Seventeen," she said. "Scan the building ahead, but start at the lowest possible frequency and modulate upward one Hertz per nanosecond."

Knowing that the new procedure could take a while, Anna walked to the nearest building away from the pyramid and sat on the paved stone just outside it. After a few minutes, she decided to call back to the ship and see how things were going there.

"Hey, Kate!" she cheerfully greeted. "How are things going back there?"

"Everything is proceeding accordingly. And there?"

"Well," Anna sighed. "I'm not making much progress. Right now, I have Seventeen doing an EM spectral scan."

"What frequency range?"

"All of them."

Kate paused before asking quizzically, "All of them?"

"Yeah."

"At what rate?"

"One hertz per nanosecond."

"I hope you don't have anything else to do for a while. You have quite a wait ahead of you."

Raising an eyebrow, Anna inquired, "How long?"

"If you scan from 1 hertz to 10^{27} hertz at that rate, according to my calculations, it would take 31,709,791,983 years, 279 days, 1 hour, 46 minutes, and 40 seconds in Earth time to complete."

Anna restrained the desire to laugh hysterically as the length of time tumbled inside her head.

"Anna? Are you there?" Kate asked, finally breaking the silence that had fallen between them.

"Uh, yeah. I'm here. Really, I didn't think it would take that long."

"I suggest you revise your parameters."

Anna resigned as she rose to her feet, "Yeah."

As she stepped toward the drone, she linked in again and stopped to think on how she could change her order to speed up the process. The only way that came to mind was to eliminate the different types of energy waves that she knew could not possibly be used to create the bubble and remove those from the request. Digging back through her collegiate studies, she sifted through what she remembered.

"Seventeen," she addressed through her wristcomp. "Modify the current order to remove the infrared, visible light, and near ultraviolet rays. Start by scanning through the radio waves for now.

"If my estimates are correct on that," muttered Anna to herself. "It should be done in a few minutes with that one."

As predicted, the drone indicated that it had finished the task on time. The results of the scan, however, proved disappointing as nothing new was discovered.

Anna sighed as she strode back to her resting place against the crumbling building, "All right. Start scanning the EUV range and move up from there at best possible speed."

Seconds after she sat down, her wristcomp signaled an incoming message.

"Scan complete."

"What?!" she cried as she read the message from Seventeen again. She pulled up the results and was astonished to find the surface scan of the pyramid on the screen along with the precise frequency at which the scan produced the result.

"Did you scan the entire EM spectrum?"

"Affirmative."

"How . . ." she wondered as she called Kate.

"Yes, Anna."

"Why didn't you tell me that the drones could scan the EM spectrum so fast?"

"You didn't ask," Kate replied. Anna pictured her smiling smugly as she answered her question.

"Just how fast CAN they scan it?"

"The last broadband scan one of them performed finished in just under 3 minutes and 46 seconds."

"Thanks," Anna grumbled before closing the channel.

She got up again and walked to her drone while instructing, "Seventeen, focus a scan on the building at the indicated frequency. Route the results to my display."

Watching the screen, her expression dropped when the scan brought back the same, blocked result. Staring at the screen in disbelief, she cried in apparent frustration, "What the hell?!"

Anna walked up to where she thought the energy field stretched across the ground and stared at the pyramid, feeling shocked and annoyed above anything else. She wanted to rip the obelisks out of their emplacements and smash them to pieces, believing that the act would solve all of her problems. As she was formulating another plan of destruction to vent her growing anger, a stray thought flashed through her mind.

Turning to face her drone, she said after taking a breath to center herself, "Seventeen, run a diagnostic on your sensors."

"I KNOW how long this will take," Anna exclaimed under her breath.

About a minute later, the results returned indicating that the sensor suite was in proper working order.

She combed her fingers through her hair as she sighed aloud, trying to figure out where the problem might be.

To the drone, she said, "Focus a full EM spectral scan at the building again."

As Seventeen began the sweep again, Anna paced back and forth until the new results appeared on the holographic screen with a different frequency listed.

"That's impossible! Scan it again!"

The third scan yielded an entirely different frequency.

"It's modulating the frequency?!" she cried in exasperation. "Are you kidding me?!"

She opened a channel and called the ship again.

"Kate, run a scan on the area and tell me what you find."

A few seconds later, the hologram replied, "I detect you, the drone, and an electromagnetic field very close to you."

"Check the sensor logs from 32 days ago and compare the results."

"Analysis complete," Kate stated several seconds later. "The results are quite different. The EM field was not there before you left for the area."

". . . which tells me that something triggered it to activate."

Kate scolded, "Couldn't be you messing with something while you were there. No, it couldn't be that."

"I'm not in the mood, Kate," Anna warned after a second's pause. "But, point taken.

"Problem now is that it seems that the EM field is continually modulating its frequency, making it virtually impossible to match and scan through it.

"Hang on!" she continued after snapping her fingers. "I have an idea. Talk to you later!"

"Anna, I . . ." Kate managed to say before being cut off by the end of the communication.

Anna turned and commanded, "Seventeen, conduct a full EM spectral scan on the building and record each frequency you find and the time interval between each one over the next three hours."

As she turned and trotted off to the woods surrounding the plaza, she whispered to herself, "Meanwhile, I'm going to think about this for a bit."

* * * * *

Anna slowly awoke to the gentle chime emanating from her wristcomp, her hair slightly mussed. Lying in the shade against a nearby tree, she stretched her arms and legs, moaning slightly as she did. Surprised that she had fallen sleep at all considering the situation at hand, she opened her eyes and turned off the alarm she had set to signal the end of Seventeen's scan. Looking around to make sure everything was clear around her, she stood, brushed off the seat of her pants, and walked back to the pyramid.

Stepping up to the drone, Anna patted its metal shell and said with a bit of cheer, "Well Seventeen, what did we find out?" Her wristcomp signaled an incoming message a few seconds later.

Reading the results, she said in a low voice, "I hope Kate can find something in all of this."

"Kate," she continued after calling the ship. "I have a list of frequencies and time intervals that Seventeen gathered over the last three hours. Can you see if you can find any sort of pattern in all of this?"

"I'll see what I can do. Send it over."

Anna transmitted the data and waited for the reply for a couple of minutes before starting to become impatient.

"Kate?"

"Everything's fine, Anna. I'm just studying the data. One moment, please."

A few more minutes elapsed before Kate finally said, "Anna, I'm sorry. I am not detecting a pattern in the information you sent me. Either the pattern is so long and complex that it cannot be determined with just three hours of information, or whatever is modulating the frequencies is doing it completely at random."

Anna frowned with disappointment but nodded her understanding.

"It's okay. Thanks for trying, Kate."

Glancing at the pyramid, she finally admitted defeat and said, "Okay, Seventeen. Let's go home."

She waited for the drone to descend to the ground, climbed onto its back and, after making sure she was securely in place, gave the order to take off. Just as the engines began to fire, they suddenly died and became silent.

Anna raised her head with a concerned look on her face and slid back to the ground. Seventeen's systems appeared to be offline. In fact, the drone seemed to be completely out of power.

"What the hell?" she asked as she examined it a little closer but found nothing wrong.

Puzzled over the sudden twist of events, she toggled her wristcomp.

"Kate?"

She received no response from the device. In fact, the wristcomp appeared to have no power.

Anna gazed at the device, and her eyes widened.

"Oh, no! No! NO!" she groaned as she pulled her hand scanner from her belt. As she swept it over Seventeen, she confirmed her suspicions when she saw the device with no power.

"Why now?!" she screamed into the air. "WHY ME?!?"

Anna returned the hand scanner to its pouch and kicked a small pebble at her feet, watching it bounce along the stone pavement for several meters.

She looked back at the drone with a sad expression and murmured, "I'm so sorry."

Taking a deep breath, she decided to hike back to the ship and ask Kate to watch the area until the field either shrank or disappeared entirely, so she could summon Seventeen home. She knew full well that she had no way of moving it under her own power, so she did not even consider that option. With a heavy sigh of defeat, she set off toward the river.

As she reached the edge of the plaza, she stopped, took one last look at the drone setting unpowered in front of the pyramid, and stepped over the ridge. Only, her foot never reached the ground. Instead, she slammed into something that knocked her to the pavement.

Stunned for only a second, Anna shook it off and peered at the air in front of her. She didn't see anything, so she got back up and tentatively reached forward with her hand. At an arm's length in front of her, she met what felt like a solid, transparent wall. Confused, she glanced around her and back at her hand pressed against this unseen barrier. Deciding to test the extent of this new obstruction, she glided her hand against it and followed it, hoping to find an edge that would allow her to slip past it.

About a half hour later, Anna had walked around the perimeter of the plaza with her hand against the invisible wall the entire time. Looking back at the drone to confirm that she had come full circle, she slumped as a feeling of dread descended over her being. Somehow, the field had expanded and solidified, trapping her with the pyramid.

Chapter 16

Anna woke up with a start. Quickly glancing around her, she took a moment to regain her senses and realize that she had fallen asleep within the chamber at the top of the pyramid. She did not know how long she was out, nor did she really know how long she had been confined within the shield wall that surrounded the immediate area.

Several hours before, she struggled to find some way of breaching the field to at least get a message sent to Kate informing her of her current predicament. She tried testing the height of the field by throwing rocks as high as she could but did not find an upper edge. She had contemplated digging her way out but quickly realized that she did not have the proper equipment to break through the paved stones. With the drone currently out of commission, she could not move any of the large rocks, either.

As she sat up, Anna winced from the sudden surge of tension in her neck. Throwing her hand to the source of the pain to massage the muscle as she popped her neck back in place, she sighed a breath of relief as the stabbing discomfort slowly subsided. After a few more seconds of massaging her neck, she walked outside and looked across the abandoned plaza.

Nothing seemed to have changed much since she went to sleep. The smaller unoccupied buildings still circled the pyramid, staring at it like lost children. The trees still stood just outside the paved area, swaying in the gentle breeze that she felt across her face. Seventeen still sat on the ground next to the pyramid, its glowing indicator lights barely visible in the sunlight.

Wait a minute . . .

With the breeze and the drone's lights present, is the shield wall gone?

Shaking the last of her drowsiness from her head before descending the stairs, Anna rushed to the ground and darted for the tree line. Tempted as she was to just run for it and hope she could make it, she skidded to a halt just in front of the opening through the wall and looked around for a pebble or some other small object. Her eyes fell upon a small stone a few meters away, which she picked up and hefted through the gate. The rock soared through the air and bounced off a nearby tree, much to Anna's delight.

She did not know how long the field had been down; she didn't care. All she thought about right now was getting back to the ship and leaving the ruins behind her for a long time.

"Seventeen!" she cried joyfully. "Let's get out of here!"

Anna sprinted toward the drone while it powered up its engines and vaulted onto its back, grabbing for one of the handles to stop herself. But, she missed her mark, slid across and over the side to land on the pavement.

Mildly irritated at her uncoordinated attempt, she laughed it off and climbed onto Seventeen's back. Once in place, she gave the order to take off and flew back to the ship without further incident.

* * * * *

Expressing joy at seeing her holographic companion again, Anna hopped out of the airlock onto the bridge a few minutes later and announced with a flourish, "I'm back!"

"Welcome home again," Kate greeted with a pleasing smile.

"Yeah, I know," replied the blonde with a smirk. "Well, don't worry. I'm not going near that place again for a long while."

"What happened with that? I noticed that the EM field grew about ten hours ago but shrank back again a few hours after that."

As she began to remove her clothes, Anna replied, "I'm thinking that whatever is controlling the energy field thought that the scanning attempts were some sort of attack and increased its defenses to stop it."

Kate watched Anna strip for a second before inquiring, "Anna, what are you doing?"

"I'm going to take a desperately-needed shower. I'll be done in about twenty minutes or so."

With a puzzled look, the hologram queried, "That's a long shower."

Dropping her pants and kicking them off next to the growing pile on the bridge floor, she said, "I plan on ... uh, relaxing while I'm in there."

Tossing her panties behind her as she retreated from the room, Anna playfully stated, "See you in a bit."

She returned to the bridge about half an hour later eating the last few bites of a sandwich. Kate, standing by the pilot's chair, turned and asked, "Better?"

With a slight laugh, Anna answered, "Much better. Thanks."

"So, what are you going to do now?"

"I . . ." said the nude technician, pausing long enough to take the last bite, chew, and swallow it. "I am going to relax on top of the ship for a little bit. After what I've been through, I think I deserve a little break."

Kate nodded and watched Anna step toward the airlock before asking, "What are you going to do about your clothes?"

Looking over her shoulder, the blonde replied, "They're filthy! I'm not going to wear them until I wash them."

"Could you not have done that during your shower?" Kate reproached, crossing her arms.

149

Anna smiled innocently and said, "Yeah, I suppose I could have. Next shower, I promise."

"But, what about the clothes now?" the avatar questioned as Anna stepped into the airlock.

"I'll pick them up later."

"Anna . . ."

"Going to relax now! Bye!" Anna interrupted after pressing the door switch, invoking a frown from Kate as the airlock closed.

After climbing out of the airlock and sitting on the hull, Anna observed the mining drones in action around the clearing. While she was visiting the pyramid this last time, the drones had leveled and plowed three decently-sized plots of land for crops and filled several containers with locally grown food. Now, they were in the process of transporting the containers out of the clearing. She guessed that they were being dropped into the river to keep them cool; that is what she would do.

At that moment, the sound of engines reached her ears. Looking over her shoulder, Anna spotted two drones descending into the clearing near the vessel's engines. She trotted aftward to watch them in action. The drones landed near the ship's fuel port, where one maneuvered behind the other and used its manipulator arm to remove the storage tanks from its partner. Impressed by Kate's ingenuity, Anna smiled approvingly and watched the other drone reciprocate the action and proceed to connect each of the 8 tanks to the ship and transfer the mined gas into the fuel tank.

"They must have finished patching the fuel tank," Anna muttered to herself. Wanting to see their handiwork for herself, she raced to the nose of the ship and across bare ground for a few meters before stopping to comfort her foot after stepping on a rock. Fortunately, she was not bleeding but suspected a small bruise may appear later. Slowing her pace, she walked the rest of the way to the engines and studied the repairs on the fuel tank.

The panel she surrendered earlier was put to good use, as the drone assigned to the task used its rarely-used cutting tool to weld the plate over the fissure in the container. With its integrity intact again, the hydrogen mined by the drones was safely stored and ready for use.

With Kate and the drones providing the lion's share of the physical labor for her, all Anna figured she had to do was make sure they remained operational. This sounded a lot like the job she had back on the station to her, but at least she would directly reap the rewards instead of passing them off to a faceless corporation back on Earth.

She lifted her arm to call Kate through her wristcomp but, finding her bare wrist instead, remembered that she left it in the head inside the ship. Smiling in spite of herself, she picked herself up and climbed back into the ship.

"Kate," said Anna as she walked out of the airlock. "I need . . ."

"You need to pick up your clothes and do something with them," Kate interrupted harshly.

Balking at the verbal attack, Anna backpedaled and replied defensively, "Now, wait a minute! I said that I was going to pick them up . . ."

"And, I don't like having to look at your dirty knickers!"

"Stop right there!" Anna yelled. "Did the real Kate Mitchum act like this, when she was alive?"

The hologram paused, contemplated the question for a second, and answered calmly, "I have no record of such behavior on file."

"Then, you need to start acting more like her and a LOT less like my mother!" Anna threatened. "Or so help me, I will shut you down.

I will not tolerate this kind of behavior from my computer. I am the human here. I am the one in charge. YOU need to respect that right here and right now. If you have a problem with me, you discuss it with me civilly, or you get over it! Understand?!"

Formally, Kate replied, "Yes, I understand."

"As for these clothes," Anna continued in the same tone. "I will move them to the back part of the ship. However, I am going to retrieve my wristcomp first. Agreed?"

"Yes, Anna."

"Thank you!"

Cursing under her breath as she moved, Anna snatched her wristcomp from where she left it on the sink and strapped it back on her wrist while walking back to the bridge.

"Now," she began after passing through the door. "The other reason why I came back in was to let you know that I want to set up a preventative maintenance schedule with the drones to keep them functioning. I want to look at Seventeen first, since it was with me at the pyramid and may have been affected by prolonged exposure to the EM field. After that, I want to inspect two drones per day . . . um, actually make that every 24 Earth hours. Please set that up."

"Yes, Anna," Kate answered passively.

Anna paused for a second as she mentally weighed the avatar's recent responses.

"Kate, I need to ask you this. Was the real woman this wishy-washy?"

Gently, the hologram asked in return, "Is this not to your liking?"

Rolling her eyes, Anna said, "Look. All I want is for you to behave as close to the real person as possible. Is that too much to ask?"

A couple of seconds passed in silence before Kate responded in a more normal tone, "No, that should not be too difficult."

"Brilliant," Anna smiled. "Thank you."

"I do have a question for you, though."

"Okay," nodded the engineer.

"Do you prefer to walk around without any clothes on?"

Anna rolled her eyes again and answered with a sigh, "Why do computers have a problem with this?"

"The act of a human remaining nude for an extended period of time is not the norm, so we do not expect it."

Replying flatly, Anna stated, "That was a rhetorical question."

"Oh, sorry."

"Up until a few months ago, I wouldn't have even dreamed of taking my clothes off except for stepping into the shower. But, I was thrust into a situation where I had to move about without wearing anything for a short time, and I found that I liked it. It gives me a feeling of freedom that I would not normally experience."

"Are you comfortable like this?"

Pausing for a second, she slowly answered, "Actually, yeah."

"Would you feel more comfortable if I also presented myself without clothes?"

Anna answered, amused by the question. "That's not necessary, Kate. I will more than likely go without for a while longer, after I inspect the drones."

"Alright."

With a smile, Anna expressed her thanks, gathered her clothes from the floor, and dropped them off in the head before grabbing a light blue T-shirt and black shorts from the pile of Ryan's discarded clothes, retrieving her tool belt, and returning outside to begin her inspection of Seventeen.

* * * * *

About an hour later, Seventeen passed its inspection surprisingly well. Only its visual receptors needed cleaning from the dust that gathered on the outer lenses, allowing Anna to breathe a sigh of relief.

"Okay, Seventeen. All done," she assured with a smile. "Go play!"

The drone lifted off from the top of the ship and flew to its previous assignment of patrolling the clearing's perimeter. Anna stood with her hands on her hips and watched it leave, smiling as it merged back into its circular flight path.

"You know, I kind of missed doing this," she said to nobody in particular.

Slipping the shop rag back into its pouch, she walked down to the ground and over to the tilled soil at the west end of her developing compound. She knelt at the edge of the plot and lifted up a handful of the soft, cool dirt. The small, dark clods easily broke apart and filtered through her fingers, exposing tiny stone bits and plant fibers mixed in with the soil. She rubbed it between her fingers for a few seconds before dropping it back to the ground.

Brushing her hands together, Anna stood back up and turned to regard the ship. As she stared at the white-hulled craft, she realized that she appreciated having it here to shelter her and aid her while marooned on the moon. Consequently, she now understood why Ryan liked it so much. But, looking at the way the ship rested on the surface made Anna feel like it was not being treated very well being left in the same position after the crash. She remembered that she had recovered one of the landing struts and thought that the others may still be out there, waiting to be found.

"Seventeen," Anna called. "Meet me at my current location. Bring the other drones from the patrol with you."

Several seconds later as the three drones rendezvoused with her, Anna mounted Seventeen and opened a channel with the ship.

"Kate, I need you to scan the area for any metal. We're going to find the landing struts and see if we can get this ship off the ground."

Chapter 17

"Remind me to wear more the next time I go up," Anna commented to herself after sliding off Seventeen's back onto the top of the ship. She combed her fingers through her blonde hair, tousled by the wind from her flight around the area, before rubbing her arms to warm them up a little.

Turning to the drone behind her, Anna thanked it and waved as it returned to its duties. She directed her gaze at her salvage now assembled on the ground a few meters from the vessel. Able to locate the two remaining landing struts and a few other pieces that had broken off during their descent, she felt confident that she could repair the damage to allow the ship to rest evenly on the ground. The dilemma at hand was to figure a way to raise the ship off the ground, so the repair work could be done. Without a drydock handy, something needed to be done to grant her access to the underbelly.

The first thought that crossed her mind was to use the drones, but she immediately knew that they did not have enough fuel to keep them running as long as she needed to work. The weight of the ship itself would crush a single drone, so using them to prop the ship up for a lengthy period of time would also be unwise.

Anna's thoughts shifted to using materials from the moon itself. The only rocks she saw in the area were the ones that created the rapids in the river and the worked stones that created the ancient pyramid, so that possibility was out.

As she contemplated the situation, she looked around the clearing at her patch of land and the line of sturdy trees that formed its boundary. The trees…wood! It had been used for countless centuries back on Earth. Why not?

Now, she just had to figure out how to cut it down. Her survival knife was too small for such a task. None of the tools on her belt were powerful enough for it. She could always shoot each tree with her laser pistol, but she would probably drain the power pack before she could effectively fell just one trunk. How she wished for a plasma cutter right now! With it, she could cut through each tree like butter without breaking a sweat. But, no such luck.

As she looked out over the cleared terrain, Anna smacked her forehead and chuckled at herself for missing what was right in front of her.

Still musing at her ability to miss the obvious, Anna called Seventeen and the other two drones on patrol with it to join her in searching the clearing behind the ship for timber.

Hours later, the four of them had brought back several logs and laid them together on the ground next to the craft. Anna believed them to be strong enough to hold the ship aloft if assembled the right way. However, the amount of timber she had brought back did not seem to be enough to raise both ends of the ship simultaneously. She figured that she would just have to prop up one end at a time, starting with the aft section.

A yawn sneaked its way through Anna's lips, reminding her that she should call it a day. Returning inside, she grabbed some food from the ship's larder and walked to the bridge, sitting in the pilot's chair while taking a bite of meat.

"Kate," Anna inquired as the avatar rezzed into existence behind her. "What music is on file?"

"All of the music on file consists of Broadway show tunes from 64 different musicals. Shall I list them for you?"

Looking over her shoulder with a confused expression on her face, Anna asked, "Show tunes?!"

"Yes, Anna. I have tracks from *Aida*, *Annie Oakley*, *Bayside Boys*, *Cats*, *Crossing Over*…"

Shaking her head in disbelief, Anna interrupted, "Yeah…never mind. I'm going to bed."

"Have I done something wrong?" Kate said as the technician walked aftward.

Stopping in the middle of the bridge, Anna turned and answered, "No, it's not you. It's just…"

She paused, collecting her thoughts, "I knew that Ryan was a lot of things, but I would have never pictured him as a lover of Broadway."

"I understand."

Lost in her thoughts, she called over her shoulder as she left the bridge, "Good night."

Several hours later, Anna woke up and looked at the shirt and shorts she wore the day before piled on the floor next to her cot. Deciding that it was time to do laundry, she gathered the garments, took them to the head, and showered, washing both sets of clothes while she did. Afterwards, she took the laundry to top of the ship and set them out to dry while she sunbathed next to them.

Her stomach grumbled after about half an hour, reminding her that she needed breakfast pretty soon. Dining on fruit and a cereal she found in her larder, she walked onto the bridge and found Kate looking outside at the drone digging rows in the tilled soil.

"Kate," Anna said. "I am going to begin reattaching the landing gear to the ship, so please don't be alarmed if you suddenly find yourself at an odd angle."

Looking over her shoulder, the hologram replied, "That's fine. Thanks for letting me know."

Anna glanced around the bridge, looking for her tool belt but not seeing it anywhere. She stepped up to the pilot seat and searched around the workstation but still did not find it lying around.

"Do you remember where I left my tool belt?" asked Anna curiously.

"I believe you left it in your cabin."

Snapping her fingers as she remembered, Anna stated, "That's right! Thanks!"

"Before you go," Kate interrupted, pointing a finger in Anna's general direction while still looking outside. "You should check this out."

Walking up to stand next to the holographic woman, Anna gazed out at the same angle but saw nothing more than the mining drones hard at work.

"I don't understand," she conceded after a few seconds with a shake of her head. "What am I supposed to be looking at?"

"This."

The control panel with the sensors display appeared in the air beside Kate, who pointed to the frozen sensor image.

"What do you make of this?"

Slightly annoyed at not noticing the image in the first place, Anna stepped back and examined the picture for a few seconds.

"If what I can tell is correct," she began while still poring over the graphical display. "It appears that another energy field has appeared around the pyramid."

"That is correct."

The blonde cocked an eyebrow and requested, "Focus on the pyramid and take the sensors log back to a couple of minutes before it appeared."

Within an instant, the image changed to a zoomed display of the area. Now, a smaller signature replaced the larger one, positioned near the edge of where it formerly showed on the holographic panel.

"Play back the logs at normal speed."

Kate complied with no visible effort, and the sensors displayed two smaller signatures separating from the larger one and move toward the location of the pyramid.

Anna's jaw dropped open as she observed the two converge on the aging structure. Several seconds passed by before the energy spike appeared and blotted out the multiple signals.

Dashing to the back part of the ship, Anna cried, "Tell Seventeen to meet me up top!"

"What are you doing?"

"I'm going back to the pyramid!"

"Again?"

"Yes!"

"Why?" Kate asked, almost sounding like she whined.

Emerging through the door with her tool belt hanging over her shoulder, Anna replied, "Somebody's there."

* * * * *

Anna jogged by herself along the river bank toward the ruins, resisting the urge to break out into a full run. She had instructed Seventeen to drop her off about a kilometer downstream from the pyramid to give her a chance to sneak in and discover the mysterious visitors without giving her presence away. Her clothes, still wet from being cleaned, clung to her body like a second layer of skin, although the flight had dried the garments a little along the way. She only had time to throw on the T-shirt and pants before the drone arrived to pick her up, so she had to wait until they landed to put her boots on her bare feet. The wind she felt as she rushed toward her destination chilled her skin despite the warm sunlight filtering through the trees.

"Are you sure this is a good idea?" Kate asked during the two-minute flight. "We don't know what they are capable of."

Anna, shouting over the wind buffeting her on top of the drone, replied, "I don't believe they're going to hurt me."

"They could, Anna. We do not know what happened to you during that month you were gone. Who is to say that they will not do it again."

"I have to take that chance, Kate. I have to take this opportunity to at least see who they are, so I know a little bit about who I'm dealing with."

"Still, I am not so sure that boldly charging in to meet an unknown being is a wise course of action."

"Why do you say that?"

"Let's look at what we do know about them. During your survey of the moon, you found no signs of civilization on the surface. You have been here for over two Earth months, and you have found no other signs of any kind of civilization with the exception of the pyramid. The mining station where you lived before has been in the station for over 100 years and received regular space traffic during that time, and not once was any kind of message or form of contact received from them during that time."

"What are you implying, Kate?"

"They don't want to be contacted!"

Anna stopped and thought about what the avatar just said. What she said was true, and all of the evidence she stated pointed to that conclusion. If these are indeed the native species to this moon and they are truly xenophobic, then she may be running into a hostile situation and putting her life in jeopardy once again. Besides, the pictures she saw inside the pyramid did show them with spears and other lethal weapons. But, why would they have healed her, when she almost died in the caves? They could have left her to die without a second thought. That is, if they are the ones that found and helped her.

"I understand, Kate. But, I have to know. I promise I won't make any contact until I know it's safe."

"Please be careful. Shall I continue to watch you, just in case?"

"I appreciate that," Anna thanked just as Seventeen touched down.

Several minutes later, Anna slowed her pace and steadied her breathing as she grew closer. Reaching the bank by the site, she took one more deep breath and cautiously stepped into the woods, making sure to not make any extra noise as she moved.

Reaching the mound that crested the wall framing the plaza, Anna dropped down, pulled out the binoculars she grabbed from the ship's locker, and spied on the area.

The first and most obvious thing she found was a vehicle parked a half-dozen meters away from the bottom of the stairs leading up the side of the pyramid. Made from what looked to be a shiny, silver metal, the transport looked to be no more than 6 or 7 meters long with a two-seat cockpit at the very front and a large, enclosed cargo area in the back. The cockpit was different than anything Anna had seen before as the seats had no back to them and seemed to be nothing more than stools. The wall behind the stools hosted a number of monitors and controls.

"What an odd place to put those," Anna remarked to herself, barely audible to her own ears.

Several minutes passed with her waiting just outside the compound for any sign of the visitors. With each passing second, she found it harder to just lie and wait. She wanted to rush in and look over the vehicle, its mere presence tantalized her curiosity. Her eyes darted between various spots around the area, looking for any sign of the craft's missing owners. She felt like she could wait no longer. Surveying the area again, she confirmed that the coast was clear, planted her feet underneath her, and prepared to sprint for the transport.

At that second, movement at the top of the pyramid caught her attention, and she dropped back to the dirt and aimed her binoculars at the visitors exiting the rooftop chamber. The two beings at first glance could easily fit into what Anna knew about the moon's ecosystem, their most noticeable feature being their three arms and three legs positioned equally around their barrel-like body much like the predator's legs. The head, if it could be called that, appeared to be not much more than a large lump on top of the torso. She could see an eye facing the direction they moved and maybe part of another over or between what would be their shoulders. What looked to be a mouth was at the very top of their heads and moved. It appeared as if they were communicating.

They each wore clothing that seemed to be rather utilitarian. The first one, which appeared to be a bit more physically fit than the other, wore khaki-colored pants and a thick harness that held an assortment of gadgets. The other one, draped in a faded blue robe of some sort, followed a few steps behind, gesturing with its hand and referring to something Anna could not understand from where she laid.

With her eyes glued to the pair as they reached the ground and stepped toward their vehicle, Anna knew that these must be the descendants of those that originally built the pyramid. She dared not move for fear of giving herself away.

The pair casually strode to the vehicle, pulled some handheld item from the back storage area, and returned to the top of the pyramid, disappearing into the dark room.

Anna watched them enter the old building. Once they were out of sight, she steadily counted to ten under her breath and, as soon as she said the last number, lunged forward and raced toward the alien conveyance. Her footfalls against the large, paved stones pounded in her ears and seemed to grow louder as she approached her target. Visions of the other two walking out and discovering her flooded her mind and fueled her fear that would force her to turn tail and run back into the woods. Fighting against the natural urge to flee, she pushed on.

Seconds later, Anna rapidly came to a halt, nearly stumbling into the cockpit as she tried to stop. Next to the doorless entry leading into the enclosed forward section, she glanced at the top of the pyramid for a brief second before glancing at the dashboard. The occupancy on what would be the port side hosted a control wheel and a myriad of screens, readouts, and meters both in front of and behind the seat showing information in a language she could not begin to fathom. The area on the starboard side featured much fewer features, the only ones that were at least recognizable were a small mirror embedded in the wall behind the seat and a button that seemed to be a switch to open a small compartment in the forward panel.

The sounds of unknown voices reached her ears, alerting her that they were returning. Knowing that she stayed out too long, Anna rapidly looked around her for somewhere to quickly duck and hide. Under the transport? No. In the back of the vehicle? No. Who knows where she would end up. Maybe one of the crumbling buildings that circled the pyramid was available? There, only a few meters behind her, and the vehicle should camouflage her escape. Without a moment of hesitation, Anna ran for the building.

Ducking through the doorway, she flattened herself against the wall just to the side and attempted to hold her breath. She listened for the voices from before but heard none. In fact, she did not hear any movement at all. Only the sounds of the wind and birds far in the distance reached her ears.

Had they heard her retreat into the ruined structure? Were they sneaking up on her now? She knew she would risk giving her position away by looking.

Despite her misgivings, Anna slowly turned her body and peered around the corner.

Chapter 18

Anna first saw the being wearing the blue robe standing next to the near side of the vehicle. She could not see the one wearing the harness, but she figured that it would not be very far away. She assumed that she had not been seen, until the robed one waved one of its three hands at her. Then, she realized that one of its eyes was staring straight at her.

Cursing herself, she cringed at her carelessness but stayed behind the brick wall. Taking a deep breath to steady her nerves, she poked her head out a little more and glanced around, locating the larger one on the other side of the vehicle, staring at her through the openings. On instinct, she ducked back behind the wall entirely.

"Wan!" one of them cried anxiously with a melodic voice, unnerving Anna. Sounds of running elevated her fears, and she drew her pistol. Her heart raced. She wanted to run and make a break for the woods. But, she knew that she would have no cover between here and the perimeter, making her a prime target if they decided to attack her.

Despite the pounding of her heart in her ears, Anna heard whispering by their transport, barely audible over the breeze blowing through the small dwelling in which she stood. From what she heard, the other's voice was deeper and gruffer than the smaller one's lyrical voice.

Several seconds passed with neither Anna nor the others making any kind of move. The whispering had ceased, and she heard no movement outside. She gripped her pistol tighter and prayed for a miracle that would get her through this.

"Gatal?" the smaller being asked in a voice that sounded more like that of an older child to Anna than a non-human. The word sounded more curious than hostile, and she started to wonder if they were going to attack.

It called out again. "Gatal?"

Anna pondered that perhaps at least one of them did not want to kill her. Then again, they could just be trying to lure her out. She had no choice; she would have to take a look. Cautiously, she craned her neck and peeked through the doorway. Both of the natives were still standing by the vehicle's cockpit. She breathed a sigh of relief and stared at the pair as they stared back.

The shorter one waved its hand toward her and said pleasantly, "Gatal! Ta monshamos va."

Anna hesitated before appearing in the doorway and responding uneasily, "H . . . hello."

"Tanso fretick," it continued, placing its hand on its torso and then on its partner. "A tansa bron."

Pointing at her, it asked, "Tansas?"

The way it spoke to her began to put her at ease, causing her to lower her guard. She still was not sure what the taller one was thinking. Perhaps it was waiting for some word from the other to attack. Then again, wouldn't they have attacked by now if they really wanted her dead?

At that second, Anna realized that she still held her pistol and was aiming it toward them. Slowly, she held her free hand in front of her and moved her arm back, intending to holster the gun. The larger being reached for something on its harness. Anna, reacting on instinct, whipped the weapon back into position again and took a step back. Both natives raised each of their three empty hands into the air as if on instinct.

"Bron," the shorter one said in a low volume. "Crav el hartan vas. Ta kamas salan mars."

The taller one grunted but made no other moves.

The leader continued to Anna, "Malas, avo el hartan. Ta monshamos va."

She studied them for a few seconds before she cautiously returned her pistol to its pouch. Once she let go of the handle, they seemed to visibly relax.

The leader said with relief in its voice, "Dranta.

"Argontamos. Ta monshamos va, en welemos ama va. Tansas?"

Anna furrowed her brow, trying to understand what it was trying to tell her. Considering what it did the last time it said that last word to her, she surmised that it was asking for her name.

Placing her hand on her chest, she said, "Anna. My name is Anna."

"An, na," it repeated, prompting a nod from her. She noticed its mouth grew tight during her nod.

Again, it placed a three-fingered, two-thumbed hand on its torso below its shoulder and intentionally enunciated, "Freh, tick. Fretick."

Anna pointed at the shorter one and mimicked, "Fretick."

"Set!"

The leader, whose name she figured to be Fretick, placed its hand on the other's chest and said emphatically, "Bron."

Pointing her finger at the larger one, Anna replied, "Bron."

"Set! Set!"

Aiming her finger at each one, Anna affirmed what she had just learned, "Fretick and Bron."

Fretick pointed back and answered, "Anna."

"Yes," she smiled, and Fretick's mouth became tight-lipped again.

Anna extended her hand, slowly took a few steps toward them, and opened her mouth to speak, but Fretick and Bron raised their hands in the air again. Her smile disappeared, until she realized that the action resembled what she did while she held her pistol.

"Oh, no!" she laughed, holding up her hands to show that they were empty. "This is a greeting."

She held both of her hands in front of her and grabbed them, demonstrating what she was trying to accomplish. Then, she pointed to Fretick's hand and held hers out again. It blinked a couple of times before cautiously closing the gap between them, reaching out with its hand as well. Gingerly, Anna grasped its hand and easily moved their clasped hands up and down in a slow handshake, smiling as she did. Unexpectedly, Bron thrust his hand out toward Anna and grunted softly. Anna stared at the hand and then at his head, unsure whether to follow through with the gesture.

"Ta monsha Bron va."

Hoping that Fretick said that the bigger one would not hurt her, she stretched her hand toward Bron, whose hand engulfed hers and slowly moved her whole arm up and down. After a few pumps, Anna managed to wriggle her hand free from its grip, prompting something that sounded like laughter from the robed native.

"Argonto," Fretick stated. "Hamano Bronsa mars."

Anna massaged her hand, attempting to return the blood to it, and smiled awkwardly. Judging from Fretick's response, she figured that its partner did not intend any harm. Perhaps Bron did not know its own strength.

Suddenly, a voice came from within the cockpit of the vehicle. Anna immediately knew that it must have been their radio, because nobody else was present. But, the sound quality was so clear, that it sounded like the person was sitting right there.

"Fretick," it said with an authoritative tone. "Shol cavan vad?"

The robed one's eyes narrowed, and it breathed ... sighed? ... before turning its feet toward their vehicle and walking to it. From her angle, Anna could see now that Fretick had three eyes around its head, much like the creatures she had encountered elsewhere on the moon.

Fretick touched something on the dashboard and replied, "Gatal lipshin. Ta rolamos. Argontamos. Welamos ama el sagadul."

"Sharan vasa ama el sagadul!" the other voice cried. "Nelamos."

"Thal krit?"

"Bik nathal."

A soft bleep told Anna that the other being ended the call. Fretick sighed again and pressed the switch on the dashboard again.

"Maras, Anna," Fretick stated anxiously. "Doras avir."

Recognizing her name, Anna blinked and cocked her head, wondering what Fretick was saying to her.

"What?" she asked uncertainly. "I'm sorry. I don't understand..."

Bron intervened by pointing to the pyramid and shouting, "Maras! Maras!"

Anna, believing she understood, ran toward the pyramid and up the stairs. Reaching the top, she stopped and turned to look at the two on the ground below. Bron handed one of the devices from its harness to its partner, who pointed it at the pyramid and pressed a button. A second later, she heard a soft pop on either side of her. She looked around for the source of the noise but found nothing. Suspecting that the obelisks had just activated again, she stepped toward one of them to examine it further.

"Anna!" Fretick called from the ground. Glancing down, she watched it wave her toward the doorway and cry, "Maras!"

Leaving the obelisk behind, Anna ducked into the chamber and sat against the back wall, waiting.

Minutes later, she heard a soft, high-pitched whine that steadily grew louder over the next several seconds. Peeking outside, she witnessed another vehicle like the first one landing several meters beyond where Fretick and Bron stood behind their transport. Two more beings of the same race stepped out of the cockpit and moved deliberately toward the pyramid. Fretick quickly intercepted the two, waving its arms and yelling something. Bron rushed to keep up.

The conversation that ensued between the four creatures could only be described as an argument from where she stood. The newcomers, wearing a harness and pants similar to Bron's, yelled a lot and pointed fingers at Anna's new friends and the pyramid. Fretick and Bron sounded as if they were doing everything in their power to keep the others away from the structure. A few minutes later, the newcomers returned to their craft, while Fretick and Bron returned to theirs. Within seconds, they lifted off and sped in a direction away from Anna's ship.

Waiting a few moments after the sounds of the crafts faded, Anna peered out and surveyed the area, finding that she was alone again. She felt bad for Fretick and Bron, as it appeared that they were rather forcefully ordered to leave.

With a visual sweep of the area, Anna casually descended the stairs and stepped clear of the pyramid, just in case the energy field was active. She pulled up the holographic screen of her wristcomp and, finding it in proper working order, called Kate.

"Send Seventeen to pick me up. I have some interesting news for you when I get back."

*****

"Are you serious?!" Kate exclaimed skeptically.

Anna nodded emphatically, "Yep! I actually got to talk with them...sort of."

"Can you describe how they looked?"

"Well," the technician began while sitting in the pilot seat. "They were taller than me, probably standing about 2 meters tall, and that was the smaller of the two. The bigger one was probably another half-meter taller! They were barrel-shaped and had three arms and three legs. They had eyes all around them, and their mouths were on top of their head . . . well, what you could conceivably call a head. It was more like a large lump on top of their torso. They had pinkish skin that looked a lot like a human's."

Kate, looking lost in thought as she listened, stood with her arms crossed, while Anna spoke. A few seconds after the description was done, the hologram asked, "Did they look anything like this?"

Another hologram appeared in the middle of the bridge that looked strikingly similar to Bron but with gray skin and not wearing any clothing.

Snapping her fingers, Anna interjected, "Yes! That's them! But, they didn't have the gray skin. It was more flesh-colored like mine."

"Anna, this is an archived illustration."

With jaw slacked, the blonde switched her gaze between the two holograms without saying a word for several seconds. Finally, she asked in disbelief, "Archived?"

Kate walked over to stand next to the other hologram and explained, "This image was in the ship's memory storage. It was located under the topic "Ancient Religions". Why we have this information in the system is unknown to me."

"I may have an idea," Anna interrupted grimly.

Kate continued as if there had been no interjection, "This image is labeled with the name 'Asag', which is also the name of an ancient

Sumerian monster dating back to around 4,000 BC. According to the myths, Asag was said to have brought great pestilence upon the land and dried up entire bodies of water. It is also said that he led an army of stone soldiers, conquered the lands with great power, and was considered by many to be invulnerable to weapons of the time, which would have primarily been an axe or spear."

Anna, impressed by the data, leaned back and contemplated the information for a moment before stating, "You know, that would make some sense, if my theory is anywhere near accurate."

"What would that theory be, Anna?"

"Suppose this race has been spacefaring for thousands of years, well before we began forming our first civilizations. If one of their ships had crashed or even just landed on Earth around where the Sumerians lived, the aftermath of that encounter would have wreaked havoc on, well, everything. We've seen evidence of meteorites messing with ecosystems when they hit. Why not a starship? If it had been a crash, the impact theoretically could have created a blast wave that evaporated lakes and scorched the land.

"If this 'Asag' monster," Anna made quotation marks in the air to illustrate her point, "was the ship's captain or a high-ranking officer, he could have led the survivors in an effort to carve out an area for them on ancient Earth. With superior weapons, armor, and technology, they would seem like an unbeatable foe.

"And, I'm willing to bet that their armor was gray, too!" Anna added, jabbing her finger at the holograms to emphasize her point.

Kate nodded and responded, "That seems like a reasonable assumption, but it is only a theory. Without any kind of concrete evidence to support your hypothesis, that is as far as it can go."

"Yeah, I know," shrugged Anna. "But, it is kind of intriguing to think that this race has had contact with humans before now."

She slid out of the chair and walked toward the airlock, when the avatar asked, "Anna, where are you going now?"

Turning around at the hatch, Anna replied with a smirk, "I need to check and see if the rest of my clothes are dry. If I am going to be making new friends, I'd might as well wear underwear."

Kate gave an understanding grin and turned to look out the forward window, while Anna entered the airlock and climbed outside.

Chapter 19

Three months had passed since Anna's encounter at the pyramid. Since then, she had neither seen nor heard from them, leaving her doubting whether they would try to contact her or visit the pyramid again.

In either case, she knew that she had to carry on with her life and focused her energies on creating a decent source of food for herself. She had since exhausted the supplies from the ship's larder and relied solely on the crops she grew and the meat she hunted during the monthly eclipse. Using the poncho to mask her presence and the night-vision setting on the binoculars to help her see in the darkness, she procured enough meat each time to last until the next cycle. Her success even gave her enough confidence to face a wandering predator when one ventured too close to her. And, she found that the meat she gained from them was quite tasty.

Her homestead now operated like a well-oiled machine and appeared to be stable. Anna owed a lot of that to Kate and the drones. Without their help, she figured that she would still be struggling with planting a small field of crops that may have not produced anything worthwhile. Starvation was not a situation she wanted to face.

The food being grown thrived under the land the drones cultivated for her. Through her foraging efforts, she located several forms of vegetation that safely satisfied her nutritional needs. She appreciated the variety her gardens gave her, but she found the craving for corn on the cob nagged her for the last few weeks. And though the tubers she transplanted to her land added some healthy starch to her diet, she resigned to the idea that they would never taste like the garlic mashed potatoes she loved so much.

The ship was still half-buried in the ground from the crash five months ago. The wood she originally obtained for the purpose of raising the ship and repairing the landing struts was diverted to building a water wheel and irrigation system for the crops. Keeping the crops alive seemed to be a higher priority than walking on a level surface inside the ship. Besides, there would be plenty of time later on to bring up more wood to build the platform. She knew full well that nobody was coming her way any time soon.

* * * * *

"Jump complete, Cap'n," uttered the scruffy-looking pilot in a thick cockney accent. Seated in the forward seat of the small cockpit, he looked over his shoulder at the tall, clean-shaven, dark-haired man standing behind him.

The captain, wearing a navy blue jacket and pants over a white T-shirt, ordered without changing his expression, "Initiate a scan of the area. I need to know where that mining station is."

The pilot jabbed his gloved finger through the switch in the holographic control panel, allowing the sensor display to appear. Seconds later, the image changed to show a large area ahead with a good number of blips.

"Well, Cap'n," the pilot said. "I'm not findin' this station of yours, but I am seein' quite a bit o' debris ahead. Maybe someone got sick o' your station and blew it to Kingdom Come."

The captain leaned closer to the display, narrowing his eyes as he studied the results. He grimaced several seconds later before standing upright again.

"Take us closer to the debris field, Robert. I need to know for sure."

"Aye, cap'n!"

The vessel, a larger, rusting freighter that had seen better days, lurched forward and coasted through the void toward the debris floating nearby.

"Cap'n," the pilot muttered, breaking the silence floating in the tiny bridge. "I'm pickin' up a smaller debris field 'bout five hundred clicks further in t'ward the sun."

"We can check on that later. Focus a scan on the larger debris and look for any indications as to what this was."

Robert's fingers flew over the controls by the sensor display. Through the forward screen, the captain watched the white sensor beam made visible by the dust floating around the debris sweep over the area several times.

A few seconds after the beam ceased, the pilot stated, "Cap'n, You migh' wanna see this."

He poked a switch by the sensors and opened a new holographic window that showed a picture of a jagged slab of metal on which were printed the letters "NING STAT" in white.

"That settles that," the dark-haired man resolved with a hint of a smile. "Set a course for the gas giant."

"Wha' 'bout that other debris field?"

"Probably the old man trying to get away from whatever destroyed the station. Ignore it. Proceed as instructed."

"Aye, Cap'n!"

Several minutes later, the freighter approached the large gaseous planet and drifted into its gravity well.

"Keep the ship moving, Robert. Establish an orbit around it," the captain said distantly while he stared out toward the planet.

"Wha' are you lookin' for?"

"Keep your eyes peeled for a moon with a breathable atmosphere."

"Colony world?"

"Actually, no," the captain assured. "It's completely uninhabited."

Robert turned around in his seat and looked at his superior officer and cried, "Are you shittin' me?! An earthlike world that ain't got nobody on it, and Earth don't know nothin' 'bout it? Sounds like a gold mine t' me."

The captain's eyes narrowed while he said smugly, "Precisely! What better place to use as our new base of operations?"

The pilot chuckled and added before turning back around and establishing an orbital path, "I like the way you think!"

Over half an hour later, the captain floated just above the walkway that traversed the cargo hold with the other four members of his crew either floating or standing nearby.

"When we find a suitable landing site, we need to offload the building materials first and begin work on making the structure as quickly as possible. If the scans from my archives still hold true, the place where we set down will be teeming with savage creatures, so we will need to . . ."

"Cap'n!" Robert's voice interrupted over the loudspeaker.

The captain sighed and cried with slight annoyance, "Yes, Robert."

"I found the moon you were talkin' 'bout and started orbitin' it. But, I need to show you som'thin'."

Sighing again, the officer replied as he pulled himself along by grabbing the handrails, "On my way."

"Shouldn't we go with you?" requested one of the men with a French accent.

Stopping for a second, the captain turned and answered, "I'm sure it's nothing."

A minute later, the officer stepped purposefully into the room and stood behind the British pilot, the expression on his stalwart face betraying his displeasure at being disturbed.

"Well, what have you found, Robert?"

Skeptically, the pilot asked, "I thought you said this place was unin'abited?"

"It is. Why?"

Toggling the sensors panel again, the pilot hit a few more buttons to produce the display.

Pointing to the image, Robert commented, "I'm pickin' up multiple electronic sources from this area east o' this lake 'ere."

The captain leaned in and stroked his chin as he scrutinized the image.

After a few seconds, he asked, "Can you zoom in on it?"

Nodding, Robert replied, "We'll be passin' over the area 'gain in a few seconds. I'll zoom in 'ere in a sec."

A brief moment passed, and the pilot locked on the location and focused in on the area. The resulting image showed the clearing around Anna's ship. Most of the seventeen drones under her control maneuvered about performing their duties maintaining the crops and patrolling the camp.

"Mining drones," the captain commented under his breath. "It looks like the old man got away after all."

Robert interrupted, "Hold on, cap! Pickin' up some movement by the ship down there."

Manipulating the image, the picture zoomed in to the vessel itself and focused to produce an image of Anna lying on her back naked, surrounded by wet clothing.

"Bloody hell!" yelled Robert. "It's a bird!"

The captain's eyes grew wide, but he said nothing as he watched the event unfold on the screen.

As the pilot ogled Anna, he yelled, "Lads, check this! She's naked!"

At that second, the other four crewmen crammed their way into the bridge, climbing over themselves to get a glimpse of the video feed.

"No way!"

"Let me see!"

"Holy shit!"

The sudden rush of extra bodies into the miniscule room nearly shoved the captain, who snapped his gaze around in time to see his crew scramble in, into the pilot's lap and through the forward window.

"'oi!" Robert yelled, irritated at the claustrophobic conditions. "I'm flyin' a ship, ya know!"

"Sorry!" the Asian crewman apologized.

Standing against the wave of bodies that suddenly flooded into the bridge, the captain bellowed, "Guys! Everyone will be able to see. Just calm down and find a spot to squeeze into."

The crew visibly calmed down and found their places in the room. At that point, all six men stared intently at the image of Anna on the screen, a couple of them with their mouths wide open. The room was deathly silent, the only sounds heard was the slight hum of the ship's engines far behind them.

One of the crewmen muttered under his breath with a Hispanic voice, "Wow! I haven't seen a woman in months!"

Robert, breaking the silence several seconds later, commented, "Yeah. Check out the jubblies on 'er bouncin' as she 'as at it!"

"I'll show you all how the French pleasure a woman," the French one announced. "We are known for our way with women."

"It takes one to know one," quipped the Asian man.

"Shut up!"

Not hearing the joke, the dark-skinned man added in a thick African accent, "I would take her from behind and try not to break her."

The first crewman cried, "Leave me an eye socket!"

The other five men stopped and turned to stare at the tanned Hispanic man standing at the back, who suddenly looked from one face to the other defensively and innocently asked, "What?"

"Paco," the French man said flatly. "A little decorum, please."

Frowning slightly, Paco apologized before they turned back to their show, "Sorry."

After several seconds, the captain interrupted, "Enough. Show's over!"

Groans from the rest of the crew evoked the captain's booming response, "We've got work to do. Move!"

After the men cleared the bridge, the captain turned to Robert and asked, "You ARE recording this, right?"

"Oh, yeah!" the pilot replied with a lusty grin.

Smiling back, the captain said, "Good! Now, shut it off and find us a good landing spot on the light side of the moon, far enough away that we can't be detected."

With a curt nod, the British crewman answered, "Aye, cap'n!"

* * * * *

Anna reclined with her eyes closed on the ship in the sun, basking in her orgasm, while lightly stroking a finger up and down the middle of her chest as she closed her legs.

"I don't think I'll ever get tired of that," she muttered to herself with a wide smile on her face.

Her wristcomp, resting next to her on the ship's hull, signaled an incoming message. Lazily, Anna picked it up and answered the call, "Yes, Kate."

"Are you finished?"

Anna instantly sobered up and asked, "Wh . . . what do you mean?"

"Anna, please," Kate answered knowingly. "I know that you have been masturbating on top of the ship every time you take your clothes up to dry. You've been doing it for months now."

Embarrassed, Anna quietly quizzed the holographic companion, "How...how?"

With an amused but annoyed tone, the avatar responded, "There are seventeen sets of eyes flying around the ship. Do you think one of them didn't happen to stop and see what you're doing?"

Anna felt as if she blushed from head to toe. She couldn't avoid admitting the truth now.

"I . . . I . . .," stammered Anna, her words unable to break through her feelings of humiliation.

Kate laughed, "Anna, it's perfectly normal. You could do it right in front of me if you wanted, and it would not matter in the least."

"Kate!" Anna cried in shock.

"You don't have to do that, of course. All I'm saying is, you don't need to feel embarrassed by it. It's perfectly natural for humans to do that."

"I . . . I know. I just . . . I feel like I've been busted by my college roommate...again."

"Well, it would seem that I've grown accustomed to your little quirks over time."

Anna laughed slightly and said, "Okay. I'm going to wait for my clothes to dry, and then I'll check up on the drones scheduled for today."

"Very good, Anna."

A short time later, the blonde technician, now fully dressed, walked across the clearing and surveyed the plants growing in the nearest farmed plot. Separated into four sections, she crouched down and lightly rubbed a large leaf of what looked like a small, dark green head of lettuce between her fingers. It felt thicker than the lettuce and cabbage she was used to eating, but Kate had assured her that it passed the health inspection and was safe to eat. And, she was right. Though a bit chewy, the vegetable tasted quite good and made a great base for the salads she ate every day. After a couple of months, she had grown tired of eating the vegetable the same way and started experimenting with different ways of preparing it.

Anna finished inspecting the crops and followed the irrigation duct to the river and the grove of fruit trees. She had tried to get them to grow near the ship but had been unsuccessful. She plucked a piece of happyfruit, the name she started calling the fruit since she did not know its true name and because of the way it lifted her spirits while she ate it, and took a large bite as she strode to the riverbank. As expected, the elated feelings emerged seconds after swallowing the first bite, and she smiled in response. She could not help but wonder if the consistent high she felt from eating it was caused by some sort of chemical naturally grown in the happyfruit but never got around to having Kate test it. Shrugging off the curious thoughts, she decided to bring it up later and just concentrate on watching the water wheel turn as the river flowed by.

The wristcomp signaled seconds after Anna took another bite. Stuffing the sliver of fruit into her cheek, she answered, "Yesh?"

"Anna… are you eating again?"

"Sho what? What do you need?"

"The sensors are acting up again. Can you take a look at them?"

She chewed and swallowed the bite and replied giddily, "I'm telling you that there is nothing wrong with the sensors. I've looked them over time and time again. The hardware is in perfect working order . . . all things considered."

"Yeah, that's the thing. The sensors still have a limited effective range of 10 kilometers. I think you're missing something."

Anna scoffed as she took another bite. "I think that you need to run a diagnoshtic on your shoftware. Maybe shomethingsh gotten corrupted and needsh to be reinshtalled."

"I would feel better if you would just look at the module again."

Swallowing the chewed bite, she replied sounding a bit perturbed, "As long as you run a diagnostic at the same time."

Kate, after a second's pause, answered, "I agree to your terms."

"Brilliant," she said still sounding a bit agitated. "On my way."

Chapter 20

After the port cargo door slid open, the boarding ramp extended out and lowered to the ground below, allowing two of the crew members to drive forklift walkers carrying large crates outside to the alien turf.

"Hey, Hikaru!" the Frenchman called as the forklifts left the ramp. "What do you think are the chances that we'll meet that woman?"

The Asian glanced over for a second as he maneuvered his lift to the side and lowered his freight before replying, "I don't know, Michel. If I had something to say about it, I'd be flying over there right now with the biggest hard-on anyone's ever seen!"

"I'd have to hold back with her," commented the Frenchman. "I'm afraid I'd kill her with my extraordinary skill in making love."

"Yeah, she'd die laughing, when she saw how small your puny schlong is."

Irritated, Michel turned his yellow walker around, pointed at Hikaru, and cried, "You need to shut up! I don't see you saying anything about fucking that woman. Maybe you prefer the other side of the fence, eh?"

The Asian laughed and answered, "I think not, my tiny friend! With me, making love is an art form, her entire body a canvas."

"So, all the women you've fucked have died of boredom while in bed with you. All the women I've made love to are breathing hard and heavy when I get done with them."

Hikaru chuckled and teased, "Yeah, probably trying to catch their breath from laughing too hard!"

"You are trying my patience, Hikaru!" cried Michel, his face turning red. "You do not defend your manhood! Perhaps . . ."

The Asian interrupted amusingly, "That's because I can at least see mine!"

"THAT'S IT!"

Michel leaped out of his walker and sprinted at Hikaru, his fist cocked in rage. Hikaru rolled his eyes and muttered, "Here we go again.

"You know, you've got anger issues."

"I will show you MY anger issues," Michel yelled as he leaped onto the other walker. "Right across your face!"

Hikaru threw open the cage around the operator's seat, slamming it into the Frenchman and throwing him to the ground. As the Asian dived at his assailant, Michel rolled to the side and watched for a second as Hikaru flopped onto the ground. Michel started to laugh but suddenly found himself under the Asian. The two scrapped for several seconds, until an energy discharge exploded in the dirt next to them and drove the two apart.

At the top of the ramp, Robert and the black-skinned man stood watching the fight, while the captain holstered his sidearm.

"You girls can play with each other later," the captain barked. "Right now, you have bigger fish to fry. Get these building materials out of the ship, or you'll be included with them. Understood?!"

"Yes, sir!" the two responded sharply before dashing back to their cargo walkers and resuming their work in silence.

"Are you sure it's a good idea to let those two blokes move this shit?" Robert asked with a smirk.

Sighing, the captain answered, "That's what they're paid to do. At least, that's what they're SUPPOSED to do. If they don't do their job, I can always throw them out the nearest airlock after we take off again."

"You could always leave them here, captain," the dark-skinned man suggested.

"No," disagreed the captain. "I wouldn't want to torture that woman we saw earlier with their incessant presence."

"Speakin' o' which, are we gonna see if we can find that bird?"

"Yes. In fact, I was getting ready to depart."

Rubbing his hands, the pilot proclaimed, "Brilliant! I'm 'bout to whet me whistle!"

"Figured you'd say that. That's why you're going with me."

"God damn, cap'n! I has a deep love in me ol' ticker for ya right 'bout now!" Robert squealed.

The captain pointed a thumb back into the cargo hold and said, "Go prep the cycles."

As the pilot skipped off gleefully, the black man turned to the captain and asked heatedly, "Why does HE get to go?"

"Because HE is good at sneaking around places . . ."

Staring down at the two cargo handlers ascending the boarding ramp in the walkers, he continued, ". . . unlike the Wonder Twins over there."

Shaking his head, the black man accused, "Sometimes, I would swear you play favorites."

Instantly, the captain grabbed the other man's throat and pushed him backward flailing against the bulkhead, where the crewman hit with a solid thud.

"Don't you EVER question my motives again," the leader threatened in a whisper while holding the black man in a tight choke hold. "Is that clear?"

The victim desperately tried in vain to peel the captain's fingers off his throat to open his windpipe again. He started to feel the effects of the hold, as his eyes bulged out and his dark skin took on a purplish hue.

"Are. We. Clear?!"

The black man managed to nod enough for his superior officer, who released his hold and dropped the crewman limply to the deck. A second later, the African harshly inhaled and began coughing to reopen his windpipe.

The officer continued with a smooth voice, "Ahmad, you are in charge until we get back. Make sure that the materials are offloaded and assembly begins by the time I return."

Ahmad wheezed and coughed for a few seconds before weakly responding, "Yes, sir."

"Good. Carry on."

The captain stiffly marched to the vacant cycle waiting just inside the entrance next to the one manned by Robert, swung his leg over the seat, and revved the engine. He placed the helmet over his head, tested the installed communicator, and glanced at the pilot. Robert flashed a thumbs-up, which the captain mirrored, and the two sped away over the trees at high speed.

A few minutes later, Robert's voice came through the helmet's audio, "So, cap'n, are you callin' dibs on 'er first?"

"No, we're not doing that."

Robert did a double-take at the captain as they flew over the endless forest and asked, "What do ya mean 'we're not doin' that'?"

"No one is going to fuck her. At least, not yet."

"Wha' are we gonna do then? Play 'opscotch?"

"Don't worry, Robert. I've got a plan. You'll get your pussy soon enough."

The pilot shook his head and added, "I sure 'ope so. My prick's been achin' to get wet for a long time now."

* * * * *

Anna lied on the grated deckplates under the bridge, staring at the sensor module in the dim light provided by her wristcomp while attempting to open the module's bottom casing.

"Something's wrong with the sensors, Anna," the blonde mocked. "Come look at the module, Anna.

"Maybe if Kate got laid every once in a while, she wouldn't be so bitchy all the time."

She paused for a second and yelled, "Are you still running that diagnostic, Kate?"

No response.

Anna smiled facetiously to herself and continued, "Answers that question."

"I would make a holographic man for her," Anna griped to herself. "Probably wouldn't do any good, though. She IS a computer, after all."

The casing suddenly dropped off the module and banged against her forehead, causing Anna to wince from the unexpected pain. Dropping her tool, her hand went straight to the wound.

"Ow! Fuck!" she repeated while she cradled the tender spot. Lying in the crawlspace for a couple of minutes tending to the pain, Anna worked to calm herself down and dissipate the troubled attitude that she created. After letting her anger subside, she rubbed away the pain and turned her attention to continuing her work, only to find that the tool she dropped tumbled over the side of the walkway and landed on the inner hull below.

"Damn it!" cursed Anna as she judged the distance. Determining that it was just at arm's length, she turned over and reached for the torque spanner, only to find that the tips of her fingers barely brushed against the handle. She stretched for it, pressing her body and resting her ear against the grating, ignoring the piercing pressure on her lobe.

While she worked to retrieve the tool, she heard a slight high-pitched whine reverberate through the deckplate. Thinking that she had not heard the sound associated with the ship before, she paused and lifted her head to listen more intently. She could not be sure, but she believed that she heard the whine die down outside the ship. Giving a look of curious concern, she decided that the spanner was not going anywhere soon and crawled back onto the bridge.

Anna hopped to the pilot station and looked outside. Nothing moved except the tree branches slowly swaying in the wind. The drones had shut down and rested on the ground, not surprising considering that Kate was offline with her diagnostic check. The area seemed too quiet, and set her on edge. She blamed her complacency with the drones being around for that.

Attempting to use the sensors would be a useless gesture, since she had to unplug the module from the ship's systems to investigate it. As a result, she knew that she would have to step outside to check the area for herself. Making sure that her pistol and knife were in place, she walked into the airlock.

Standing on top of the vessel next to the dorsal hatch, nothing looked out of the ordinary with the exception of the silence that filled her ears again like when she first arrived on Paradise. But, Anna could not help the feeling that something was not right. She glanced all around her for anything that appeared unfamiliar. Nothing. Walking to the aft section, she stood next to the tail fin above the engine assembly and searched again. This time, she caught the glint of something in the woods a fair distance behind the ship. She pulled the binoculars out of her belt and hunted for the source of the reflected light.

A few seconds later, Anna located what looked to be an air cycle parked about a hundred meters back just beyond the tree line. No, she saw two of them there. But, where were the drivers? They had to be somewhere, and why didn't they make themselves known? Any company would be welcome at this point. Scratch that. Any company would be good, as long as they weren't trying to kill her.

Was that movement ahead?

Before she had a chance to find out, she felt a sharp blow on the back of her head, and everything went black.

"Night, love!" said Robert happily as he holstered his pistol. His eyes ran lustfully up and down Anna's athletic frame, and a little smile formed on his bearded face.

"Man, you are fit, aren't ya?"

A beep from his belt told Robert to retrieve the communicator and answer the call.

"Yeah?"

The captain asked through the line, "Well?"

"Yep! I go' 'er. Dropped like a stone."

"Bring her here. We'll take her back to the ship."

Robert sighed and replied, "Aye, sir."

He looked longingly at her unconscious form again and mumbled, "Ya know, I may have to take ya back to the cap'n, but 'e didn't say anythin' about coppin' a feel while I do."

He knelt down and unfastened her tool belt, letting the straps slide off her waist onto the hull. He easily lifted her up and draped her over his shoulder. As he walked toward the nose of the vessel, he clapped a hand onto a butt cheek and gently squeezed it.

"Ya like that, love?" he asked. "I do, too."

* * * * *

Anna woke up some time later feeling groggy and with a splitting headache. The back of her skull throbbed from where she had been struck. She tried to place her hand over the source of the pain but discovered that she could not move it. Turning her head, she blearily stared at her hand, barely able to see that somebody had bound her hand to the bedpost. Looking to the other side confirmed that her other hand was tied there as well. She tugged on the cloth strips that confined her in place, but she was held fast and not going anywhere anytime soon.

She turned and looked down at the end of the bed and found that her feet were not bound. However, panic began to rise within her, as she realized that whoever had abducted her took the liberty of removing most of her clothes. She was now wearing only her T-shirt and panties; her bra, pants, boots, and wristcomp were nowhere to be seen.

Her head cleared after a while, allowing her to better examine her surroundings. The room where she was confined appeared to be a small cabin, perhaps within a spaceship of some sort. From what she could tell, the accommodations were spartan at best, so this room was either thrown together for her or the people that resided here didn't have much to their name.

Despite not having any knowledge on how long she had been unconscious, the pressure building in her bladder told her that she had been out for a while. She hoped that somebody would come along soon and let her use the head.

Anna stopped upon hearing voices outside the door. She leaned her head closer to help her make out what they were saying.

"Man!" the first voice exclaimed with an Asian accent. "That ham really sucked tonight! What was Michel thinking?"

The other one, sounding Hispanic, replied, "I know! I think he undercooked it or something."

"Something. At least he tries to add a little variety to what we eat. All you make are tamales!"

"At least I make them right."

"Yeah. If you make one thing long enough, you're bound to get it right sooner or later."

"I don't see you making anything besides sushi and yakisoba. Can't you at least cook the fish first?"

The Asian man answered in a calm tone, "First off, if I cooked it, it wouldn't be sushi. Second, by Japanese cuisine, it's an art form."

Before the other one said anything, the Asian man continued, "Hey, there's the room. When do you think the captain's going to let us at her?"

"I don't know," the other said after a second's pause. "I hope it's soon. I can't wait to see her."

"See her? I can't wait to fuck her."

Chapter 21

Anna's eyes snapped open wide from the remark, panic sweeping over her. They meant for her to be their sex slave. That explains her current state of dress. Pushing thoughts of what might have already happened to her while she was unconscious out of her mind, she wanted more than ever to break her bonds and flee. She knew she couldn't try now for fear of the men outside hearing her. Though her heart racing in her chest beat loudly in her ears, she tried to listen again, but the two men had walked away from the door. She listened for a few seconds more, hoping the silence on the other side of the door meant the coast was clear.

Praying that nobody was outside her door, Anna tested the straps that confined her to the bed. She twisted and tugged, trying to find some way of wriggling free, but her efforts were fruitless. Frustrated, she searched the room for anything that might help her out of her plight. Besides the bed, desk, and dresser, nothing was visible. The desk did have a drawer without a lock on it, but it was out of reach.

Or, was it?

Swinging her legs toward the side of the bed, Anna carefully squirmed her way to where she could set her feet on the floor. Her position, bending her back to keep from stretching the wrist farthest from her feet, was uncomfortable, but she felt that she was making progress.

She stretched out with her leg toward the desk drawer. Not close enough. Walking her feet toward her target, she turned on her side and reached out with her leg again. Despite stretching her shoulder to the limit, her foot did seem to get a little closer to the drawer handle but was still not close enough to grab it.

At that second, Anna heard footsteps outside the room. She scrambled back onto the bed and, despite the relief on her back and shoulder, cursed under her breath just before the door opened.

A Hispanic man wearing an orange shirt and black pants looked into the room and, upon seeing Anna lying on the bed, smiled broadly before entering with a tray of food.

"Hola!" he said, his smile not fading while he spoke. "You're pretty."

Anna stared coldly back at him without saying a word, anger flaring in her eyes at her captor.

"I don't blame you for not wanting to talk," he continued with a sigh as he set the tray onto the desk. "But, don't worry. I'm here to help care for you. The captain said it was my turn to be your caretaker."

He continued cheerfully, "My name is Paco. What's yours?"

Again, Anna did not respond, electing only to stare daggers at his captor.

After a moment, Paco stated, "I see. You're going to be one of those non-talking types. That's okay. I'll give you a name, then."

He looked her over from head to toe several times and slowly uttered, "An…"

Anna raised her eyebrows at the attempt, suggesting to her that maybe he knew her true identity.

Finally, he proclaimed, "You look like an Angelina to me, a pretty name for a pretty lady. Is that your real name?"

No response.

"Okay, it's settled then. Your name will be Angelina.

"Now that that's settled, I brought your dinner. I hope you like it. We have baked ham, scalloped potatoes and green beans. I'll warn you, though. I think the ham's a little undercooked, but you might like it. Or, would you like some water first? I don't think you've had anything to drink since you got here. Let's do that first."

Lifting the empty glass, Paco poured some water in from the short plastic pitcher next to it and walked over to the bed. Sitting on the edge of the bed, he held the glass in front of her face, encouraging her to open her mouth and drink.

Anna merely looked at the glass and back at her server. She was trying to decide to quench her dry throat or abstain, suspecting that they may have slipped a drug into the drink.

"Oh, it's okay," Paco assured. "I filled the pitcher myself. See?"

He took a sip of water in front of her and gulped it down before offering it back to her. Again, Anna merely stared at the drink.

A few seconds later, he stood and stepped by the desk again, saying while he moved, "Perhaps you'll be thirsty later."

As he returned the glass to the tray, Anna noticed the sidearm holstered on his hip. It seemed kind of small, but having it in her hands would give her some power in this situation.

"Paco," she finally said, her voice crackling a bit. She cleared her throat and continued trying to sound gentle, "I really need to use the bathroom, and I'd really hate to wet the bed. Can you help me and let me out of these straps?"

The man turned around with a smile on his face and replied, "I like your voice. It is very sweet, too.

"I have just the thing for you. Be right back."

Paco swept out the door, barely closing it behind him. The instant he was gone, Anna struggled against the restraints again. But, the attempt only lasted a few seconds, as he emerged through the door again with a bedpan in hand.

"Here! You can use this. That way, you don't have to wet the bed."

Anna rolled her eyes and sighed in frustration.

He stepped up to the bed and set the bedpan on the mattress next to her. Sorely tempted to swing her leg up and knee him in the jaw, Anna tensed her leg to strike. At the last second, she changed her tactics. What if Paco was not imposing himself on her and was trying to be nice? She decided that winning his favor may actually be more beneficial to helping her escape rather than attacking him, especially considering that she would still be bound to the bed if she knocked him out.

Anna looked at the bedpan and back up at him standing over her, staring at her body. With an annoyed glare, she asked, "Can you find it in your heart to loosen my hands, so I can at least relieve myself without, you know, going through my panties?"

"Hmmm?" he replied absentmindedly before breaking his trance. "Oh! Sorry. Yes, I can help you with that."

Smiling in response, Anna wiggled her fingers, anticipating her freedom. Instead, Paco hooked his fingers under the waistband of her panties.

"What are you doing?!" she cried in shocked disbelief.

Looking at her face while he spoke, he responded in a confused tone, "I'm doing what you asked. I'm removing your panties. This way, you can't get them wet when you pee."

"I'm not a 2-year-old!"

"No, you aren't. But, I can't untie you. Sorry."

As he pulled her panties down over her hips, she yelled while she tried to squirm away from him, "God damn it! Stop!"

Despite her resistance, Paco pulled the garment past her hips, pausing long enough to stare at her exposed crotch for a long second, and off her legs.

"Wow!" he said with a smirk, observing the assorted stains in the formerly white pair of panties. "You really need some new underwear, Angelina."

"Fuck you!" Anna spat as she stared harshly back at him.

Paco looked dejected for a second and apologized, "I'm really sorry that I had to do that. But, I have my orders. I cannot untie your hands."

Anna stared at him but asked frantically as he dropped her underwear into the top dresser drawer, "What are you doing?"

"Since I can't untie you and you may need to take a piss again, it might be better for you if you kept these off. That way, you won't wet yourself waiting for me to come check on you."

"So, I'm supposed to lie here like this?!"

Paco shrugged, "I guess so."

Anna shook her head as if by doing so would somehow wake her from the nightmare she was now living in.

"Well," he suggested. "You should probably go ahead and pee, so I can clean the bedpan."

Anna fumed while she contemplated her choices. She could relieve herself and get it over with, or she could delay the whole thing just to test his limits. On the one hand, she would finally release the building pressure she felt and maybe finally get him out of here. Yet, she could hold out and maybe get her panties back or even get him to untie her out of sheer impatience. However, that could have the nasty side effect of him deciding to get physically violent with her, and that would more than likely have the net result of her wetting the bed involuntarily.

With a little effort, she managed to scoot back toward the headboard and sit up on the flat pillow. She pulled the bedpan toward her with her foot and positioned it in front of her. She moved forward but accidentally bumped the bedpan away from her.

"Here, let me . . ." Paco began as he moved forward, stopping when he saw Anna glaring back at him.

She again pulled the bedpan back into position and successfully mounted it the second time. Taking a deep breath, she prepared to relax but saw him out of the corner of her eye watching her.

Turning her head, she demanded, "For fuck's sake, a little privacy, please?!"

Paco frowned but begrudgingly turned to face the wall.

Keeping an eye on him, Anna did her best to relax, taking deep breaths and take her mind off the fact that a strange man was in the room with her. She even tried visualizing a huge waterfall, doing her best to conjure the sounds of rushing water in her mind's ear.

After a couple of minutes with no results, Paco asked impatiently, "What's taking so long?"

"You know what?" Anna replied, irritated by the question. "Let me trade with you. Why don't you try doing this with your hands bound and a stranger in the room with you."

Throwing his arms in the air, Paco cried, "Fine! I'll step out."

Before she had a chance to say anything more, the door shut behind him, leaving her alone.

"Finally!" she exclaimed through a whisper.

A couple of minutes later, Paco lingered outside the door, leaning against the opposite wall with his arms crossed and scowling as he waited.

"'oi!"

He turned to see Robert pacing down the corridor toward him. The pilot was carrying a pool cue with him and wearing a big smile on his face.

"'ow's it goin'?"

"Okay," Paco replied, sounding a little down. "Just waiting for her to get done."

"Waitin' for 'er? What's she doin'?"

Hesitantly, the Hispanic said, "She's, uh, relieving herself."

"Is she now?" Robert affirmed with a smile.

"Robert, wait!"

The pilot opened the door and found Anna sitting on top of the bedpan as she just finished. Hearing the door whoosh open, she snapped her gaze to the doorway and, upon seeing Robert standing there, yelled, "Hey!"

Robert chuckled and greeted, "'ello, love! Excited to see me?"

"Get out!"

Paco, standing right behind the Brit, pleaded, "Come on, Robert! Leave her alone."

Turning around, Robert questioned teasingly, "What's the matter, Paco? You gettin' soft for 'er? Don't tell me you're smitten' with the li'l bitch?"

"No! That's not it!"

"I think you're fallin' for 'er, aren't ya? Well, you know what? Get over it! All you are is 'er nursemaid. An' if you do your job right, maybe you can get wha'ever is left o' 'er after the rest of us are done."

"Now, hold on . . ."

"No," Robert forcefully interrupted. "You need to remember your place in this 'ere crew! Just because you 'elp keep the ship runnin' and got stuck wit' bein' 'er nanny doesn't mean that you can have any dibs above me an' every other scumbag on this boat. You do what the cap'n tells you an' like it!"

"So, why should I listen to you? Last time I checked, you ain't the captain!"

Before Anna could say anything, Robert cocked his arm back and slugged Paco across the jaw, sending the tan-skinned man sprawling across the corridor. Paco slammed into the metal wall with a solid thud, and the pilot was on him again.

"Robert!" a voice yelled from down the hall from a person Anna could not see. "Stand down!"

Releasing her caregiver, Robert stood to attention and cried, "Aye, cap'n!"

"Get back to the bridge and check our fuel levels. Make sure we have enough to take off again."

"Aye, aye!" Robert yelped and ran off.

"Paco!" the captain barked. "Get up!"

He stood to attention in front of the door, saluted, and replied sharply, "Yes, sir!"

"How is our guest doing?"

Glancing into the room for a brief second, he answered, "Fine, sir. Just finishing up."

"Good. Finish the job, and make it quick. I want a word with her when you're done."

"Aye, sir!"

Paco stepped into the room, and the door slid shut behind him. Immediately, Anna could see the red welt developing on his chin. She actually felt kind of bad for him. He stepped up to defend her and took a punch for it. Maybe he did care for her, however little it may be.

Impatiently, he asked, "Are you done?"

She moved off the bedpan, "Yes, I'm done."

Snatching up the bedpan, he quickly steadied it to prevent the liquid within from sloshing around. On reflex, he looked into the container and back up at Anna with narrowed eyes. After a few seconds, he walked to the door and passed through after it swished open.

A couple of minutes later, Paco returned with the empty bedpan, set it at the foot of the bed, and turned to grab the tray when the door opened again.

In the doorway stood a tall, thin man with short brown hair wearing a white collared shirt and navy blue pants along with a long navy blue trench coat. Anna could only assume that this was the captain Robert and Paco mentioned earlier.

"Done?" he asked sternly with a clear American accent.

Standing tall, the Hispanic man replied, "Yes, sir. I was just about to . . ."

"Leave the tray," the captain ordered with a simple wave of his hand.

"Yes, sir."

The captain nodded his head back and added, "Leave us."

Without uttering another word, Paco quickly exited the room, leaving the captain alone with Anna. A second later, the door closed with a slight hiss.

Once the door was securely shut, he looked at her and asked, "Anna Foster, right?"

Surprised upon hearing her name, she replied quizzically, "How did you . . ."

"I hacked into your wristcomp. Nice little device, I might add. But, never mind that. I'm not here to ask about your belongings. I'm here to ask about you."

Anna clamped her mouth shut, determined not to help him with any of his questions. He had already broken into her wristcomp files. What more could he possibly want to know?

"First," he began. "Let me extend an act of good faith."

The captain strode purposefully to the dresser in the back corner, opened the bottom drawer and pulled out a white linen sheet, which he then unfolded and draped over Anna's nude hips and legs.

Surprised at the act of kindness, she watched the sheet float down upon her and then looked back at the captain.

"I am James Renfro, captain of the *Resolute*. Did you tell Paco your name?"

Anna merely shook her head negatively.

"He picked out a name for you."

Reluctantly, she nodded.

James shook his head, humored by the situation before he responded with a slight laugh, "Let me guess. Angelina?"

Anna meekly nodded.

"Well . . . 'Angelina', I need you to help my crew."

"You can help ME by untying my hands. I'm afraid I can't be much help confined to the bed."

"No. A few questions first. Are you a good cook?"

Surprised by the question, Anna did a double take and asked confusedly, "What?"

"Are you a good cook?"

"Why?"

The captain answered as he removed his trenchcoat and laid it across the top of the dresser, "I already have a ship's engineer and his assistant, so I don't need another technician aboard. I need to find if you fit in here."

Anna furrowed her brow and asked, "And, why would I want to stay aboard?"

"You don't have a choice."

Before Anna could respond, James continued, "Answer the question, please."

"I'm not much of a cook."

"Domestic cleaning?"

"No. Is this all you expect out of a woman: to be a homemaker?"

"Well," James sighed as he stepped next to the bed. "If you can't do any of that, then the only role you can perform on this ship is 'Morale Officer'."

Anna cocked an eyebrow and asked through clenched teeth, "What does THAT entail?"

James responded by whipping the sheet off of Anna, exposing her lower body again.

"I believe it's time to check your qualifications."

Anna's eyes widened, as the captain unbuckled his belt and unfastened his pants.

"Go to hell!" she threatened as she pulled back her leg and kicked him squarely in the crotch. James doubled over from the blow. Anna drew back again and smashed her foot across his jaw. The captain tumbled to the floor beside the bed with a slight groan.

Within seconds, he rose to his feet and stared coldly at her while rubbing his jaw. Anna prepared to launch another assault.

"Hellcat," he stated. "We'll see how long that lasts."

James lunged at her with a hand stretched toward her. Anna kicked again, but he blocked the attack with his forearm. Before she could react, he was upon her, his hand raised to strike.

Several minutes later, James walked out of the room to find the rest of the crew waiting in the corridor. He looked at their faces, each of them waiting anxiously. The captain intentionally paused, reveling in the attention.

After several seconds had passed, he breathed deeply and stated, "Next."

Chapter 22

"Smooth as silk," Hikaru commented with a smile at the breakfast table the next morning.

"You can say that again!" added Michel as he served a plate of scrambled eggs to the Asian man. "Eat up!"

Staring at the food, Hikaru asked as he poked a pink cube with his fork, "Is this the ham from last night's dinner mixed in here?"

"Just eat it. It's not that bad this time," Paco suggested from across the table.

Pointing his fork at the Hispanic man, Hikaru shot back, "Easy for you to say. You eat everything."

Paco shrugged.

Hikaru grumbled and ate a bite of the eggs.

"Mornin', boys!" Robert greeted cheerfully as he hopped into the galley. "'ow's everyone feelin'?"

Michel looked over his shoulder for a second and stated enthusiastically, "Better now that I am sure I'm a far superior lover than all of you combined."

Robert and Hikaru emphatically agreed, but Paco continued eating his eggs without a word.

"Whatsa matter, Paco?" the pilot teased. "You're not cheerin'. Did you not get to shag 'er last night?"

Paco sank deeper in his chair and took another bite of his eggs without replying.

"Aw, no! 'e didn't wet 'is willy last night!"

The other two chuckled at Robert's comment while he continued to pester Paco.

"Were you afraid of 'urtin' 'er, or were you just not gettin' it up?"

209

Hikaru interjected, "Maybe she didn't turn him on?"

"Wha' are you sayin'?" Robert gasped. "You sayin' that 'e's a pillow biter?"

"I'm not gay," Paco mumbled.

Robert leaned in and asked, "Eh? What's that?"

"I'm not gay!"

Chuckling, Robert added, "I don't know. Come to think o' it, you do seem a wee bi' girly."

Paco shot up to his feet, pushing the chair back against the wall in the process. Pressing his finger into the pilot's chest with each word, he growled, "I'm . . . not . . . gay!"

Dropping his humored expression, Robert straightened up and quietly threatened, "I don't like your tone, poofter. Shall we 'ave another go?"

"Robert!"

The captain's voice broke the tension in the air, and everyone came to attention. James walked into the room and looked over each of the crewmen for a few seconds.

"Paco, go check on our guest."

The Hispanic man wordlessly bolted from the room, grabbing the plate of food Michel had just filled on his way out.

"Where's Ahmad?"

As Robert shrugged his shoulders, Michel interrupted, "He was in here earlier. He said something about checking the engines after shoveling down his food. He has the table manners of a goat. I'm surprised if he tasted anything."

Ignoring the complaint, James turned on his heel and left the galley, making a beeline toward the engine room.

* * * * *

Paco poked his head into Anna's room to find her silently curled up in as much of a fetal position as she could manage while still tied to the headboard. Her wrists appeared pinched and bright red from the cloth restraints tightening during last night's ordeal. He set the plate of cooling eggs on the desk after the door closed behind him and watched her for several seconds before clearing his throat.

"How are you holding up?" he asked, hoping for a response. But, she remained motionless and said nothing.

He glanced at the floor as he struggled to find something that would help provide her with some comfort.

"I . . ." he stuttered. "I brought you some breakfast. You must be hungry. Would you like some eggs?"

Anna still did not respond.

"They have bits of ham in them. It's really pretty good. Michel outdid himself this morning. Of course, it doesn't take much."

Paco looked at her again, hoping that his attempt at humor would be enough to ease the tension in the room. He lifted the plate, carried it over to the bed, and sat on the floor next to her. Scooping up a forkful of eggs, he eased the bite toward Anna encouragingly.

"Here. Take a bite. You need to eat."

Anna did not stir.

"Please?"

She turned her head away from him.

Setting the fork back on the plate, Paco set it aside on the floor by the bedpost. He leaned up on his knees and gently placed a hand on her side. Anna violently pulled away, but the movement stretched her arm even more, causing her to flinch in pain.

"Don't!" she mumbled intensely, her body trembling violently.

Realizing the error, Paco settled back onto the floor and stared at her back for a few more minutes.

After a short while, Anna whispered, "Go away."

"What?"

"Go away!" she repeated, still no more than a whisper.

He sighed, "I'm supposed to feed you breakfast. Please eat."

Anna fell silent again.

"You haven't eaten in almost a day. You need to eat."

Again, she said nothing.

Slightly frustrated, Paco sympathetically asked, "Is there anything I can do?"

"Let me go," she pleaded.

"The captain would kill me if I did. He doesn't want you going anywhere."

Anna paused a few seconds before replying, "Untie my hands?"

Paco weighed his options. On the one hand, he could release her hands, easing her pain and probably win her favor for his kindness, but he would probably be punished for disobeying the captain's orders. Considering he was the newest member of the crew, doing so would more than likely not cast him in a good light with the others. However, he could keep her tied up, running the risk of permanent damage to her hands, and nothing would really change with how he got along with everyone else aboard.

Rising to his knees, Paco tenderly grabbed the knot and worked at loosening it. About a minute later, he untied the strap around her wrist, and she weakly pulled her arm to her side.

"Thank you," she whispered, the words barely reaching his ears.

He reached for the strap around her other hand but could not get the leverage he needed to effectively undo the knot.

"I'm sorry," informed Paco after attempting for several seconds. "But, I need to get on the bed to release your other hand."

Since she said nothing in reply, he planted one knee on the bed by her shoulder blades and straddled over her. As he worked the knot, Anna glanced up. Seeing him positioned above her flooded her mind with memories of the previous night. Consumed by the violent imagery, tears burned her eyes and streamed quietly down her face.

After releasing her and watching her arm flop onto the mattress, Paco looked down into her face and innocently asked, "Did I hurt you?"

Anna continued to weep without answering.

"What is it?" he questioned, leaning down toward her.

She muttered between sobs, "Please..."

Confused, he asked, "What?"

"No more, please..." sobbed Anna, shoving him with her forearm. Lacking the strength to push him off the bed, she only managed to nudge him toward the edge.

Paco climbed off the bed and watched her sorrowfully as she wrapped her arms about her body. After thinking about her reaction, he replied, "I am really...truly sorry."

Silently, he left the room, leaving Anna with her grief.

* * * * *

Zooming over the treetops some time later, Ahmad drove his skycycle toward his destination. Grumbling about having to perform the task the captain gave him about half an hour before, he vowed to finish the work as quickly as he could and get back to the ship to finish checking the engines. As much as he liked shore leave, spending that time on a world without any form of civilization was not his idea of fun.

After flying for several more minutes, Ahmad reached the clearing where Anna's ship had crashed. The dozen or so drones that flittered about the area seemed to pay him no mind as he landed the cycle behind the vessel's engines and dismounted. He rounded the corner and walked along the starboard side toward the nose of the ship, watching the drones' activity as he moved. Surprised to find them farming and tending the land instead of mining, he shook his head in disbelief, shocked and impressed with the resourcefulness of their prisoner at the same time.

Ahmad reached the front of the ship and climbed up to the dorsal hatch, pausing when he spotted the keypad lock. He knelt next to it and punched in a random code, confirming its operation when the red bar appeared above the buttons.

Whipping out the communicator from his belt, Ahmad called his ship, "*Resolute*, this is Ahmad. Get me the captain."

Seconds later, the voice of the captain came through the communicator, "What is it, Ahmad?"

"The ship has a keypad lock on the top hatch. I need the passcode."

"Understood," James replied after a short pause. "I'll call you back."

Back on the ship, the captain marched off the bridge straight down to Anna's room. The door whisked open, and he walked in with a grim look on his face that turned to surprise upon seeing her sitting up and rubbing her red, swollen wrists.

He lunged forward, giving Anna barely enough time to flinch as he backhanded her across the face. As she hit the mattress, he screamed, "HOW DID YOU GET LOOSE?!"

When Anna only answered with a muffled whimper, James grabbed her by the hair and pulled her up, making her cry out in pain as he did.

"Give me the code to your ship," seethed James, his face inches away from hers.

Despite the pain, Anna scratched his face near his mouth and answered, "Fuck you!"

The captain pulled back and punched her in the gut. The blow knocked the wind from her, and she collapsed onto the bed doubled over in agony after he released her hair.

"GIVE ME THE CODE!"

Anna groaned, "Go to hell!"

Feeling a sting of pain coming from his lip, James lightly touched his fingertip to the wound and looked at the drops of blood that coated it. The sight set the fire in his eyes ablaze. He grabbed her by the hair again, slugged her across the jaw, and threw her onto the bed again.

"NOW!!!"

Out in the hall, Robert, Paco, Michel, and Hiraku loitered outside Anna's door, listening to the tirade on the other side.

Paco cringed as the sound of her being hit again reverberated through the wall and pleaded softly, "Answer him."

Anna's scream pierced the metal wall, causing both Paco and Hiraku to flinch.

Michel inquired to the group, "Is he going to kill her, too?"

Shaking his head, Robert solemnly answered, "Dunno. Maybe."

"She'll make the fourth girl he's killed like this," the Frenchman sighed. "Why does he do this?"

"Mommy issues?" suggested Hiraku.

As everyone else looked at him, some with curiosity and others with annoyance, he shrugged and added, "Makes sense to me."

The sounds of violence stopped suddenly, and all eyes turned back to the door. Paco turned pale as he feared the worst. Michel shook his head again.

Suddenly, the door opened, and James stepped out, stopping in the doorway while he stared at the four men waiting outside.

Several seconds later, he asked, "Who wants her?"

Michel and Robert quickly raised his hand, earning a nod from the captain.

"She's all yours, Michel," James said just before marching down the hall.

As the Frenchman stepped through the doorway, Robert protested, "Wha'?! Michel, you bloomin' wankstain!"

"Michel, don't do this!" pleaded Paco. "She's just been beat up."

Before anyone else could object, the door slid shut.

Turning around to face the bed, Michel paused as he took in what his captain had done. Anna was still alive, but she had been severely battered. She lied crumpled on the bed over her knees, wearing only her white T-shirt. Her face was red from being slapped multiple times, and a bruise was already forming on her jaw.

Michel watched her slowly try to curl herself up into a fetal position.

Shaking his head again, Michel muttered to nobody in particular, "Why does he do this?"

A few seconds later, he walked toward her.

* * * * *

Ahmad keyed in the code he just heard from the captain, and the hatch slid open without a problem.

"That worked, captain," he said through the communicator. "Anything else I should know?"

James replied, "Nothing I am aware of. Hope you find some useful stuff in there."

The black man smiled and added, "Will do. Ahmad out."

He returned the communicator back to his belt and climbed into the airlock. As his feet touched the floor of the airlock, the upper hatch closed, plunging the cramped room into darkness.

"Hello," a female voice greeted with a British accent through the airlock door. "Who are you?"

"Uh," Ahmad started. "I am Ahmad. I didn't know anyone was here."

"Hello, Ahmad. I am here. Why are you here?"

"Who are you?" he asked.

"I am the one asking questions right now, Ahmad. Why are you here?"

"Angelina sent me to pick up some supplies."

"Angelina?"

"Yes," he nodded in the dark. "The owner of this ship?"

The woman's voice did not respond for a few seconds. Finally, she said with mock enlightenment, "Oh, right! Angelina! Yeah.

"What supplies did she want you to pick up," the voice continued, her tone turning serious.

"Um . . . she needed . . . her toiletries! Yeah! Her shampoo and conditioner, stuff like that."

Ahmad felt pretty good about coming up with an answer so quickly, especially since he knew that he couldn't lie very well.

"I see," she stated flatly. "What is the password, please?"

"Password?" he remarked, his happy expression melting away. "Um . . ."

"You have 10 seconds to give the password," she warned.

"Or what?"

"You're wasting time."

"Um . . . um . . ." Ahmad stuttered, unable to come up with an answer. After several seconds had passed, he finally guessed, "Uh . . . please?"

"I'm sorry," she said with fake sorrow. "That is an incorrect answer."

"So, what's going to happen?"

With a serious tone, Kate answered, "I regret to inform you that I am not letting you in."

Ahmad sighed, "I kind of figured that."

"I'm not letting you out, either."

He paused for a few seconds before yelling, "WHAT?!"

"You might as well settle in, because you're not going anywhere!"

Chapter 23

"Why hasn't anyone thought of removing the captain from command?" Paco asked quietly while he, Robert, and Hikaru walked down the boarding ramp outside.

"Oh, they 'ave, Paco," Robert answered. "You can bet on that."

With a curious expression, Paco continued, "What happened?"

Hikaru said, "The mutiny died real quick. The captain got wind of it, killed the ringleader in front of the rest of the crew, and stuffed his corpse into the nearest airlock. It wasn't pretty, either."

"Yeah," Robert added with a gruesome smile. "'e gave 'im a necktie, if ya ge' my meanin'."

He mimicked the action with his thumb.

Paco shuddered as he imagined the scene unfolding.

"Yeah, 'e's a bi' on the crazy side, but 'e's one damn good pirate. Best loot we ever got was under 'is command."

"Speaking of which," Hikaru interrupted. "We need to get this latest batch offloaded and secured soon if we're going to take off again without earning the captain's wrath. He's already on edge as it is."

Grabbing a handle to climb into a cargo walker, Paco turned back and inquired, "He does seem a bit more irritable these days. Why is that?"

"Dunno. Don' get paid to care."

"Well, Dr. Takahashi," Paco teased lightly. "Any insights?"

Hikaru took a deep breath before answering from inside his walker, "If you ask me, I think it's because your girlfriend is a bit stronger-willed than the others we've acquired."

Paco started his walker after climbing inside, put on the headset, and asked, "Do you think the captain hates her?"

The Japanese man paused for a moment before stating, "I don't think so. I think he just has issues with women in general. I'm not going to ask him about it. That's a good way to get yourself killed."

Paco nodded grimly but said nothing.

"You should be proud, Paco," Hikaru assured as his walker stepped forward. "You found yourself a good one! She's managed to survive longer than the others."

The Hispanic nodded again and said under his breath, "I don't feel proud about this, not in the least."

On the bridge of the *Resolute*, James pressed the communicator button and paged, "Ahmad, come in."

No response.

"Ahmad, do you read me?"

Still no response.

James frowned, holding back the anger welling up inside, and called again, "Ahmad, are you . . ."

"Yes, captain. Ahmad here."

"Where are you?" the captain asked, his voice betraying his frustration.

"I'm inside the airlock of Angelina's ship."

"Why aren't you inside the ship itself?"

After a second, Ahmad replied, "Because the other woman won't let me in."

James' eyes grew wide as the thought of somebody else standing in his way came to light. The last thing he wanted was another unknown variable thrown in the mix.

"What other woman?" he asked slowly.

Ahmad replied, "I don't know. I'm stuck in the airlock."

Growing more frustrated, James asked, "Did you get her name?"

"No. But, she's British, and she's a pain in the ass."

The captain took a breath, trying futilely to compose himself, "Did you bring your tools with you? Maybe you can find a panel to open and . . ."

"Um, no. I left my tools on the bike."

James took several deep breaths, his nostrils flaring with each one that grew louder than the one before.

"WHAT?!"

Ahmad pleaded, "It won't happen again."

"You're damn right it won't happen again," fumed James. "Because if you do, I will kill you myself!"

He slapped the switch to close the channel and stormed off the bridge. A minute later, he stomped into Anna's room and stared for a second at Michel sitting on the bed beside her.

The captain threatened. "Out!"

The Frenchman looked back at him dumbfounded and stammered, "But, but captain . . ."

"I SAID GET OUT!!"

Michel paused, looking between James and Anna. A couple of seconds later, James impatiently threw the man off the bed. Michel yelped as he hit the floor.

The captain shoved Anna against the wall, leaned toward her, and demanded, "Who's the other woman?"

Stunned from the impact, she merely moaned in pain.

"WHO'S THE OTHER WOMAN?!"

Regaining some semblance of her senses, Anna mumbled, "I don't know what you're talking about."

Straightening his posture, he warned, "Really? Let me refresh your memory…"

He grabbed her by the front of her shirt, jerked her up, and harshly slapped her across the face twice while screaming, "THE

OTHER WOMAN HOLDING MY CREWMAN PRISONER IN YOUR SHIP! THAT OTHER WOMAN!"

"Captain!" Michel pleaded from behind Anna's assailant.

James slapped her again, splitting her lip.

"WHO IS SHE?!"

"Captain, you're going to kill her!"

He stopped his assault and looked at Michel over his shoulder. A look of insane aggression consumed his visage.

"What good is she to you dead?"

James's expression hardened, as the Frenchman's words sank in. He turned back to Anna and threw her onto the bed. She landed in a heap and did not stir as blood oozed from her mouth onto the dirty white sheet.

As he turned on his heel and marched from the room, the captain ordered, "Clean her up."

* * * * *

Over half an hour later, James landed the second skycycle about a dozen meters from where Ahmad had left his. Quickly dismounting and drawing his pistol, he dashed forward and braced himself against the hull, waiting for some kind of response from inside the vessel. Several seconds passed, and the only movement he saw was about a dozen drones going about their business tending the area. Occasionally, one would pause, look his way, and go back to its task. James raised an eyebrow as he watched the drone, as if it was curious about him. He quickly dismissed the thought and switched his focus back to why he was there.

After glancing around the ship and confirming that the coast was clear, James sprinted to the ship's nose and slid to a halt, staying as quiet as possible while listening for anything that sounded out of the ordinary. Satisfied that he was still undetected, he crawled on his belly up the front hull to the forward windscreen and peeked in.

Next to the pilot seat stood Kate, wearing what James recognized as the dark green uniform of the British Star Fleet. In one hand, she held a pistol, while she entered a series of commands with the other into the holographic keyboard floating between her and the window. With her brown hair tied back in a bun, she looked every part the highly trained and efficient naval officer.

James dropped back down before she could see him and lay against the hull on his back. He had not anticipated his prisoner's partner being armed and in the military. Quickly concluding that he had little chance of taking her in a fight and that other ships in the British fleet would arrive fairly soon to find her, he started formulating a plan of negotiation with her to free Ahmad.

Then, he turned his head and watched the drones at work. The tilled fields appeared to be growing a fair amount of plant life pretty well and promised a good harvest when they bore fruit. If his estimates were correct, those plants had been growing for a couple of months, and the two ladies have been stranded on the moon for a while. Perhaps those ships wouldn't be coming after all.

James did not know what their story was. He didn't care. He wanted to get his head engineer back, and he had an idea how.

"Hey!" he called out, staying down and out of sight.

A few seconds later, she responded through the window, "Who are you?"

"I'm an associate of the man you have trapped in your airlock. I've come to negotiate his release."

Kate smiled to herself.

"Let's discuss terms," he offered.

"That depends," she replied. "You have an associate of mine named Angelina. Do you not?"

"Angelina? Never heard of her."

"Really? That is very curious, as that is not what Ahmad tells me."

"How do you mean?"

"When he first arrived, he told me that he needed to pick up some supplies for her and wanted me to let him in."

James cursed under his breath and conceded, "Oh, Angelina! My mistake…yes, she is back at our ship."

"What is her condition?"

"She's fine. Perfect health."

"I'm very glad to hear that," Kate stated. "I want her returned here, still in perfect health. Once she is returned, I will release Ahmad to you."

James looked around the area as he considered the proposal. As he did, his eyes fell upon a drone near the edge of the clearing observing him several meters away. What was it with these drones? Why did they keep watching him? They would have to have some force behind it directing it to do so. Unless . . .

"All right," he called out. "I would be willing to do that. Why don't you come outside, and we will secure the deal?"

"I'm afraid that's not possible," Kate stated.

James asked skeptically, "And, why is that?"

"Your man is in my airlock. What's to prevent him from attacking me, once I open it to get out? And, if I let him out before me, what's to prevent the two of you from departing before I get Angelina back?"

James seethed with loathing, as she was not going to fall for his pretense. Why couldn't he just break Ahmad out and flee back to his ship while keeping his pretty blonde prisoner?

He yelled, "We have a deal. But, I would like to talk to my associate first to verify his well being."

Kate paused a few seconds and answered, "Fair enough. You may talk with him through the closed hatch. Once you are done, bring Angelina back here as trade for your man."

James nodded, climbed to his feet, and walked up the ship to the dorsal hatch. He took a quick look around the clearing and called out, "Ahmad, climb up to the top of the airlock, so I can hear you better?"

"Captain?"

"Just do it."

A few seconds later, the response came from below the portal, "I'm here."

"Wait right there."

Without hesitation, James shot the keypad. Fanning the smoke away and ignoring the sparks spitting out of the newly-created hole, he dropped to his knees and looked around again, his firearm following his line of sight.

As he expected, six of the drones immediately turned from their duties and flew toward him, extending their grasper arms as they moved. He took quick aim and shot the closest machine. The blast penetrated its outer casing and sent it to the ground. He picked off a second and a third before the other three came within range, forcing him to move fast. James jumped to his feet and bolted for the bow of the ship, shooting while he moved.

At that point, James discovered three more drones coming toward him from the other side. He rushed down the forward window and fired twice. He shot down one of the new drones and damaged another. He flipped around and found two of the original robots bearing down on him. James fired a shot into the front of the closest one, but the second one grabbed him and lifted him off the ground. He placed the muzzle of his gun against the metal arm shaft and blasted it off its frame, dropping him a couple of meters to the ground below.

Ripping the lifeless grasper off his clothes, he turned again and fired into the one above him. The impact created sparks from within and sent it careening into the woods. A glance toward the tilled land showed the last four drones turning and rushing toward him. James pivoted to run around the port side of the vessel, when the last nearby drone seized him from behind and rocketed him skyward.

James turned enough to aim his weapon at the drone's chassis but noticed an oddity about this one. Crudely-formed handholds had been welded to the back of this one, and their presence gave him an idea.

Grabbing the arm shaft tight, James blasted the area between him and his hand, letting the fragment fall away and leaving him dangling from the drone in flight. He holstered his gun and firmly grasped the robot with his new free hand. The drone spun wildly, trying to buck him off, but James barely managed to keep hold. As he lifted himself onto its back, he spied the remaining four flying within range.

Now several dozen meters above the ground, James took hold of one of the handholds and planted his feet in the metal tabs he assumed were footholds. Pulling out his pistol again, he fired at the incoming drone, while the one he rode continued to attempt to throw him off. Due to the bucking drone, his aim was off, and his shot passed harmlessly by.

Growing impatient with the robot he rode, James pointed his firearm at the drone and fired point-blank, creating a smoking hole in the middle of its back. Holstering and securing the pistol, he reached in, grabbed several cords, and yanked hard, ripping them out of place. The drone shuddered in mid-air and dropped like a rock.

"Oh, shit!" said James, realizing his error.

The drone slammed into the ground near the tree line, throwing him into the forest. He hit the ground and rolled several more meters before coming to a stop at the base of a thin tree. He came to a few seconds later, just as two of the remaining drones flew nearer.

James groaned as he checked himself for injuries. His left arm felt like it might be broken, and he was having difficulty breathing, too. Maybe a cracked rib?

He spotted the advancing drones as his head cleared, and he drew his pistol again. Despite his shaky hand, he hit one after a couple of shots and brought it down into the dirt. The other one loomed over him and reached its arm down. He shifted his aim and fired into it. The impact of the blast triggered something inside it, as it suddenly zipped away and rammed into a nearby tree, exploding on impact.

Climbing to his feet, James looked around for the last two drones. He heard them in flight but could not spot them. He kept his weapon ready as he slowly walked back to the ship.

Kneeling next to where the keypad used to be, he grabbed a couple of wires and placed the exposed ends together. Nothing. He dropped one of the wires and grabbed another, repeating the action. This time, the hatch slid open, and Ahmad scrambled out of the airlock.

"Thank you, captain," the black man elated.

James glared at him and said, "Shut up. Get to your skycycle."

The two men moved as fast as they could off the ship and to their vehicles. As the captain mounted his and started the engine, he spotted the two remaining drones floating above the trees, watching him.

Without another word, James and Ahmad lifted off and sped back to their ship.

Chapter 24

Anna awoke in a lot of pain. Her face felt as if something had been dropped on it from several meters up. Her mouth stung every time she moved it. Her back and arms felt bruised and battered. Death would be a welcome change.

Hoping that it was all a bad dream, she slowly opened her eyes. Reality sank in as she confirmed that she was still in the same tiny room with the Frenchman standing next to her.

"How are you?" Michel asked.

Anna groaned again and whispered while wincing, "Go away."

He smiled and commented, "Almost back to normal, it would seem."

She stared at him, wishing he would spontaneously combust.

"You are lucky, Angelina. Nothing is broken. You have several bruises that will take some time to fade, and your lip is split. I'm sorry the captain did this to you."

Narrowing her eyes at him, she said nothing until she reached over to touch her shoulder and found she was no longer wearing her shirt. Stopping for a second, she feebly lifted her head to find that she was lying completely naked on the bed.

"What is wrong with you? Why can't you leave me alone?" she asked angrily.

Michel sighed and answered, "Cherie, I had to remove the remainder of your clothes to give you a thorough medical examination."

As Anna slowly covered herself with a bedsheet, she chided, "Right…Sure you did."

He smiled at her scolding in spite of himself.

"Can I have my shirt and panties back?"

With a nod, he replied, "As soon as they are properly laundered. They were very soiled. Don't you have cleaning facilities aboard your ship?"

She laughed in spite of herself before the pain in her face stopped her.

Michel leaned down to check her face. As he reached up to brush a lock of her hair away from her face, she pathetically tried to stop his hand and softly warned, "Don't!"

Ignoring her gesture, he brushed the hair aside and examined her cheeks and lips. As he did, Anna squeezed her eyes shut and started to sob. He pulled back after a few seconds, overwhelmed with remorse. Silently, he stepped back and left the room, leaving her alone with her physical and mental anguish.

Several minutes later, Ahmad and the captain landed outside the ship. During the flight back, James concluded that his arm was not indeed broken but would be sore for a while. His breathing cleared up pretty quick after discovering that one of his muscles got pinched under a rib, and stretching pulled it painfully back into place.

After stretching his arm again to keep it from getting stiff, the two riders looked over the progress the others had made. The sheet metal outer walls of the square structure had been erected and secured in place on the ground several meters from the edge of the boarding ramp. But, it was far from complete. Paco, manning one of the walkers, carried the doors off the ship. Robert and Hiraku had been sitting in the grass nearby engaged in some form of conversation, but sprang to their feet upon sighting the incoming skycycles.

Activating his communicator headset, James barked, "Paco!"

As the walker came to a halt at the bottom of the ramp, the captain continued, "Get out of the walker. Robert, take over. Hiraku, help get that building finished."

Paco clamored out of the cockpit, but Robert slumped and whined, "I'm no good at drivin' one o' those!"

"You'd better get that way," James cried. "Because if that shelter is not done within half an hour, I'm flogging both of you!"

Instantly, Robert ran for the walker and shoved Paco out of the way just as he set foot on the ground. Within seconds, the walker stepped toward the half-constructed building.

Turning to Ahmad with a look of disgust, James stated before driving the cycle into the ship, "Make sure they get it done."

"Aye, sir!"

"Paco, follow me."

Inside the cargo hold, the Hispanic man jogged up to where James had parked the skycycle.

"Yes, sir?"

"Paco, you work way too hard around here. It's time you take a break. Go spend half an hour with our Morale Officer."

With a hesitant smile, Paco replied, "Um, thank you, sir!"

As he turned to leave, James continued, "In fact, I'm going to come with you."

Turning around mid-stride, the young crewman asked, "Sir?"

"I've had a stressful morning myself. So, I think my morale could be raised, too, if you catch my meaning."

"Well," Paco stammered.

"Do you have a problem with that?"

"It's just that I'm not used to having an audience. You know?"

Paco had no intention of touching Anna, let alone forcing himself upon her. He wanted to check on her and make sure she was okay. Now with the captain wanting to be present during his proposed break, he knew that he would be expected to perform.

Waving away the concern, James assured, "Don't mind me. You won't even know I'm there."

At that point, Michel casually strode into the cargo bay with his hands in his pockets and appearing lost in thought.

"Michel!" James cried. "Come over here."

The Frenchman hustled to the skycycle where the captain and Paco had assembled.

"Yes, captain?"

Clapping the young man's shoulder, James said cheerfully, "Paco here needs to spend some quality time with our female guest. Is she all gussied up and ready to go?"

"Actually, captain . . ."

Losing his happy demeanor, the captain sternly asked, "You DID clean her up, didn't you?"

"Oh, yes! Yes, I did, captain," Michel answered rapidly. "Of course."

"Is there a problem?"

"Honestly, sir, she's in bad shape. Her face, arms, and back are all bruised up. She has a split lip. We've been a bit too rough with her. I would suggest that we let her recuperate a bit."

In his mind, Paco thanked the powers-that-be for the French man's intervention. The captain, however, had different thoughts.

"I don't think so," he stated as he stepped purposefully from the cargo hold with Michel and Paco hot on his heels, both crewmen looking at each other with concern.

A minute later, the three men burst into Anna's room, where she lay trying to rest. James reached the edge of the bed and snatched the covers away from her, exposing her nude body to the air and instantly waking her.

"Oh, god!" she cried as the fog of exhaustion quickly dissipated.

James grabbed her legs and lifted her hips off the mattress, sending Anna flailing for the headboard or something to grab hold.

"Captain, what are you doing?" Michel yelled.

Paco protested, "Captain, don't! Please!"

Anna, weak and exhausted, tried in vain to escape his grip.

Ignoring their pleas, James spread her legs, slid a finger into her, and probed around for a second. Anna cried out in horror and pain. After pulling his finger back out, he dropped her roughly onto the bed and stated, "She's a little dry, but she should be fine. Just spit on your cock."

"Captain!" the Hispanic man shot back. "With all due respect . . ."

Sternly pointing a finger at Anna, the captain ordered, "You'd better get over here and fuck her . . ."

"Captain, please!" Michel interrupted. "It will do us no good to kill her. If you want her to be around for a while, we need her to regain her strength."

"She doesn't need her strength! All she needs to do is lie on her back and let us fuck her!"

Standing tall, Paco proclaimed, "Sir! With all due respect, I am not going to fuck her, not like this!"

Without pause, James punched Paco in the jaw, sending the younger man sprawling into the dresser.

Grabbing his superior by the shoulder, Michel yelled, "Captain, listen to reason! We can't continue to treat her this way!"

James pushed the Frenchman away and screamed, "I WILL HAVE YOU TWO EXECUTED FOR INSUBORDINATION!"

"Captain!" Michel pleaded. "We've all grown attached to her."

"She's only been with us for a day!"

"So?"

"WHAT MAKES THIS BITCH DIFFERENT FROM THE OTHER COUNTLESS WHORES I'VE BROUGHT ON BOARD FOR US?!"

"I DON'T KNOW!" Michel screamed back before sitting on top of the desk. "I don't know. But, I do know that none of us wants to see her die. Yet, you seem to be going out of your way to try and kill her."

"What did you say?" James angrily questioned, getting in Michel's face as he asked. The captain grabbed the Frenchman's shirt and reeled his fist back.

Michel continued, "Sir, a good leader knows when to express mercy. Please show some mercy! Extend some simple kindness, and she will grace us with her presence longer which will keep us all in better spirits and operate as a better and more efficient crew."

James stopped, weighing the Frenchman's words. He glanced at Paco, who was leaning back against the dresser and listening as he massaged his jaw. He looked over his shoulder at Anna, who lied sprawled out on the bed shaking profusely. This last act of abuse had been too much for her in her current condition.

The captain relaxed his stance, as the sudden realization that he was polarizing his own crew dawned on him. Wondering where he had gone wrong, he let go of Michel's shirt and wordlessly left the room.

As soon as he was gone, Paco leaped forward, scooped up the sheet from the floor, and covered Anna with it. He wanted to offer her some comfort but was afraid to touch her.

As the sheet touched her flesh, she screamed through her tears, "GET AWAY! DON'T! JUST LEAVE ME ALONE! PLEASE! NO MORE!"

Paco and Michel looked at each other, ashamed that they could not have done more for her. As they left the room, Paco paused and whispered, "I'm sorry. . ." But, words failed him.

Without another word, the two men departed, her sobs ringing in the hall as the door closed.

* * * * *

The two remaining drones scrutinized the wreckages of the eleven that had been shot down earlier in an attempt to see if they could possibly be repaired or salvaged. From what Kate saw through their electronic eyes so far, most of the parts could be used to get at least half of the drones working again. But, she feared that about five or six would have no use except for parts to keep the others going. Number 14, whose navigational system was damaged at point-blank range at the tree line, had met its end in a fireball against a solid trunk.

Kate replayed the incident over and over, sifting it through the tactical software that Ryan had installed when the ship was first granted to him by the company. After several attempts at trying to find where she went wrong with her plan to stop the intruder, she could not pinpoint where the flaw existed. Was it that the drones were too slow? Could it have been something to do with the amount of time it took the drones to respond to her commands? Should she have tried another way of subduing him?

An incoming signal told her that the four drones sent to mine more hydrogen from the gas giant were returning with full tanks ready to deposit. Kate transmitted instructions to them to divert from mining duty to farming, seeing as how most of her work force was currently out of commission, and the crops needed to be maintained.

Through it all, Kate continued to evolve a plan to rescue Anna from her captors and return her home. With only six drones operational and sensors offline since Anna had been abducted, her options were severely limited. But, she would not abandon the technician. She had to come up with something and fast.

One of the drones approached Seventeen and began its examination. The gaping hole in its back with its power conduits dangling out immediately told Kate that the internal damage it endured would not be easy to fix, especially if severing its power feed caused additional damage to its power supply or motherboard. But, she knew that Anna would be extremely upset if she came back and found it inoperative.

After the first two of the four droids had deposited their harvest into the fuel tank, she ordered them to join the others in gathering the damaged drones and placing them in a central area in the middle of the clearing.

Kate began replaying footage of the incident and analyzing it again for another hour.

* * * * *

"Gawd!" Robert exclaimed over his bowl of chili. "I can't believe 'ow 'oppin mad the cap'n got over that! 'e was so red in th' face, that 'e looked just like that bloody tomato over there!"

Laughing, Ahmad chimed in, "And, you can believe that it will happen again! His temper is so short . . ."

"How short is it?" interrupted Hikaru.

Ahmad glanced over his shoulder at the Asian man before continuing, "It's so short, that Dylan McDonald, you know…the comedian, looks like a giant compared to it!"

"That's short!" Hikaru added after swallowing his spoonful of chili. "How tall is he anyway? What, 40 centimeters?"

Robert chuckled, "Nobody is tha' fuckin' short!"

Michel stepped into the galley and, without greeting his fellow crewmates, picked up an empty bowl and scooped some lunch into it.

Looking at the two others sitting at the table with him and back at the new arrival, Robert greeted, "'ey, Frog! 'ow's it goin'?"

Glumly, Michel answered, "Fine. You?"

Robert glanced at Ahmad and Hikaru again before continuing, "What's eatin' you?"

"Gentlemen," the Frenchman uttered before downing a spoonful. "We need to let Angelina be for a while."

All three men at the table snapped their gazes at him.

"What?!"

"Yes. She's not doing so well and needs time to recover."

Flabbergasted, Robert retorted, "Aw, c'mon now! She's a tough bird. She can 'andle it!"

Michel shook his head and replied, "No, I do not think so, not with what the captain has just put her through."

Ahmad and Hikaru looked at each other across the table with grim expressions before returning to their lunch.

Looking back and forth between the two of them, Robert protested, "You goddamn tossers, going soft on 'er! Fuck the lot of you! I'll shag her if I want to."

"No. Not anytime soon, you're not," Paco interjected as he walked in.

Robert stared at the young crewman in disbelief and objected, "Bloody 'ell! You can't be serious. She was gonna suck my cock tonight."

Michel shook his head and calmly said, "Looks like it will be Rosie for you tonight, my friend."

Ahmad and Hikaru chuckled at the comment, prompting a look of astonishment from the Englishman.

"Does the cap'n know 'bout this?"

Both Paco and Michel nodded.

Slapping his hands on the table, Robert pushed his chair away from the table and announced, "We'll see 'bout this!"

As he started to rise from his chair, he turned to the doorway and found Anna standing there, wrapped in a bed sheet with trails of tears gliding down her bruised cheeks.

Chapter 25

"Bloody 'ell!" Robert cried as he flinched, almost tripping backward over his chair.

The rest of the men turned and, finding Anna standing in the doorway, exhibited similar reactions.

Blinking, Hikaru asked, "How did she get out?"

Oblivious to their stares, she stepped into the galley and stole the bowl of chili that Paco had just dished up for himself. Dropping a spoon into the bowl, she gathered the sheet closer around her body, lifted the bowl with her free hand, turned, and exited the room.

The men looked at each other for a moment before surging forward and shoving themselves through the door to follow her, fighting each other to be the first one out. Finally squeezing through, they stopped and stared as Anna walked through the door at the far end of the corridor that led into her room, the bottom of her makeshift dress trailing on the floor behind her.

They moved down the hall as a group and opened the door in time to see her sitting in the corner of the room on the floor with her bowl of food in hand. She started to let the sheet slip down but caught it in time just as the door opened.

"What do you want?" asked Anna sharply, not looking up from her bowl.

With a snicker, Robert prodded, "What are you gonna do with that sheet, love?"

She gathered the sheet closer to her and took a bite of her chili without responding, keeping the linen pinned to her body with her elbow while she ate.

"We're not going to hurt you," Hikaru offered, hoping for a positive response.

The pilot snorted and rolled his eyes. Robert's response earned him a dark look from Paco.

Anna still did not respond, keeping her face down while she ate.

After a few seconds of silence, Paco stepped in front of the others and knelt down carefully to not get too close, "Is there anything I can get you?"

Setting her spoon into the bowl, she softly answered after a few more seconds, "My clothes."

Robert leaned in and, cupping a hand to his ear, mocked, "I'm sorry, love. I didn't quite get that."

With a tortured expression, Anna screamed, "MY FUCKING CLOTHES!"

Her face fell with grief as she turned to look back at the men. A second later, a single tear rolled down her cheek.

The men said nothing. Paco and Hiraku hung their heads in shame, while Ahmad looked away. Michel dashed away from the door.

Robert, on the other hand, observed with a hint of a laugh, "You look real cute when you're cryin' like that. I got a pacifier for ya."

"Christ, Robert!" Hiraku interrupted as he and the others turned to look at the pilot. "You're a dick."

"You know what? You can be . . ."

Ahmad jumped in, "That's enough!"

All eyes turned to the African man. While Paco and Hiraku regarded him normally, Robert gazed at him incredulously.

"'oo the 'ell do you think you are? No one pu' you in charge."

"I did!"

The captain's voice filled the hallway as he stepped through the door from the cargo hold.

Robert looked upward and whispered a curse before James joined the group at Anna's door.

Forcefully dropping a hand on the pilot's shoulder, the captain questioned, "Don't you all have something better to do?"

Wordlessly, Paco, Ahmad, and Hiraku departed. As Robert began to leave, James held him back and uttered, "Robert, a moment, please."

Robert's face drooped as the captain continued, "To the bridge."

James glanced into the room at Anna, who had returned her attention to her bowl, and escorted the Englishman to the front of the ship.

After finishing her lunch, Anna wrapped herself in the sheet again and looked out the door to make sure the coast was clear. The corridor was unoccupied, making her wonder where everybody was. She heard a voice from further back in the ship but could not confirm its owner or the content of the conversation.

She hurriedly made the short trip to the galley, also empty of occupants. She set the bowl on the table that filled most of the room and gazed out the forward-facing window at the dense forest just a few meters away. The sunlight outside beamed strongly across the land and beckoned for her to join it again.

Anna's thoughts wandered back to the ship that she had called home over the last several months. Her mind dwelt on Kate and conjectured about how she and the drones were doing. Without her wristcomp, she had no way of reaching her to find out. Perhaps she could find a way to sneak onto the bridge, wherever it was.

Come to think of it, Anna did not even know where she was. The only detail she could confirm about her location was that she was still on the daylight side of Paradise. Without getting a clear, unobstructed view of the sky, she had to satisfy herself with the knowledge that she would get back to her ship one day, though she could not comprehend when that might be. All she wanted to do was get away from the men aboard this vessel and leave them far behind.

The men. Thinking of them immediately opened the flood gates and sent the memories of the atrocities toward her to the forefront of her mind. The visions of the beatings and the sexual onslaught tormented her. She was abused, violated, and in despair. Frustrated that she had no control over her predicament, she could not hold back the tears any longer and fled from the galley.

Anna ran down the hall, not able to see clearly through her tear-filled eyes. She came to the door to her room and passed through it, stopping when she realized that she had entered the wrong cabin. This one held a bunk bed and two foot lockers against the far wall. The wall opposite the beds was decorated with color and monochrome holograms of scantily-clad and naked women in various sexual positions. Repulsed by the photos, she fled from the room.

On the opposite side of the hallway from where she exited was the door clearly marked "Lavatory". Without a second thought, Anna charged through the door and locked it behind her. Spying the shower facilities within, she dropped the sheet and rushed into the hot water. She needed to get clean, not for the actual physical cleanliness but for her psyche. What had been done to her over the last couple of days made her unclean, and she had to attempt to wash it away.

Sometime later, Anna awoke to the sound of loud pounding on the door.

"Open the damn door!"

"Come on! How long are you going to use it?"

"Typical woman always takin' up the bathroom."

"I'm about to burst!"

"What's going on?"

Anna recognized the captain's voice but did not want to move. The shower had made her feel safe.

Seconds later, the door burst violently open and slammed against the wall. As it slowly drew closed, James slapped it open again and stared fuming at Anna sitting curled up in a ball naked on the shower floor, the spray of the water deluging her drenched hair.

"WHAT THE HELL ARE YOU DOING?!" screamed the captain.

As he stormed toward her, Anna crawled away to the back of the stall, pleading with outstretched arms, "No! Please don't!"

James grabbed her by the wrist and jerked her out of the stall and through the door in one fluid motion. Her wet feet slid out from under her, causing her to stumble across the hall and hit the cabin door a split second before it could automatically open. She tumbled headfirst into the dark quarters beyond after they finally opened. He had traversed half of the hall, when Paco called out to him from the lavatory entrance, "Please, sir! She was only trying to take a shower."

The captain stopped mid-stride, slowly turned toward the younger crewman with a look mirroring wild hatred, and moved toward Paco with clenched fists. Overcome with fear, the Hispanic man cowered before his commanding officer. James just watched with contempt and turned his attention back to Anna.

Michel, standing on the other side of the doorway, mildly struggled to get his superior's attention.

"Captain?"

James turned and stared through the French man.

"Captain!"

"WHAT?"

The sharp response surprised Michel, causing him to stumble over his words for a few seconds.

"Um," he started slowly. "Perhaps, we should consider why she was in the shower."

James closed the gap between him and Michel and stood toe-to-toe with him, staring straight into his eyes.

"Why? Why was she in the shower, Michel? Was it to get clean?" the captain asked with an angry sarcasm.

"It has been a couple of days since she got here. She has only had a bedpan available as her only means of maintaining any form of hygiene. She has had no way of cleaning herself, brushing her teeth, or anything to make herself presentable to us."

"Do you take me for a fool, Michel?"

Shaking his head, the French man replied, "Never! But, does that not make the most sense?"

James crossed his arms and asked skeptically, "Why would she make herself presentable to us?"

Michel shrugged and suggested, "Perhaps she has decided that it is to her benefit?"

The captain dropped his aggressive stance and cocked his head as he contemplated the French man's rationale. In his experiences, he had never seen a woman on his ship decide to be a willing participant. After the treatment she had received, it did not seem likely to him that she would now.

Looking back at his crewman, James said matter-of-factly, "You know, Michel. That is the biggest crock of shit I've ever heard."

Pointing to the open cabin door, the captain continued, "Here's what I'm going to do. I'm going to go over there, and I'm going to beat the holy fuck out of her. That will teach her to stay out of areas where she does not belong."

"If you keep this up, you will kill her."

"Well then, you can add her to the list," James interjected spitefully. "I am the captain here! I am the one in command! YOU DO WHAT I SAY! UNDERSTAND?"

Michel nodded his head rapidly.

"AND IF YOU HAVE A PROBLEM WITH THE WAY I RUN THIS SHIP, FEEL FREE TO LEAVE AND PRAY I DON'T SHOOT YOU AS YOU WALK DOWN THE BOARDING RAMP! I DON'T NEED YOUR MORALITY ON ME! SO, SHUT YOUR FUCKING HOLE! GOT IT?!"

Michel grimaced, nodded, and hastily moved toward the cargo hold.

The captain watched him retreat and turned his attention back to the closed cabin door. He paused for a second, trying to remember if the door was open or not. Dismissing the thought, he opened the door to find the room unoccupied. Surprised, he rifled through the quarters, upturning mattresses and furniture as he searched for her. After a minute, he gave up upon not finding her and walked straight to the room where she had been held.

The door whisked open to find Anna sitting on the bed without a stitch of clothing on or around her. Immediately, she threw her hands in front of her and cried, "Wait! I can explain!"

James surged forward, pushed her hands aside, and threw a right cross against her jaw, knocking her flat on the mattress. He threw off his jacket and had dropped his pants when she came to.

"No! Not again! Please!" she pleaded as he pushed his way between her legs.

Leaning down toward her, he screamed, "Yes again! You are going to learn one way or another that I am your master now, and you don't have free reign here! One way or another."

Anna kicked at him and scrambled to get away, grabbing the headboard and pulling herself toward the wall. He reacted too quickly for her, seized her legs, and jerked her back toward him. She continued to plead for mercy, but her pleas quickly turned to sobs.

A couple of hours later, Anna lied on her uncovered bed curled up in a fetal position facing away from the door. She stared blankly at the wall, emotionless after crying for a straight hour. The trauma that the pirates, their captain in particular, continuously inflicted upon her was more than she could bear.

She knew that she had to get away from them one way or another. But, how could she escape? Where could she go? Returning to her ship would be the easiest choice, but that would be easily determined by her captors. She could hide out in the forest, but she would have no defenses and could be found with their sensors during the day cycle. The eclipse would increase her chances of getting away, but she would be vulnerable to the indigenous predators and had no way to protect herself. The only other place that came to mind was the pyramid. If she could reach the pyramid, she would have a better chance of defending herself.

Anna knew that she could not get there without finding out where she was first. She did not have her wristcomp and had no clue as to its whereabouts. Thinking about where it could be reminded her that the captain had hacked into it to learn her name. In that case, chances were good that it would be in his quarters, provided he kept it.

The only other option that she could think of was to somehow use their ship's sensors to locate hers. For that, she would have to snoop around the vessel without anyone noticing, especially the captain. Doing that would be difficult at best.

Anna rolled over and sat up. Refusing to let the trauma she had endured stop her, she instead focused on what she felt she must do. Although she was successful for the most part, she could not push the memories of the captain's brutality aside. She felt the tears welling up in her eyes. No! She would not let him win. She forced herself to relive her last encounter, until her fear transformed into a fiery rage. She no longer wanted to just escape; she wanted him dead.

In that moment, Anna noticed something odd about the dresser. The second drawer was slightly ajar. Had it been opened before? Perhaps it slid open when Paco fell against it after the captain punched him. She did not remember it being open before.

Anna stood and slowly opened the drawer. Uncertain of what she would find, her discovery brought a cold smile to her face, the first smile she had given willingly in days.

Chapter 26

Her clothes! How did they get into the dresser? Were they here all along? No, she checked the dresser after they untied her and left her alone in the cabin. Someone brought them here for her.

Anna lifted her T-shirt out and examined it. It shined a bright white again under the lights, and all of the lubricant stains were gone. Whoever had washed her things had gone out of his way, considering that everybody else's clothing looked a bit on the grimy side.

Draping the shirt over her bare shoulder, she gently pulled her sports bra out and felt pleased to find the same result. Never in over the past six and a half years had she looked forward to putting the restrictive undergarment on, until now.

Her panties were next and surprised her the most. Not only were they a bright white again, but the stains were mostly faded and gone. Anna was almost touched by the attention given to her things. She tossed the shirt and bra onto the bed and immediately put her panties on. Though made from a flimsy cotton-like material, they felt to her like armor.

Finally, she picked up her pants, folded neatly at the bottom of the drawer, and let them drape down toward the floor while she held the waistband. As she had hoped, these also were free of the mud and lubricant stains, leaving the garment looking its cleanest since her time aboard the mining station.

With the feeling of security each item gave her inspiring her to put on another article of clothing, Anna quickly got dressed and found that she only lacked her socks and boots. Nevertheless, being clothed had never felt so good. If she had any control over it, she would do what she must to keep them on as long as possible from now on.

She searched the other drawers and, not finding her footwear, figured that they were probably mixed with the supplies for the crew. Adding it to her list of items to find, Anna began devising her exodus.

A short time later, Anna emerged from her quarters into an empty hall. From what she remembered during her short stint in one of the other cabins, at least two crewmen stayed in each berth. She also remembered that the door to the head was labeled, which should help make her search easier.

Checking the doors on her level revealed that the laundry equipment was installed in the storage room right next to the lavatory across the hall. Getting in was easy, since the entryway was unlocked, and she quickly found her socks and boots.

As Anna was about to leave the laundry room, she heard voices outside the door. Listening closely, she pressed her ear to the door.

"Are you sure that's going to be a problem," Paco asked. "I mean, I've seen ships run on less maintenance and get by fine."

"That may be fine for civilian cruisers," scolded Ahmad. "But, this is a pirate vessel. If we are to succeed at what we do, we need to be stronger and faster than the ships we attack, meaning we . . ."

". . . we need to stay on top of the engines and keep them in tip-top shape!" Paco tiredly repeated with the black man. "I know. I know."

The head engineer chuckled, "Well, then, you should also know that we have to keep them running their best."

The wheels in Anna's brain turned furiously upon hearing this bit of news. Her escape plan had just developed a new addition to her agenda.

The Hispanic man sighed, "Let me go check on Angelina, and then I'll meet you back in Engineering to finish the maintenance."

"Okay, but make it fast. This isn't play time. You can do that later tonight with the rest of us."

"Don't worry," Paco replied with a spiteful tone. "I'll keep my dick in my pants."

A second later, the larger door at the end of the hall opened and shut just before a smaller door whooshed open.

"Oh, shit!" muttered Paco.

Suddenly realizing that he had discovered her missing from her room, Anna felt the need to work fast to keep her plan intact. She rushed out the laundry room door and across the hall to her quarters, where she nearly ran into her nursemaid coming back out. The two ran into each other, and the impact forced him to drop the wrench in his hand. He attempted to catch her before she hit the floor but only managed to deflect her enough to make her land on her butt instead.

As the two recovered from their accident, Paco smiled nervously and lowly uttered as he extended his hand to help her up, "Sorry about that."

Anna, refusing his hand, sternly responded, "I got it."

"Oh, sorry!"

He dropped his hands as she got up off the floor. After she stood, she pushed him into the room and let the door shut behind them.

"Hey!" he cried as he reeled backwards. "What gives?

"Hey, you found your clothes! I was hoping…"

Anna, ignoring his attempt at conversation, stated, "Not now. I need a favor."

Paco's eyebrows shot up on his forehead upon hearing the request of a favor. He was willing to do just about anything for her.

"Of course."

Her mind raced on what to say, she knew that she had to find an advantage. Paco seemed to be her best bet. She quickly decided and said, "If I'm going to be aboard the ship for a while, I figure that I should get my bearings. So, I was looking around to get a feel for where everything is."

Nodding, Paco agreed, "That makes sense."

"So, do you think you could keep my excursion between us?" Anna requested, attempting to turn on the charm.

"Uh, sure! It'll be our little secret!" Paco responded, relieved at the thought of finally being of use to her.

Anna genuinely smiled and said, "Thanks."

With a wide smile, Anna continued, "So, I was going to finish my tour. Where is everybody else? I don't want to get either of us in trouble."

"Uh," he stuttered uncomfortably. "The captain, Michel, and Hikaru are outside securing the storage building. Ahmad went back to Engineering to work on the engines, and I think Robert is on the bridge."

"Thank you. I mean it. Thank you." She smiled again in earnest.

Grateful to have an ally, Anna congratulated herself for her first victory and opened the door leading into the cargo hold. The vast compartment rose at least three stories within the hull, and she heard the sounds of construction filtering in through the large entryway on what she figured was the ship's port side. One floor above her, a metal catwalk extended along the length of the hold from the front to the back, and the access ladder to it was in the near corner against the port wall.

Since the galley was at the front end of the ship on this level, Anna deduced that the bridge and the captain's quarters must be one floor up and stealthily dashed to the ladder. Within seconds, she had climbed to the second level. She noticed that the far end of the catwalk ended at another door. She could not tell where it led but estimated that Engineering was on the other side. As quiet as she could manage, she moved to the nearest door and passed through.

As she expected, another short corridor stretched forward with doors flanking the passageway to the single door at the far end. Carefully, she moved along, checking the door labels as she walked. She found a few more storage rooms and doors leading to areas such as avionics and computer hardware. Several more were unmarked, piquing her curiosity, but she forced herself to move on. At the far end of the corridor were the pilot's cabin, the captain's quarters, and the bridge.

Glancing down the hall and finding nobody behind her, she attempted to open the door to the captain's room. Surprisingly, the door slid open. She quickly entered and let the hatch slide shut.

James's room was decorated differently, since he had it all to himself. The single bed was covered in luxurious-looking blankets and a large, soft pillow. The tall wardrobe in the far corner appeared to be an antique, made of a dark, lacquered wood. The desk next to the door, crafted similarly to the wardrobe, hosted a small computer with a holographic keyboard and screen, and next to it sat her wristcomp, still intact. Snatching up the device without a second thought, she stuffed it in her pants pocket and quickly exited the room.

Back in the hall, Anna eyed the door to the bridge for a few seconds. Hoping to reach the sensors and find her ship, she stepped up to the door and hit the button to open it.

Her luck had run out.

As the door swished open, Anna saw Robert sitting in the lone pilot's seat eyeing a display on the holographic panel floating in front of him. Not wanting to deal with the brash man due a strong dislike of his crude behavior, she tried to back away from the door. His head turned before she could retreat, and he smiled upon seeing her.

"Well, 'ello there!" he welcomed, his broad smile revealing several gold teeth. "Wha' brings you 'ere, love?"

In the seconds it took for him to turn and acknowledge her presence, Anna spotted the active sensor display and decided that, since he knew she was there, taking advantage of the situation would be best.

Anna forced herself to smile and replied, "I was actually looking for you."

Robert's eyes snapped open wide. Doubtfully, he asked while pointing to himself, "Were ya now?"

Her nod affirmed the question as she fought to hide her revulsion.

"Well, then. Come on in!" he invited boisterously. Patting his thigh, he added, "Sit yourself right 'ere!"

Apprehensively, Anna walked in and gently sat on his knee. Robert instantly wrapped his arm around her waist and pulled her in closer. She could smell an odd combination of whiskey and onions on his breath. She forced herself not to vomit and flee.

"You're lookin' fit today! I'd say your jubblies look pre'y nice up close!"

Guessing that what he said was a compliment of sorts, Anna smiled as best she could and said, "Thanks."

"So, why are you lookin' for me?"

Taking a deep breath, she stated, "Well, I was thinking that, if I am going to be with you boys for a while, I'd might as well learn about the ship a little more. Besides, being cooped up in that small room gives me cabin fever."

Deciding to play the 'dumb' card, she continued, "So, I thought that, since a ship, like, flies, that the pilot might be a good place to start."

Robert beamed, "You made the right choice, love. 'cause nothin' beats flyin' by the seat o' your pants in a ship through space, dodgin' ast'roids n' comets n' all the other ships flyin' after you."

"How exciting!" Anna exclaimed, trying to sound enthusiastic.

"First thing you need to do is learn the controls of the ship you're gonna fly."

He wheeled the chair around, pressing Anna against the metal frame that housed the holographic projectors.

"Now, are you familiar with holographic controls?"

Hesitantly extending her arm, Anna slowly answered, "I, think so. You just touch them like this, right?"

She jabbed her finger through the key that initiated a focused scan. The prompt appeared on the sensor display, waiting for the intended target.

Robert chuckled, "Yeah, that's right! In fact, that's the sensors readout you just touched there. The sensors are probably one o' the most important things a pilot needs to fly the ship. It 'elps you see where you're goin'."

Hamming it up, Anna looked at the window and asked, "Then, why did they put a window there?"

Laughing out loud, the pilot said, "We still need to see where we're going with our eyes, but the sensors allow us to see further."

"So," Anna inquired while studying the sensors panel. "What's that dot . . . there?"

She jabbed the lone signal on the screen near its upper-right edge. After a couple of seconds, the focused scan completed and produced the pop-up result which read:

Identify: Vessel, Arrow-class Transport
Distance: 102.45km
Relative Direction: 44.73 mark 359.00

Robert perused the information and announced, "Oh! That would be where your ol' ship crashed. This li'l window tells you what it is, how far away it is, and what direction it is from you.

"According to this, it's about a hundred clicks that way," he indicated by pointing out the forward window to the right.

Anna commented with a smile, "So, what does this console do?"

As she reached for the communicator button, Robert intercepted her hand and gently tugged it away while saying, "That's enough of the pilotin' lessons for now. Why don't we do somethin' fun?"

Dreading what he was about to suggest, Anna asked with a semblance of a grin, "What do you have in mind?"

Chapter 27

Before she knew it, Robert had pulled Anna's head toward him and planted his mouth on hers. Stunned at first by the sudden action, she resisted after a second, struggling to break free of his strong hold on her neck. The taste of whiskey and onions from his breath almost induced vomiting. She planted both hands on his chest and pushed as hard as she could, finally breaking through his grip.

Taking a second to catch a breath of clean air, Anna said while sounding winded, "Wow! That was . . . some kiss."

"If you think THAT was good, wait 'till I get me pants off!"

Giving a nervous chuckle, Anna slid off his lap and replied, "You're moving awfully fast, Robert."

"Pilot! I like movin' fast. I like fast ships and fast women. C'mere!"

As Anna backed against the wall, Robert lunged for her right when the door swished open. Standing on the other side was the captain with a fiercely stern look on his face. Robert froze with his hands against the wall on either side of Anna's head.

"There you are!" James cried, staring right at her.

Glancing at the captain and back at the pilot, Anna smiled sheepishly and muttered, "Guess we'll have to finish this later."

She ducked under his arm and lightly stepped off the bridge past the captain, not looking back as she made a beeline for the door leading to the cargo hold.

"Angelina!" the captain called out. Anna stopped in her tracks and turned around to face him, praying that he was in a forgiving mood.

"The next time that Robert wants some . . . attention from you, insist that he stay in your room to do so."

Relief washed over her as she replied, "Yes, sir."

Without waiting for anything else from him, she turned back around, but he called to her again.

"I need to see you for a moment, before you return to your room."

Her stomach twisted into knots upon hearing his words. She wanted to run and hope she could sprint all the way back to her ship, but she remained frozen in her tracks and waited for his inevitable approach. She heard him and Robert discussing something, but their voices were low enough to make details difficult to discern.

A minute later, James stepped up behind her and placed his hands on her shoulders. She tensed from head to toe, waiting for the strike that would knock her off her feet. But, the blow never came.

"Anna," he began emotionlessly. "Ahmad is having an issue with the engines not firing properly. Go see if you can help him fix it without being obvious about it."

Her jaw dropped open. She never expected to hear this coming out of his mouth and speculated on what ulterior motive inspired this change in him. She did not trust him, and this difference in his outward attitude changed nothing.

Anna turned around and looked into his face staring back at her. She cocked an eyebrow and asked suspiciously, "Why? I thought all I was good for was lying on my back and spreading my legs?"

"Don't worry. You'll still be doing that. Let's just say that I want to see what other . . . talents you possess. You say you're a technician. Prove it."

Anna narrowed her eyes at him, slowly turned on her heel, and wordlessly walked to the back of the ship at a hurried pace.

Walking through the door to Engineering permitted Anna a true view of the condition of the ship's systems. She originally thought the mining station's systems were bad, but what she saw made the station look pristine in comparison. The paneling had visible rust corrosion, and some were not even hanging properly in place anymore. Cords and conduits hung suspended across the room, exposing meters of potentially lethal wiring and tubes within easy reach of anyone walking underneath them. The throbbing sound coming from the power core sounded sickly. Ahmad sat on top of a large, cubical casing hitting what appeared to her to be a plasma conduit with a hammer.

Anna was severely tempted to state her hypothesis that the ship could not even break orbit, let alone fly to another star system, and drastically questioned his technical training. However, she bit her tongue and decided to play the dumb blonde again.

"Hi!" she yelled, waving her hand delicately at Ahmad.

Looking up from his work, he waved back with a smile but quickly lost his balance and fell off the conduit to the deck. Since the drop was only a couple of meters, Anna was not too concerned for his safety, but she played the part and rushed to his side.

"Are you okay?" she inquired while trying to sound compassionate.

Ahmad shook his head and rubbed his arm before replying, "Yeah, I'm okay. You should not be in here. Engineering is a dangerous place. You could get hurt."

Anna agreed, considering the condition of the place and not the reason she assumed he was thinking. She helped him to his feet, where he brushed himself off and looked her over.

"Hey!" he looked at her confused. "There's something different about you.

He paused, "You got clothes on!"

She refrained from punching him in the face and tried to smile instead, testing the limits of both her acting skills and her temper.

"Is it okay if I watch you work?" Anna inquired. "I'm learning about the ship and figured that I could maybe learn a tip or two from you."

The black man looked around the room and sighed aloud. Unsure of where to start, he simply said, "That's fine. Just follow me, and I'll see what I can do."

Over the next hour, Ahmad worked on recalibrating the engines with Anna watching him over his shoulder. She easily picked out half a dozen steps he skipped in trying to complete the process. Despite her desire to point out what he missed, she stayed quiet and let him work.

During that time, he gave a few suggestions to her on how to properly maintain ship engines. Some of the tips were decent, but she realized that the others would only work for a short time before causing other problems elsewhere.

Maintaining her façade, Anna queried near the end of the calibration, "So, what happens if you aren't able to get the engines cali . . . calib . . ."

"Calibrated."

"Yes," she smiled sheepishly. "That's the word. Calibrated."

"We don't take off. If the engines don't fire correctly, then we won't be able to get off the ground. We'd be stuck here."

Anna pouted, "That's not good. I hope you can get it fixed."

"Me, too. Thanks for tagging along, Angelina. I enjoyed your company."

"Maybe we can do it again sometime?"

Ahmad grinned, "Anytime."

She smiled back, though she felt disgusted with herself for doing so.

"Okay," he added, dropping the spanner into his tool box. "Break time. Want to join me in the galley?"

"Actually, I was hoping to walk outside for a little bit. I haven't breathed fresh air in days."

"Get used to that, once we take off."

"All the better to enjoy it while I can," she pleasantly shot back.

Agreeing with a nod, Ahmad said, "All right, then. Enjoy the sunshine. I'm getting a cup of coffee."

After he turned and walked a few steps, Anna glanced to the access panel next to her and, spying a few modules plugged into the system, hastily pulled one out of its socket and pocketed the part before leaving the area.

A couple of minutes later, she casually strolled down the boarding ramp, basking in the sunlight and ignoring the noisy construction ahead. She relished the warm rays that tickled her face and wanted to disappear into the woods for hours. The sight of James standing at the base of the ramp negated the thought all too quickly.

Turning to look at her over his shoulder, the captain gruffly asked, "What are you doing out here?"

"Ahmad is taking a break," she replied. "So, I thought I would, too. Would it hurt to let me out once in a while? I'm a person, too, you know."

"You don't have any right to be out here. You're not one of the crew."

"Get over yourself!" she mumbled.

James backhanded her across the cheek, flaring new pain in her bruised face. The act distracted Michel's and Hiraku's attention from their work for a couple of seconds.

"Don't EVER speak to me like that again, or those words will be your last. Understand?!"

While caressing her cheek, Anna nodded.

"Now," he continued in a tone made calm so suddenly that it scared her. "What happened in Engineering?"

"Ahmad is not an efficient engineer. I'm surprised your ship hasn't had problems before."

"Can he get the engines calibrated?"

"Maybe in a couple of weeks."

"And if you help him?"

Anna stopped and pointed to herself, "Me? You want me working on your ship?"

"You want out of here, don't you?"

"Maybe. Why?"

"If you can get the engines running, we'll leave you here with your drones and your computer friend."

"My computer friend? I don't understand."

Smirking smugly, James admitted, "Your friend Kate is a hologram."

Anna shifted her weight on one leg, and probed, "What makes you think that?"

"While I was rescuing Ahmad, I noticed the drones continuously watching me. Why would drones do that on their own? Additionally, Kate did not even try to get out of the ship to shoot at us as we flew away. I would think that, if she were a living, breathing human, she would have tried to stop us to get you back. Your friend is a hologram!"

Anna's heart skipped a beat. His powers of deduction were quite astute to come to that conclusion after so little exposure to her home. If he believed that her ship was defenseless, nothing could stop him from destroying everything, leaving her either stranded with nothing or forced to join his band of pirates as their "morale officer". Neither option appealed to her. Perhaps she could still salvage the situation.

A smile formed on Anna's face, and she acted as if she was stifling a giggle. James's expression changed and hardened slightly as he stared at her reaction of amusement.

"What's so funny?" he asked, irritated by her reaction.

Sensing that she may have overplayed her bluff, Anna lightly teased, "Captain, you're so funny. A hologram? I'll have to remember that one."

James crossed his arms and, staring hard at her, prodded, "What's so funny about that?"

"Maybe we had set up the drones to act as security cameras? What better way to hide your surveillance equipment than as workers? Who would suspect drones of being security cameras while they're working?

"Silly captain, Kate's British! She doesn't like shooting people! She's got that whole honor thing going on. Besides, she probably figured that discretion was better, since you outnumbered her two to one."

James's face turned bright red. He clenched his fists again and again, as Anna pointed out the flaws of his conclusion. Coupled with the tone with which she spoke, he was on the verge of blowing his top.

Anna giggled, failing to note the drastic change in his disposition. "Looks like P.I. is out if you ever decide to give up all this."

That did it.

Before Anna could react, James slammed his fist across her face, driving her hard to the ground. Despite the pain surging through her cheek and jaw, Anna would no longer put up with his violent behavior. If she was going down, she was going to at least put up a fight.

As he loomed over her, James reached down to grab her shirt. Suddenly, Anna rolled onto her back and launched her foot into his scrotum. The hard blow to his privates caught him off-guard, and he cried out in agonizing pain as he doubled over and cupped his crotch with his hands.

Across the clearing, Hiraku turned his cargo walker to lift another palate, when he noticed Anna's swift kick. His eyes lit up, and he announced through his microphone, "Michel, check it out!"

Michel whipped his walker around and grinned at seeing Anna fight back.

Anna rolled back on her shoulders and drove her foot into James's chin, pushing him forward to where he lost his balance and dropped. Despite her best attempt, she was unable to get out of the way fast enough, and he landed on her, pinning her down in a jack-knife position.

James recovered his wits, ignoring the burning pain in his pants, and propped himself up with his hands, a look of utter rage on his face. He grabbed Anna's leg and pushed her to her side, giving her the clearance to punch him hard across his nose. The blow distracted him long enough to let her roll away and rise up to her knees before he reacted.

Tasting something salty, he brushed his hand across his mouth and found blood coating his lip, confirming that she had broken his nose.

"You're dead!" he growled, rising to his feet as he wiped away the blood gushing down his face from his nose.

Anna swept his feet out from under him with her leg and replied as he hit the ground with a thud, "Fuck you!"

She leaped on top of him, pinning him down on the boarding ramp, and threw several fists down on his face. He squeezed an arm free from her leg, reached up between her arms, and seized one of her breasts in a crushing grip. Anna screamed from the unbearable pain, stopping her assault and giving him enough time to throw her off. She rolled down the ramp to the dirt below, where she got on her hands and knees while cringing from the pain in her breast. James scrambled to his feet and bolted down the ramp. Reaching Anna before she could get to her feet, he kicked her in the ribs. She howled in pain and collapsed on the ground, and he stepped back to admire his handiwork.

"Had enough?" he smirked in an arrogant tone.

Anna rose to her knees and replied with a swift punch to his abdomen. As he lurched over from the blow, she sprang to her feet and smashed her knee into his face, spraying more blood from his nose, followed by a downward punch across his jaw. James blocked her strike at his face and landed a counterstrike into her gut. Back in his fighting stance, he threw several punches at her face and abdomen. The first one caught Anna off-guard, but she blocked the next few and returned with her heel into his knee. The unexpected riposte buckled his leg, and he staggered toward the ground. Anna reared back and kicked James in the chin. As he fell forward, she moved closer to him, hoping to strike the final blow. Countering, he quickly raised his leg and planted his foot in her solar plexus, knocking the wind out of her. Anna groaned and fell to the ground, gasping for breath. James regained his footing and grabbed her, taking a handful of her hair. He pulled her upright to ensure he would see the look on her face, as he cocked his arm back and punched her in the face. The force of the blow to her cheek bone and jaw fell her to the ground. With a sneer, James kicked Anna in the head, knocking her out cold.

"Michel!" barked the captain. "Get over here!"

Without delay, the French man climbed out of the walker and jogged up to James, while the captain ascended the ramp into the ship. Michel paused by Anna long enough to cast a sympathetic glance her direction.

Reaching the cargo hold, James looked around and saw Paco maintaining one of the sky cycles. His blood boiled, suspecting that the Hispanic man was the one that released Anna.

"PACO!" bellowed the captain. Paco bumped his head on the cycle, dropped the tool in his hand, and sprang to his feet.

"Yes, sir?"

"GET THAT BITCH BACK IN HER ROOM AND TIE HER UP!" James threatened. "IF SHE GETS OUT AGAIN, I'LL KILL YOU AFTER I KILL HER!"

Chapter 28

Paco had finished securing the last of the strips around Anna's wrists, when she groaned softly. He sighed in relief that she was regaining consciousness and stepped back to give her some space.

Anna moaned again and opened her eyes, immediately regretting doing so, and shut them again. She did catch a glimpse of Paco's legs and said, "I'm tied up."

Hanging his head, he answered, "Yes, you are. Sorry!"

She sighed and slowly opened her eyes again to look around her. Back in the same, cramped room, Anna looked around to see if anything had changed.

"Well," she commented tiredly after taking in her surroundings. "At least I'm still dressed."

"May I ask you something?" Paco dropped to his knees at her bedside. "Why did you fight back? You can't win against him. No one can."

Anna lolled her head to one side and looked at him for a second before stating, "I probably have brain damage by now.

"By the way, thanks for bringing my clothes to me."

Paco looked stunned and shifted his gaze around the room several times before turning back to her and confessing, "I . . . didn't . . . bring you your clothes."

Waking up a bit more, Anna's eyes narrowed upon hearing the news, prompting her to ask after a few seconds of contemplation, "Then, who did?"

With a shrug, Paco admitted, "The only one I can think of is maybe Michel. He does the laundry whenever he gets the chance."

Anna nodded, "Remind me to thank him later. Okay?

"Hey, Paco. Why doesn't anyone stand up to the captain?"

"Like I said," he repeated. "He can't be beaten. I heard about the last mutiny attempt, before I joined the crew. What I . . ."

"Why did you join the crew anyway?" interrupted the blonde.

Paco flinched at her question. Not wanting to answer her, he continued, "Later. What I heard about the last attempt is that the captain got wind of the coup, dragged the ring leader out of his quarters in the middle of the night, slit his throat, and threw him out the nearest airlock."

"Was everyone sided against him that time?"

"I don't think so. From what I heard, they were evenly split."

"What about the current crew?"

Paco's jaw dropped open, and he quickly responded in hushed tones, "What are you trying to do? Get us both killed? There is no way that we could pull off a mutiny!"

Anna rolled her eyes and flatly said, "Seriously? Answer the question."

Stammering, he stated, "I . . . I don't think . . . I . . . uh."

Rising to his feet, Paco paced around the room while contemplating her query.

"Answer the damn question!" Anna demanded a little louder than before.

Paco stopped, took a deep breath, and quietly stated, "Give me a second. Okay?"

Anna nodded and gestured for him to sit on the edge of the bed.

He breathed again after sitting down and continued, "From what I can tell, we're fairly evenly split. I know that I don't like him too much, and neither does Michel or Hiraku. Robert will side with the captain. I'm not sure about Ahmad, though."

The sudden pounding on the wall outside the room interrupted the conversation, followed by Robert demanding, "'ey you two! 'urry up in there! I wanna turn with 'er!"

"For the love of God!" Anna whispered. "I can't! Do something, please!"

"What? I'm the lowest guy on the totem pole around here!"

"I don't know. Think of something, please!" she begged.

After a few seconds of thought, he jumped up and went out the door.

"About time!" teased Robert. "Now, let me in there!"

Hiraku, who appeared to be waiting outside with Michel, held up his hand and stated, "Hold on a sec! Why are you next?"

The British man glared at Hiraku and declared, "'cause I'm the fuckin' pilot! I fly your sorry asses all over the bloody galaxy!"

"You haven't been doing it for the last couple of days," the Asian responded. "In fact, you haven't been doing much of anything for the last couple of days."

"Bollocks! I'm the one that brought 'er pretty li'l ass 'ere in the first place! In fact, if it 'adn't been for me, we wouldn't 'ave found 'er in the first place!"

Hiraku snorted, "One lone human on the entire moon. Doesn't sound too hard to do. You were probably jacking off while you were watching her before you even called for anyone else."

"You git!" Robert shot back. "The cap'n was in there, too!"

With a smirk, Hiraku said, "Oh! I knew you and the cap were close."

"Wha'? Oh, fuck you! I ain't no bloody poofter!"

"So, now you want to fuck me? I guess that means you gave up your spot in line for Angelina then. I'm next!"

"Oh, no! You ain't goin' nowhere!"

Robert reeled back and slugged Hiraku across the jaw, sending him stumbling back into Michel who had watched the whole scene unfold.

"Hey!" the French man cried as he and the Asian fell to the floor.

"Serves you right!" Robert accused as he shook the pain from his knuckles. Before the Brit could do anything else, Hiraku sprang to his feet and dived at him, tackling him against the metal wall.

As the fist fight ensued, Paco yelled, "Nobody is having sex with Angelina tonight!"

All eyes turned to him, giving Hiraku a chance for one last punch to Robert's jaw before he diverted his attention to the junior crewman.

"What do you mean?" Michel asked anxiously.

"Why not?" questioned Robert as he pushed Hiraku off of him.

Paco paused for a second, giving the pilot the opportunity to force the issue, "Why ain't we 'aving our bit o' fun with Angelina tonight?"

"Because...she's on her period."

"What?!" cried Michel.

Hiraku moaned, "Oh, man!"

Robert smiled and proclaimed, "Not my first set of red wings."

Michel turned to Robert and chided, "You, sir, are perverted!"

Smiling back at him, the pilot replied, "Thank you!

"So, what about you, Mexi-boy! Is your willy a nice, bright scarlet now?"

Paco twisted his face to show his revulsion and responded with disgust, "Oh, god! No! Eww!"

"Or maybe," nodded Robert. "Maybe you just want 'er all to yourself tonight. Is that it, Paco?"

As the British man jabbed his finger into the younger one's chest, he replied, "Uh, no."

"I think it is! We all know you're googly-eyed over 'er. You know wha' I think? I think you want your night o' romance with 'er, while she's still breathin'."

"No, that's not it!"

The pilot grabbed a handful of Paco's hair and knocked his head back against the wall.

"Don't lie to me, boy!"

"I'M NOT!"

"I'm gonna . . ."

"Robert!" called James as he walked in from the cargo hold. "Let him go!"

The English man slapped Paco's head against the wall as he released his hold, pointed two fingers at his own eyes, then at the younger man while saying, "I'm watchin' you!"

The captain stepped forward and asked, "What is all of this?"

"Li'l Taco 'ere says we can't fuck Angelina tonight!"

James snapped his head over to Paco and asked with trepidation, "Why not?"

Meekly, Paco replied while looking at the floor, "She's on her period, sir."

"Hmmm..." the captain paused for a few seconds. "Well, that would explain her behavior earlier.

"Sorry, boys. No party tonight!"

The sounds of complaining and bellyaching from the rest of the crew filled the corridor, until they vacated the area and left Paco alone with the captain standing next to him.

"Is she really on her period?"

Nodding, Paco answered, "Yes, sir."

"Okay," James sighed. "I'll take your word for it. But, be warned. You're on everyone's shit list for now."

"Yes, sir."

"Carry on," the American ordered as he stoically walked into the cargo hold again.

Breathing a sigh of relief, Paco entered Anna's room and smiled to her. She smiled back and asked, "You were brilliant! Quick thinking. Hey, can you untie my hands? This is really uncomfortable."

He frowned, "I can't. I want to. Believe me! I do. But, if the captain finds out . . ."

"You're really scared of him."

"Scared?" Paco replied defensively. "No! I'm not . . ."

Anna's skeptical expression forced him to pause and confess, "Okay, yeah…maybe. But, what's to keep him from turning around and killing me for doing something stupid or just for breathing when he's in one of his states?"

"That's why you need to band together with the others and stop him. Otherwise, you all could be dead someday."

He bowed his head, considering her words carefully, and nodded in agreement.

* * * * *

About an hour later after Paco had left, Anna sat up and rubbed her jaw. It still felt tender from the captain's blow earlier, but she knew she would recover. It was the same with her wrists, especially since Paco had not tied them too tight this time.

Anna stood and fished the engine part out of her pocket. Looking it over, she recognized it as a fuel igniter, cheap and easy to replace if any spares were around, and its removal probably would just slow it down a bit and not prevent the ship from taking off. But judging from the way Engineering looked, she doubted that they had any spare parts readily available. If they did, they would be lucky if they worked.

Anna dropped the part into the bottom drawer of the dresser and carefully shut it. Taking a deep breath, she cautiously moved over to the door and looked out into the corridor. Nobody was moving about, and the sounds of the men still carrying on in the galley provided a little comfort. She ducked back in, hopped onto the bed, and pulled her wristcomp out of her pocket. Praying for a miracle, she activated the screen.

Everything seemed to operate like before, but she could not be sure exactly what the captain had done while digging around inside it. Could she afford to take a chance with it? Right now, she did not have much choice. After a second's pause, she called Kate.

A couple of seconds later, the familiar British voice clearly cut through the silence, "Anna?"

"Kate, it's me," Anna stated with a smile and sigh of relief.

"Are you all right?"

In hushed but anxious tones, the blonde replied, "No. I'm being held prisoner. I've been repeatedly beaten and raped. Kate, please help get me out of here."

"I cannot tell you how far away you are. The sensors are still offline."

"We can work around that. I know where you are, and I have an idea on how to get back. But, it may be a few hours before I try. If I can manage to get back, I'll try to bring the sensors back online."

Kate said enthusiastically, "I would appreciate that. I feel blind."

"What about the drones? You should be able to 'see' through them."

Kate did not respond.

"Kate, what's wrong?"

"Oh, Anna. I'm so sorry."

Anna's brows knitted with concern, "What happened to the drones, Kate?"

"When your captor arrived to rescue his friend, he either damaged or destroyed most of the drones in the process."

Anna's face drained of color.

"How many drones were damaged?"

"I was trying to arrange for your release, and . . ."

"How many, Kate?"

"He managed to free his comrade, and . . ."

"HOW MANY, KATE?"

"Eleven," the hologram confessed after a short pause. "Eleven drones were damaged or destroyed."

In shock, Anna sat back on the bed, trying to envision the clearing around the ship littered with the smoldering wrecks that used to be her workforce and how she was going to be able to maintain the fields they had worked for her.

"Anna? Anna, are you there?"

Snapping out of her thoughts, she replied, "Yes, I'm still here, Kate. Did Seventeen survive?"

A couple of seconds passed before Kate answered, "No. Seventeen was severely damaged during the fight. I do not believe it can be salvaged."

Anna reflected on the turn of events for a few seconds more and questioned, "Who did it?"

"The man Ahmad referred to as the captain."

James did this! Her anger swelled as she fit his image into her visualization of the event as it occurred in her head. She pictured him running, diving, and firing at her drones as they converged on his position, taking them down one by one.

With her hand clenched and trembling from rage, Anna vowed quietly, "I swear he will pay for this...for everything!"

"Anna, what are you proposing?"

Calming down with a few deep breaths, she relayed to Kate what the captain had done to her since her arrival at the pirates' ship.

"Oh, Anna! I'm so sorry. Why would..." Kate sympathized.

Anna shrugged and cut her off, "I don't know, nor do I care. I can't take much more of this. I have to get out of here."

"I could send one of the drones, but I do not think it wise to risk losing any more than we already have."

"No, I wouldn't want you to do that anyway," reassured Anna. "In fact, tell the drones to fly to the pyramid and scan it."

"Won't that . . ."

Anna interrupted, "Yes, it will. That's why I want them to do it."

"Anna, please don't..."

"I'll be careful. I have an idea. You're going to have to trust me on this."

* * * * *

A few hours later, Anna emerged from her room again to a quiet hallway. The party in the galley died down an hour before, when the captain had ordered everyone to quarters. To increase her chances of success at her plan, she had to wait for everyone to fall asleep. She counted four of the crewman retiring to their cabins, and Robert and James walked into the cargo hold, presumably to climb to the upper deck and retire in their respective rooms.

Stepping out quietly in her bare feet, Anna tiptoed to the door leading to the cargo hold. The door whisked open, sounding louder than usual in her ears, and prompted her to cringe and listen for any movement. After none came, she quickly moved into the hold and wasted no time in rushing to the ladder as quietly as she could manage. Surveying the large chamber that was still open to the brightly-lit clearing outside, the hold still had some of the containers left to be offloaded but was mostly clear. The walkway directly above her as well as the one that stretched back to Engineering was unoccupied and ready for her to move without obstruction. Anna ascended the ladder and slinked across the catwalks to the aft entryway into Engineering. With one last look around her to make sure the coast was clear, she entered the room.

The sound of the power core's constant hum accompanied Anna's footfalls as she moved toward the engine. She reached the part of the engine where her tour with Ahmad ended and threw open the panel where 7 fuel igniters were still plugged in. Without hesitation, she pulled the first of the igniters from its socket and stuffed it into her pocket. Even though she knew that the crew slept as she performed her act of thievery, her heart felt as if it had leaped into her throat and pounded in her ears. The palms of her hands became sweaty, making it harder to pull each successive igniter out. Afraid that someone would step through the door and catch her in the act, she worked faster and fumbled over her fingers even more, which only served to heighten her anxiety.

Finally, Anna pulled the last one loose and thrust it into her pocket. She took a deep breath to calm her racing heart and rushed to the door. Pushing her way through the opening door, she slinked speedily across the catwalk. As she approached the end of the catwalk, she froze in fear as the door leading to the front part of the ship suddenly opened.

Chapter 29

Robert walked through the door wearing a gray tank top and white boxers. Scratching his rear, he appeared groggy and sluggish, but his eyes grew wide when he saw Anna standing in front of him in the cargo hold.

As the door shut behind him, he pointed to her and exclaimed, "You can't be out 'ere! You're tied up!"

Thinking on her feet, Anna replied in a low voice, "That's right, Robert. I am tied up downstairs."

"Then," he asked after glancing around himself. "'ow did you get up 'ere?"

"I'm not. I'm still tied up downstairs."

Robert scratched his head and mumbled, "I don't understand."

Anna smiled and suggested, "You're dreaming, Robert. You're actually still in bed."

"I am?"

"Yes, Robert. You are."

Scratching his head again, Robert thought for a second until a smile formed on his face.

"This can't be a dream," he concluded. "If I was, you'd be naked and playin' with your jubblies or somethin'."

Anna gently shook her head like a school teacher to her student, "No, Robert. Dreams don't work that way. It's your mind telling you something."

"What's it tryin' to tell me?"

With a smile, she answered, "It's telling you to go back to bed and sleep for the rest of the night."

Furrowing his brow, he queried, "Go back to bed?"

Anna nodded.

"Shouldn't I shag you or somethin'?"

Anna shook her head negatively.

"Can't I just . . ."

"To bed, Robert."

Slowly, he turned around while rubbing his eyes and sleepily walked through the door toward his quarters, leaving Anna in disbelief. After the door had shut, she sped to the ladder, slid down its length, and shot for the door leading to her room, when the upper door opened again. Anna froze.

Robert gradually came out again, saying, "Angelina. . ."

When he saw that she wasn't there anymore, he looked around until he saw her almost directly under him.

"'ow did you get down there?"

"Remember, Robert? You're dreaming. Things don't make sense in dreams."

He nodded drowsily, before she gently told him, "Go back to bed now."

With another nod, he passed through the door again. Anna dashed back to her room and hastily put her boots and socks back on. She retrieved her wristcomp from under the bed, strapped it on, and grabbed the igniter she hid in her room earlier. Feeling complete, she left the room again and dashed for the two skycycles parked in the far corner of the cargo hold. Mounting the first one, she looked over the controls and determined that they would be easy enough to use. Without wasting another moment, she started the cycle.

The roar of the engine filled the cargo hold, immediately telling Anna that she had little time to make her escape. She prayed that she could take off before anyone could reach her. As she feared, both the upper and lower doors leading forward opened within seconds. James and Robert stood next to each other up above, while the rest of the crew stared at her on the lower level. The captain yelled something that she could barely make out, but the group of men below did not move. Robert, on the other hand, sprang into action and sprinted for the access ladder.

At that second, the ready light blinked on in front of her, and Anna hit the accelerator, speeding out of the ship into the sunlight. Out of the corner of her eye, she saw Robert skid to a halt and scream something while shaking his fist at her. Not caring what he said, she steered the skycycle in the direction of her ship and began her flight home. As she left the clearing at high speed, she pulled the fuel igniters out of her pockets and tossed them into the woods below, one at a time.

* * * * *

"HOW THE FUCK DID SHE GET OUT?!" the captain ranted. "HOW?"

When nobody responded, he continued his tirade, "GOD DAMNED IDIOTS! ROBERT, TAKE THE OTHER SKYCYCLE AND BRING HER BACK HERE! MICHEL, GO CHECK HER ROOM AND FIND OUT HOW SHE GOT OUT! PACO, GET YOUR ASS UP HERE NOW!!!"

As the British pilot sprinted to the remaining skycycle, Paco rushed to the ladder, while the rest of the crew retreated into the forward section of the ship. The Latino skidded to a halt about a meter in front of James and saluted as he stood at attention.

"How did she get out, Paco?" demanded James at a normal volume.

With a shrug, Paco replied, "I don't know."

The captain stepped forward and, as he grew more enraged, stated firmly, "You were the one responsible for tying her up. So, I'm going to ask you again. How did she get out?!"

"I don't know, sir!"

"You're lying!" accused James as he continued his approach. "You were in there with her for over an hour! You must have helped her. There is no other explanation."

Trembling with fear, Paco pleaded, "No, captain! I . . ."

Placing a hand on the junior crewman's shoulder, the captain lowered his head and stared right into Paco's eyes.

"I warned you," he murmured. "There is a price for failure aboard my ship."

The Hispanic man lurched forward with his eyes bulging out of his face. As his face filled with horror, he looked down in time to see James pull his knife out of his chest, its blade coated with fresh blood. Unbearable pain from the wound that pierced all the way to his heart consumed the young man, and Paco grabbed his commander's jacket in a futile attempt to remain standing. As the pain increased, he fell to his knees, releasing his death grip on his killer's garment, and stayed upright for a second before dropping in a heap on the catwalk.

James wiped his blade clean on Paco's pants and returned it to its sheath inside his jacket. He scowled in disgust at the dead crewman in front of him and calmly walked through the doors that led to the ship's bridge.

A few seconds later, Michel burst through the lower doors, crying, "Captain! Captain!"

The French man fell silent upon seeing the blood dripping onto the deck from the catwalk above. Slowly, he lifted his gaze and stared in horror at Paco's body. He shook his head in disbelief and dashed to the ladder. Within seconds, he was by the dying man's side.

"Paco!" Michel exclaimed as he rolled him over and assessed the damage. "What happened?"

Weakly, the young man whispered, "Captain . . . thought I . . . helped her escape."

Pausing for a second, the medic winced upon seeing the entry wound just below his ribs. With blood pouring out of his gut, Michel knew that he did not have much time or blood left.

"Did you?" he asked.

Paco gently shook his head and coughed a few times. Tears fell silently from his eyes.

"I don't want to die!" he labored, each breath spilling more blood out of his chest.

Michel leaned over him and whispered, "You're going to be fine, Paco."

"Really?" the younger man asked, wanting to believe the lie.

Nodding, the French man continued, "Yeah. Angelina came back. She's waiting for you in her quarters. She said she couldn't leave without you."

"She is?" smiled Paco.

His body convulsed, each breath shallow and rapid. His gaze shot upward, fixed on some unseen object. Michel grabbed his hand and squeezed it, offering Paco assurance that he would not die alone. Seconds later, death rattled through Paco's body.

As the French pirate bowed his head, he spied Hiraku standing just inside the doorway, watching the scene unfold. The Asian man turned and slowly walked away from the hatch. Michel closed Paco's eyes, laid the young man's hand to his chest, and followed after his crewmate.

* * * * *

Speeding across the treetops, Anna relaxed and prepared to call Kate, when a burst of energy zipped past the bike. Quickly glancing behind her, she spotted another vehicle far in the distance, just as another bolt of lethal energy lanced the air near her head and flew past her. Turning forward again, she lowered herself as close to the cycle as she could manage, increasing her speed as fast as it would go. Realizing that she had been in flight for only a few minutes, she knew that she had a long way to go before she reached her ship.

Another shot flew past, dangerously close to striking the skycycle. Anna glanced back again and could swear that her pursuer was narrowing the gap. Wishing that she had a firearm on her, she cursed under her breath and resorted to swerving the vehicle back and forth, hoping to make her a more difficult target to hit.

Several more blasts raced past her over the next few minutes, each one making Anna more and more nervous. She worked to randomize the intervals at which she would shift the other direction and felt that she was succeeding, since each shot that threatened her appeared to be several meters away.

A single shot slammed into the back of her ride near the landing base. The impact shook the cycle and nearly threw her off, but her white-knuckled grip on the flight controls kept her in place. The vehicle shuddered again. She diverted her gaze to the panel before her, confirming that her speed was decreasing. Anxiety and fear washed over her, and her mind raced to find another way to avoid being taken back to the hell that was the pirates' starship.

A fair distance ahead, Anna spotted a clearing in the forest canopy. As she avoided another menacing shot that narrowly missed her, she steered her skycycle toward the break in the treetops and dived into the forest seconds later.

She had only seconds to drop the speeding vehicle to skim the ground and penetrate the tree line, letting the trees provide her with extra cover. With all of her strength, she directed the cycle between two large trees and left the clearing as quickly as she entered it.

Seconds later, Robert dove into the clearing atop his skycycle and, not finding Anna anywhere in sight, balked at pursuing her through the trees.

"Oh, shit!" he spat as he pulled back on the flight control bar. He was not fast enough to climb out of the clearing. However, he managed to direct the bike into the woods unscathed. He doubled his efforts and surged forward, cutting through the trees as he chased after his prey.

At first, Anna was terrified as she sped between the trees, afraid that she would accidentally turn the wrong way and smash against a solid trunk, prematurely ending her flight. After several seconds had passed, her fears subsided, and she directed the bike easily through the woods.

A moment later, she caught movement out of the corner of her eye. Turning her head for a second, she saw Robert on the other skycycle. She knew that his look of anger and frustration was directed solely at her.

Robert touched the switch on his headset and radioed the ship.

"Cap'n. I got 'er in me sights, but she's still flyin'."

He listened for a couple of seconds and asked, "You sure?"

After a few more seconds, he nodded and confirmed, "Aye, cap'n."

He touched the switch again and leveled his pistol at Anna. She glanced over and, seeing the weapon being brought to bear, nudged the accelerator a little. Her cycle pushed ahead quickly enough to cause him to miss her by centimeters. He pulled his arm back in, dodging a low-hanging branch, and took aim again. Just as he was about to fire, Anna swooped past a small tree that directed her to a slightly different path, and he held his shot.

Several seconds later, Robert closed the distance and brought his gun to bear again. He tensed his finger to pull the trigger, but an approaching tree forced him to evade the trunk at the last second. By the time he recovered, Anna had positioned a few more rows of trees between them.

Robert grumbled as he attempted to maneuver his cycle closer to her. Without difficulty, he brought his bike alongside of hers. He smiled evilly at her as he gripped and raised the weapon. As he lifted his sidearm, Anna reared back and kicked his vehicle, sending him off course and scrambling to regain control. However, the force of her defensive action took her off course as well. She steered the cycle back on track but not before the vehicle skimmed a thick tree and bent the forward leg guard in a bit.

Recovering his position, the rogue raised his pistol and prepared to fire. Focused solely on his target, he failed to spot the incoming branch in time, and the strike against his lower arm threw the firearm out of his grip and to the forest floor below. He cried out in pain and glanced at his arm, seeing the welt on his forearm change to a brighter crimson with each passing second.

Over her shoulder, Anna yelled, "Serves you right!"

"Fuck you!" he screamed back.

"Leave me alone!"

"Cap'n's orders! If I don't bring you back, 'e'll skin me alive!"

Unsure why James wanted her back so badly, she asked, "What does your captain want with me?"

"Don't know! Don't care!"

Anna scowled at his response and maneuvered her cycle further away, narrowly missing a fallen tree in the process. Her vision shifted around her as she piloted through the forest, trying to find a way to lose her pursuer. Dodging another tree, Anna viewed an upcoming opportunity and steered her vehicle in its direction.

To her surprise, Robert flew his bike through an opening in the trees and matched her position. As soon as he matched her course and speed, he reached across the gap and grabbed her shirt, growling as he did. Though she tried to avoid the attempt, his hand was too quick. She slapped at his hand while trying to maintain control of her own bike, but her strikes did nothing to deter his grip. After a couple of seconds, he pulled on her, trying to rip her away from her seat. She tightened her hold on the control bar and slapped at his face and arm, but he held fast and yanked harder.

Anna heard the first of several tears coming from her T-shirt, encouraging her to strike harder. A few seconds later, the garment split and pulled off of her torso, leaving only her arm caught in the damaged clothing. She quickly slipped her arm out, tossing him backward in his seat with only the ragged cloth in his hand. With a look of frustration, he threw the useless shirt over his shoulder and reached for her again. His fingers brushed against the skin of her shoulder, but he could not get a hold on her. She glanced over her shoulder at him for a second and turned her cycle away, putting some trees between them again. He swore and urged his bike forward through the next opening, tapping the two skycycles against each other. At the second of impact, he stretched forth his hand and grabbed her upper arm.

"Gotcha!" he yelled, inciting a short scream from Anna.

Instantly, she maneuvered her vehicle away from his, but his firm grip on her arm pulled her away from the controls as she did so, forcing her to keep the ride in place.

"C'mon! Get over 'ere!" he grunted as he tugged on her arm while she fought against him and pulled herself back the other way.

At first, they were caught in a deadlock, neither of them giving way. But, Anna felt her fingers sliding off the handlegrip.

Catching sight of another divergence ahead, Anna gathered her strength into refusing to release her hold of the control bar until, at the last possible second, she lurched to the side and dragged him toward her into the gap. Without a chance to react, Robert's head and upper chest slammed into a thick trunk, plucking him off of his bike while it sped onward into another tree several meters away and exploded on impact.

Anna felt the surge of heat against her exposed back, and she quickly looked over her shoulder at the fireball that engulfed several trees around it. Not wanting to risk getting caught in a fire or worse, she continued on her way without looking back.

Chapter 30

A few seconds later, Anna noticed the headset resting in its niche on the control bar indicating an incoming message. She directed the vehicle into a nearby clearing, lifted the earpiece to her ear, and opened the channel without responding.

"Did you get her?" James's voice asked through the headset.

Anna smirked and replied, "Not so much."

A second of silence separated her statement from his response, "You bitch! Where is he?"

"Robert found a spot in the woods to rest. I don't think you'll be seeing him for a while."

"You will pay for this, Anna!" he threatened with apparent anger in his voice.

"I already have," she sneered before closing the channel. "If you insist on continuing after me, you're going to have to catch me first."

Back on the *Resolute*, James slammed his fist against the communicator switch.

"FUCK!" he screamed, frustrated over the loss of his pilot and friend. He vowed to get revenge on her one way or another, and hopped into the seat and started the ship's pre-flight routine. A few seconds into the systems activations, red lights lit up on one section of the board. A quick examination told him that the engines were offline. Furious over the turn of events, he stormed out of the bridge, stood in the corridor, and shrieked at the top of his lungs. After a few seconds, he turned on his heel and returned to the bridge, where he activated the internal broadcast system.

"AHMAD!" bellowed the captain. "WHY WON'T THE ENGINES START?!"

Several seconds went by, until the engineer answered through the intercom, "I don't know! On my way to Engineering!"

James slapped the switch and closed the channel. He clenched his fists, trembling with unabated rage. He burst through the bridge doors and stomped all the way to Engineering, arriving several seconds after Ahmad, who had already begun inspecting the drive systems.

Barely a minute passed before the captain berated, "What's the problem?!"

The black man threw open a panel as he replied, "I'm moving as fast as I can, sir!"

"You are as slow as you are incompetent! Find it and fix it!"

A couple of minutes later with James staring over his shoulder, Ahmad found the source of the problem.

"All of the igniters are gone! The engines can't start, because there isn't any way to create fire."

The captain nodded and commented with a peculiar calm in his voice, "So, we're stranded."

He turned away and strode toward the door. As he took the last few steps before the hatch opened, he yelled furiously, "That BITCH!!!"

Stepping onto the catwalk, James spotted Michel and Hiraku standing at the port cargo door discussing something. Pointing at his crewmen, he roared, "YOU TWO! SCOUR THE SHIP AND FIND THE MISSING FUEL IGNITERS! WE CAN'T TAKE OFF WITHOUT THEM!"

The two crewmen ran to the doors leading forward without giving a response, while the captain moved forward to search the upper deck. He strode purposefully toward the upper doors, not noticing the missing body that had rested on the catwalk earlier.

* * * * *

Anna's resumed course did not take her directly to her clearing as she had hoped. But, she did locate the river and followed it upstream, until she located the crashed ship. She could not help but smile upon seeing it and reflected on how she never thought she would be so glad to see the place again.

Her emotional response quickly adjusted from elation to horror, as she saw the mechanical wreckage littering the clearing. The hulks of the eleven drones still sat where they had landed after being shot by James during his rescue mission. She circled the area, studying the results of his carnage, until she found Seventeen still sitting motionless near the northern tree line.

She landed the skycycle next to the ship and sprinted toward her favored drone, tears flowing down her cheeks. Reaching the machine, she collapsed onto its back and wailed in anguish over her loss. A couple of minutes later, her wristcomp signaled an incoming message. Wiping the tears away, she answered the call.

"Anna?" Kate questioned.

Anna sniffed, "Yes, Kate. It's me."

"I'm glad you made it back safely. Are you being pursued?"

Giving a slight laugh through her tears, she replied, "I don't believe so. I lost the one that was chasing me, and the others shouldn't be able to follow any time soon."

"No offense, Anna, but that does not give me much comfort. I would feel better if the sensors were back online."

Nodding her understanding, she tearfully answered, "I'll be right there."

Forcing herself to stop crying, she dashed to the ship but stopped abruptly when she caught sight of the crater in the hull where the keypad was destroyed.

"Um, Kate?" she called out. "How am I going to get in?"

Through the still open channel, the hologram informed her, "Touch the blue and green wires together."

Following the instructions, the hatch opened as expected, letting her climb in. As soon as she stepped through the inner airlock door and looked upon Kate, Anna smiled and started crying again. Facing the door, the avatar smiled and warmly greeted, "Welcome home, Anna."

Staggering forward, the blonde technician stated while sobbing, "I wish I could hug you."

"I know, Anna," Kate replied. "I know."

Anna dropped to her knees and buried her face in her hands, letting the tears flow unchecked. The hologram moved next to her and crouched down to her level.

"Anna," said Kate softly. "I understand that you have been through a highly traumatic experience, and I want to help you through it. But first, we need to get the sensors back online. We must know if anyone is approaching. We cannot take any chances."

Taking a deep breath to calm herself, the blonde nodded and wiped her eyes with the back of her hand.

"Where's my tool belt?"

"It is inside Seventeen's storage tank. Since your abductors left it behind when they took you, I saw no reason for it to continue to be exposed to the elements."

Nodding again, Anna rose to her feet and dashed out of the airlock. Within a minute, she stood behind the fallen drone and reached for the storage tanks.

"Even in death, you are helping to save me, Seventeen," she muttered as she released the safety catch and tugged on the container. Seconds later, she pulled the tank to the ground and opened the metal cylinder, locating her tool belt and all of her equipment. Withdrawing the belt and fastening it around her waist, she reached in and pulled out the sidearm that had slipped out of its makeshift holster. Remembering her former fear of its use, she now felt empowered with the weapon in her hand, and she gripped it confidently before returning it to its pocket and rushing back to the ship.

As soon as she hit the floor of the airlock, Anna pushed her way through the hatch and moved straight to the maintenance panel that was still open from the time she was taken. Dropping through, she crawled to the sensor array and began reassembling the unit. In no time, the array was together again and secured in place.

"Ah!" exclaimed Kate with relief as soon as the sensors came back online. "That's much better!"

Poking her head through the opening, Anna asked, "What do you see?"

A few seconds later, the avatar stated with disappointment while pointing outside, "That misreading is still there."

"Ignore it for now," Anna dismissed, waving her hand as if trying to shoo the comment away. "What else do you see?"

"The area is clear, Anna," Kate assured as the technician climbed to the deck through the maintenance hatch.

Anna sighed, "Good. I don't expect them for quite a while."

"Why is that?"

With a smirk, she answered, "Because I took all of their fuel igniters and scattered them in the woods. They are going to have to concentrate on that before they even think about coming after me."

* * * * *

"Why are we even looking out here?" complained Hiraku as he walked through the woods outside the pirates' ship. "She obviously took them with her, and we need to find a way to get them."

"Do you really feel like walking over a hundred kilometers to get a handful of fuel igniters?" Michel asked through the headset. "Ahmad didn't find any spares, and both skycycles are gone."

Rolling his eyes, the Asian commented, "Don't remind me! I liked those skycycles! They were fun to ride."

"I know. Remember the time we flew over the USS Barack Obama coming in for a landing on Aldrin?"

"And almost getting shot down? Yeah! I remember that! Good times, Michel. Good times."

"Enough of the chatter!" the captain interrupted over the channel. "Find those igniters, or I'll be using your eyeballs in their place!"

As the French man sighed, Hiraku responded, "I don't think that would work very well, sir."

"Do you want to find out?!" threatened James.

"Not particularly."

"Then, shut up and find those damn igniters!"

Hiraku frowned and replied solemnly, "Yes, sir."

Over the next several minutes, the only noise heard in the area was the sound of feet moving through the underbrush.

"Men," the captain announced through the headset. "I've recalibrated the sensors. Scanning now."

A few seconds elapses before he continued, "Hiraku! Move about thirty meters ahead. I have a metal source there."

Jogging ahead, Hiraku came to a halt at the base of a large tree. He looked up the length of the trunk into the branches that beckoned him to climb up.

"Well?" asked the captain harshly. "Did you find it?"

"I have to climb a tree first."

"What?! God, damn it! Climb the fucking tree!"

After rubbing his hands together, the Asian jumped up, grabbed the lowest branch, and hefted himself into the tree. He spent several minutes scouring the vegetation and returned to the ground empty-handed. Disappointed, he sighed and looked down as he called, "Captain."

As James acknowledged him, Hiraku spotted a glint of metal half-buried in some low-lying plants at the base of the tree. Kneeling down, he picked up one of the missing fuel igniters. Smiling, he declared, "I've found it!"

"What do you want?" the captain responded facetiously. "A goddamn medal?

"GET YOUR SORRY ASS UP HERE AND PLUG IT INTO THE DRIVE!"

A few minutes later, Ahmad, looking as if he had just barely survived a heavyweight boxing match, took the igniter from Hiraku's hand and slowly walked toward the compartment where the part belonged. The engineer's face, bloody and bruised from the battering he recently received, made the Japanese man cringe when he saw it.

"Are you okay, Ahmad?" asked Hiraku compassionately.

Ahmad only nodded as he opened the panel.

"Why did you let him do this to you?"

As the igniter slid into place, the black man responded, "He'd kill me if I resisted."

"He'll kill you if you don't!" warned Hiraku. "You should not allow him to do this to you."

"He's the captain."

Ahmad stepped up to the intercom on the wall by the door and toggled the switch, "The igniter's in place, captain. Give it a shot."

He turned and gazed at the engine as the start cycle began. A few seconds later, the drive roared to life.

"Good job, Ahmad!" James congratulated through the speaker. "Strap in! We're going on a little trip."

The ship shuddered a bit while the men found seats nearby. After a short moment, the shaking ceased, and they felt themselves rise into the air. The direction of thrust shifted several seconds later, and the vessel lurched forward.

"Michel! Hiraku! Get to the turrets!" ordered the captain over the intercom.

Turning back to the engineer, Hiraku urged as he rose from his seat, "You must do what you feel is right, of course. But, please remember how he has mistreated you. Do you really want to put up with that for the rest of your life?"

Ahmad remained silent as the other two crewmen departed.

Meeting at the forward end of the catwalk, Michel handed Hiraku a pistol and his sheathed katana. After nodding to each other, both men walked through the door with a look of grim determination on their faces.

* * * * *

"Anna," Kate warned. "I am detecting an anomaly on the sensors to the southeast, approaching fairly quickly."

Slumped in the pilot's chair, the blonde woman regarded the hologram over her shoulder and asked, "Can you lock on it?"

A few seconds later, an image of the pirates' ship appeared in a display from the front control panel.

"Hull configuration is identified as a Boeing-Lockheed 9469 medium transport."

With a nod, Anna confirmed, "That's them. ETA?"

"Four minutes and 36 seconds."

"And, the drones are at the pyramid?"

"The EM field has been up for the past 40 minutes. They should be safe."

Anna sighed, "And, I don't have time to repair Seventeen. I'm going to have to do this the hard and apparently the suicidal way.

"Thanks for everything, Kate," she added with a somber smile.

Kate returned the smile and replied, "It was the least that I could do for you."

After a few seconds, Anna entered the airlock and climbed to the top of the ladder, poking her head out and looking to the southeast. Far in the distance, she located the *Resolute* approaching. Suppressing her fear, she breathed deeply, secured herself to the ladder with a safety strap, and drew her pistol.

"I wish I could turn the ship around and fire the cannons at them. At least then, I would stand a chance.

"Oh, Kate!" cried Anna down the airlock. "Close the solar panels, too!"

Aboard the pirate vessel, Michel and Hiraku stopped outside the bridge with firearms in hand. They looked at each other again for reassurance. They both nodded at the same time, prompting Michel to hit the switch.

The door to the bridge opened to show James flying the ship over the trees. Glancing over his shoulder, the captain barked, "Why aren't you in the turret?"

"We're not going," Hiraku said defiantly. "There is no logical reason why you should pursue Angelina. She can't go anywhere. Leave her alone."

Setting the ship on autopilot, the captain stood and turned to face his crew, who instantly raised their guns at him. Judging from their fierce expressions, he quickly deduced that they were serious about this new endeavor.

Chapter 31

"What exactly do you hope to accomplish with this mutiny?" James demanded, seething through his teeth.

Shaking his head, Michel responded sternly, "That is irrelevant. You won't be around to see it."

Slowly approaching the duo, the commander questioned, "So, you mean to kill me then."

"No," Hiraku stated. "Throwing you in the same room where you kept Angelina confined should be sufficient."

James smirked, "Is this your attempt to win the lady's favor? I've got news for you. She doesn't give a rat's ass about you. She hates you. She hates all of us. She'd rather see us all dead at her feet."

Michel snapped, "I don't believe you!"

"Why do you think she stole the fuel igniters? She'd rather us remain stranded here and die, just like she's going to do after she runs out of supplies."

Noticing their heads shaking, he continued, "That's right. She's hoping we kill ourselves, so she can steal our food and supplies."

"You lie!" cried the French crewman. "She wouldn't do that!"

"She already has. In fact, she's now set up to attack us when we arrive."

"Lies!" accused Hiraku.

With a flourish of his arm, he directed the men to the bridge door and offered, "See for yourself!"

The two conspirators looked at each other for a few seconds, contemplating the captain's statement. Although they did not believe what he told them, a seed of doubt rested in their minds. He was right about the taking of the igniters. Could he be right about this, too?

"Cover him," Hiraku ordered. With a nod, Michel asserted his position by adjusting his aim at James. With the way clear, the Asian man entered the bridge.

Through the forward viewport, he saw that the ship was coasting closer to a large clearing where a white-hulled transport and numerous smaller mechanical or robotic devices were present. He recognized one of their skycycles parked next to the white ship and found the woman he knew as Angelina standing halfway out of the vessel's upper airlock with a firearm in hand.

"She's really there," Hiraku muttered, surprised at the truth of James's statement.

Michel stepped onto the bridge and, looking over the other man's shoulder, asked, "Really?"

Pointing out the window, Hiraku confirmed, "Yeah. See her?"

As the two men stared out the window, the captain stealthily maneuvered behind them, withdrew his knife from its sheath within his jacket, and plunged it into Michel's back. As the French man cried out in pain, James snatched the pistol from his hand. Hiraku turned and raised his sidearm, firing a shot at the captain but missing by mere centimeters. The shot was enough to force James to make a hasty retreat from the bridge after pulling his knife back out of Michel and throwing the wounded man to the deck.

As Hiraku emerged in the doorway in pursuit, the captain fired back, hoping for a quick end to the rebellion aboard his ship. But, his hurried movements skewed his aim, and the blast impacted against the wall next to the Asian man who fired again as he ducked back for cover. The second shot flew wide and hit against the far wall at the opposite end of the hallway. Retaliating quickly, James fired again. His shot was closer, but Hiraku found cover behind the wall in time.

The commander fired again, shooting through the doorway and smashing one of the bridge's control panels.

Rapidly, Hiraku peeked around the corner, locating the leader standing by the doorway leading to one of the turrets. The attempt invoked another couple of shots from James, one of which came close to flying into the bridge. Feeling trapped, Hiraku was on the verge of surrender, when a groan from Michel reminded him that his partner was still alive and brought to light again the reason why they fought against their captain in the first place. The Japanese man steeled his resolve, peeked again, and fired one true shot that shattered the weapon in the American's hand.

Dropping the ruined weapon, James ignored the shards of heated plastic and steel embedded in the back of his hand and sheathed his knife inside his jacket.

"Hiraku!" he cried out. "Cease fire! I'm unarmed."

Poking his head out, Hiraku demonstrated a look of odd curiosity and inquired, "What do you mean? You always carry a backup firearm."

"Only during boarding actions. I didn't think I'd have to after the last mutiny.

"But since you have me at a disadvantage, I see no point in prolonging the inevitable and surrender," James stated as he raised his empty hands up in front of his chest.

Stepping through the doorway into the hall, Hiraku pointed the pistol at the captain's chest and ordered, "Turn around and put your hands on your head."

James slowly placed his hands atop his head but did not turn.

"I have to hand it to you, Hiraku. I didn't think you had it in you."

Hiraku cocked his head and looked upon James with a skeptical expression as he continued.

"I'm impressed. You've certainly proven that you have the balls and can obviously stand up for yourself," the captain said. "How would you like to be my first mate?"

James stepped forward and extended his hand with an expecting smile, waiting for the Japanese man to respond.

Hiraku snorted, "Seriously? Why would I trust you?"

As his smile melted away, James replied while retracting his hand, "I know exactly where you're coming from. That's how I reacted when I took command of the ship from the previous captain."

"Step back."

"If you are going to take over as the new captain," the American added. "Your first responsibility has to be taking care of the crew."

Still lying on the floor, Michel groaned as he stirred.

"And, it might be a good idea to see to your medic as well. You don't have another one."

Hiraku turned to look at his compatriot on the floor next to him. Blood was pooling on the floor from beneath his shoulder.

"Michel," asked Hiraku. "Michel, you all right?"

In a blurring motion, James drew his knife and plunged it into Hiraku's hand. As Hiraku screamed in pain, his hand relaxed its hold on the pistol, and James quickly snatched it away. Turning the weapon around, James pointed the weapon at Hiraku's eye and pulled the trigger, splattering the back of the Asian man's head on the wall behind him. The captain casually retrieved his knife as Hiraku's mutilated body twitched and dropped to the floor.

Ignoring the sputtering and smoldering controls from within the bridge, James stepped over to Michel and pressed his boot against the man's wounded shoulder, pinning him to the floor. Screaming from the pain created by the aggravated wound, Michel rolled onto his side, attempting to get away from the source of his misery. Aiming the pistol in his hand at the wounded medic's head, James gently squeezed the trigger.

Throwing the weapon down the corridor, the captain mumbled as he stepped over the dead body at his feet, "God damn crew! Always got to do it myself!"

* * * * *

Anna's heart raced within her chest as the rusted pirate vessel came to a halt in midair and shifted to vertical thrust, allowing it to hover in place. Afraid that the ship would unleash something that would kill her in a second, she prepared to drop into the airlock for some semblance of protection.

But, nothing came. The ship floated in place, doing nothing as if it was trying to stare her down.

Anna stared hard at the ship, expecting something to happen. A second later, a brief flash of light from the front of the vessel caught her eye. The light flashed again several times a few seconds later but dimmer than before. Not recognizing what may have caused them, she grew more and more nervous with each passing second. She would have thought that the captain would have done something by now. With her palms moist with perspiration, her pistol nearly slipped out of her hands as she flexed her fingers around the grip of the gun again and again.

Suddenly, a panel opened on the side of the pirates' transport on the same level as the bridge. Out of the new opening came a transparent globe with some sort of nozzle on one end, all of which was held within a dark gray circular frame. Sitting at a small control panel inside the clear orb was the captain, staring at her the entire time. After the sphere extended out all the way, it rotated around to point the nozzle in her direction. James appeared to be laughing inside his sealed chamber.

As it suddenly hit Anna what he was doing, she cried, "Oh god!" Fear overtook her bravado, and she dropped into the airlock.

A split second later, the pirate captain opened fire. A rapid barrage of energy bursts cut through the air and slammed into the white ship's upper hull, exploding on impact and shaking the entire ship. Anna screamed in fright as one of the last shots hit just outside the entrance to the airlock.

Through the wristcomp, Kate declared, "Anna, the hull is withstanding the attack. The white hull plating appears to be not just for aesthetics. It seems to have reflective qualities that reflects a good portion of the energy from the shots away."

"No wonder Ryan was so attached to this ship," Anna whispered to herself before responding to the hologram. "Does that mean that he can't do anything to us?"

Kate replied grimly, "No, Anna. Although the energy is harmlessly reflected away, the impact of each shot is damaging the hull. If he keeps it up, the energy will eventually get through."

Anna looked skyward through the open hatch and prayed for a miracle as she climbed back to the top of the ladder. Just before she poked her head through, another volley of energy bolts rained across the top of the ship. She held fast to the ladder as it shuddered from the hits.

"Anna," Kate called to her. "We are being hailed."

She sighed and requested, "Patch him through to my wristcomp."

A split second later, James's voice filled the air, "Anna, I find you in a rather precarious situation. Tell you what. I've got a deal for you. Surrender and join my crew, or be destroyed. It's your choice. You have 60 seconds."

Anna's jaw dropped open, and the pit in her stomach returned in full force. She did not have the power to properly defend herself against his vessel's weaponry. Her resolve sank into despair, and she slid down the ladder and walked onto the bridge for what she felt was the last time.

"Kate," Anna groaned. "I . . ."

Holding up a hand, the hologram stated, "Anna, I know that this is difficult. Whichever decision you make, do it for yourself. Do not concern yourself with me. I'm only a computer interface. Your life is far more important than me, this ship, or anything else here."

Speechless, Anna stared at Kate for several seconds, unable to respond. Finally, she collected her thoughts and uneasily said, "Thank you, Kate. For what it's worth, you've been the best holographic friend a person could have.

"I know what I have to do."

Anna ran back into the airlock without waiting for a response.

Clambering up the ladder, she paused at the hatch long enough to look outside at the ship floating nearby. Several seconds passed with no visible action coming from the ship.

"Anna," Kate said from the bridge. "The minute has passed."

Looking back at the pirate's ship, she saw that it continued to dauntingly hover. No announcement came, no weapons fired, nothing happened.

Anna pulled the binoculars from her belt and peered at the turret. From what she could tell, James' attention was focused on something inside the ship.

"What is he looking at?" she muttered just as an idea struck her.

303

Aboard the pirate vessel half a minute before, James finished counting down the seconds, his patience extremely thin. As he gripped the fire control stick to resume fire, the power in the turret failed without warning.

In shock, James yelled, "What?! What's going on?"

"Captain!"

The leader looked over his shoulder to find Ahmad standing in the doorway. In his hand, the black man held Hiraku's pistol aimed at the turret's power cable that he had just shot.

"What are you doing?!" the captain cried out.

With a deadpan expression, Ahmad answered, "Your reign of terror is over, sir."

Aiming the weapon at his commander, he continued, "Goodbye, sir."

"NO!" screamed James as a look of horror crossed his face, and he threw his hands up in front of him.

Back on the ground, Anna pulled the pistol from her belt, positioned the binoculars on top of it, and aimed at the distant turret through her makeshift scope while resting the butt of the weapon on the hull. As she prepared to fire at the bubble, she noticed James lean away from the controls with his arms crossed before his face.

On the ship, Ahmad moved in with his gun, took a deep breath, and fired a shot at the turret. But, his shot reflected off the orb and hit the ceiling. Staring in disbelief, he raised his weapon and fired again, but the result was the same.

Realizing that he was safe from small arms fire, James looked back at Ahmad with a smug smile on his face.

Suddenly, several bolts of energy slipped through the opening, some of which impacted against one of the orb's support struts. The blast jostled the turret, alarming James of the change in his predicament. Turning, he saw Anna squeeze off another shot from her pistol, which smashed through the rest of the support strut. The turret, released from one of its restraints, bounced on its remaining supports for a second before stabilizing.

"STOP SHOOTING!" screamed James from within the protective orb.

Without changing her position, Anna responded with her middle finger before shifting her aim and firing another shot that penetrated the second of the turret's two upper support beams.

James turned his gaze back into the ship and, with a horrified expression, pleaded, "Ahmad, help!"

Appearing weary, Ahmad nodded and replied, "I'll be happy to, sir."

The engineer opened a small panel in the wall near the doorway, glanced back at his commander, and pressed the large, red eject button.

The spherical turret launched away from the ship, carrying the screaming pirate captain in a large arc toward the ground meters below.

Seeing the turret launch away from the ship, Anna straightened her posture and watched the orb descend to the ground near the far edge of the clearing. Certain that the captain could not survive the fall, she wanted to breathe a sigh of relief and return inside her home. But, she knew that she could not afford to take any chances. With the pirate ship making no hostile moves, she put the binoculars back into her belt, climbed out of the airlock, and sprinted toward the fallen turret, traversing the last several meters cautiously.

Anna looked upon the shattered sphere, shards of metal and plastic peppered the area around the point of impact. In the middle of the ball lay James's bloodied and broken body.

Stepping up to the wreckage with her pistol in hand, she gazed upon the captain, seething with contempt.

James suddenly stirred, slowly blinking his eyes open and cringed as pain wracked every inch of his body. Catching Anna out of the corner of his eye, he slowly turned his head and looked upon her with bloodied eyes. He tried to lift his trembling hand, only managing to raise it a couple of centimeters.

"Help me," he croaked, barely audible over the sound of his ship's engines.

Through narrowed eyes, Anna looked down upon him, aimed her weapon at his face, and firmly replied, "Death first."

She pulled the trigger, and his body jerked one final time.

Chapter 32

In the sky above her, the sound of an explosion grabbed Anna's attention. Looking that way, she caught the sight of a fireball dissipating from the front of the *Resolute*. Deciding not to take any chances, she sprinted back to her ship.

Aboard the hovering craft, Ahmad, despite exhaustion threatening to overtake his body, snapped his gaze through the doorway behind him, as the deafening roar assaulted his ears. He quickly mustered the strength and ran into the hallway to see the bridge engulfed in flames.

"Gotta set the ship down!" he cried as his adrenaline-fueled legs took him back to Engineering.

Reaching the engine room, he quickly glanced at the internal systems analysis to see that the guidance systems were offline. He instinctively rushed to the override system to find the auxiliary system was offline as well. As panic set in, he felt the floor sloping and grabbed the console to keep from sliding down.

On the ground, Anna reached the nose of her ship and turned to look at the other vessel. The airborne ship listed to starboard and slowly veered away from her, while flames licked at the hull above the bridge. She climbed into the airlock far enough to be able to drop to safety in case something catastrophic happened to the other craft.

Inside, Kate called, "Anna! I'm picking up an energy spike coming from the other ship!"

A second fireball erupted from the bridge, followed by another from the stern several seconds later.

With her gaze fixed on the *Resolute*, Anna called out, "How bad is it, Kate?"

"The guidance systems are offline, and I detect multiple fires aboard, particularly around the bridge and within Engineering. I am also picking up one life form aboard."

"One?" asked Anna incredulously. She inquired to herself, "What happened to the others?"

Another explosion ripped through the hull above the engines. Seconds later, its exterior lights flickered and went out. The pirate ship hung for a brief moment as if suspended in the air. Anna held her breath. Suddenly, the *Resolute* dropped. The doomed craft hit the ground, creating a cloud of dust and splintered wood. The ship and the earth beneath it shuddered from the impact, and Anna gripped the top rung of the access ladder to keep from falling. As the rumbling ceased, the sounds of small particles raining onto the hull reached her ears.

"Kate!" cried Anna as she looked at the plumes of smoke rising from the trees. "Scan the ship. I want to see how well it stayed intact."

"What do you have in mind?"

"I'm hoping I can salvage parts and repair our ship to get us off the ground again. There might be some fuel left and maybe even…"

"Anna," Kate interrupted. "I'm detecting another energy spike above the crash site."

Before Anna could respond, a large hexagonal spacecraft faded into view over the trees. The size of the ship dwarfed her own and cast a dark shadow over a good portion of the forest below. Its grayish-white hull framed a circular aperture, its center glowed a soft, blue light. A deep hum emanated from within it, filling the air with its resonance.

Instantly, a bluish-purple beam shot from the underside of the hexagon toward the *Resolute*. A second later, the flaming wreckage rose into the air, engulfed by the light produced by the huge vessel.

Anna, her eyes glued to the scene unfolding between the giant ship and the *Resolute*, said in a calm tone, "Kate, scan the other ship."

"I'm trying, but the sensors are not able to penetrate its hull. I sense that it is there but I get nothing more."

A couple of seconds later, the vessel lifted skyward, taking the pirates' ship with it in tow. Awed by its presence, Anna could do nothing more than watch.

The light intensified just as the pirate vessel exploded inside the energy bubble that surrounded it. Nonplussed, the other ship ascended out of sight along with the fiery debris, leaving the area as quiet as before with only the sound of the wind blowing through the trees.

Anna stared dumbfounded at the sky, trying to process what had just happened. The reality of the events that she witnessed washed over her.

She rushed to the starboard edge of the ship, waving her arms frantically, and yelled, "HEY! WAIT! I'M STILL HERE!"

"Anna," Kate replied softly after the engineer waved for several seconds. "They're gone."

"Are you sure?"

"My sensor range allows me to scan the areas of the upper atmosphere directly above us, and I am not detecting the other vessel anymore."

Glancing towards where the *Resolute* crashed, she inquired, "What about the crash site? Maybe the one person got out?"

"No, Anna. I'm sorry."

Dropping her arms to her sides while still staring into the sky, Anna whispered while fighting back the tears that came with the knowledge that she had been left alone once more, "I know."

"I'm sorry?"

Anna sniffed and repeated, "I know, Kate. They're gone."

Kate spoke through her wristcomp, "There is a bit of good news. Do you remember the sensors problem I kept asking you to fix? It's gone. It was focused on where the larger ship used to be."

"Yeah, that's good," she sighed.

The two fell silent for a moment. Anna stood at the top of the ladder, her mind playing back through the last few days. She climbed into the airlock and pressed her back against the wall opposite the door. With one last glance skyward, the memories of her recent experience filled her mind. She sobbed uncontrollably. Her legs gave way, and she slid down the wall to sit on the floor.

Seconds later, the airlock door opened, revealing Kate standing on the opposite side, grief for the young woman on her face. She watched Anna curl into a fetal position while she wept, saying nothing.

"Anna," Kate said after several minutes. "I am so sorry. I wish I could comfort you. I wish there was something I could do for you"

Her crying subsided, Anna wiped away her tears with the back of her hand, sniffled, and sat up.

"It's okay, Kate. There isn't anything to say. I can't talk about it, not yet. But when I'm ready, do you think…"

"Anna, it would be my honor."

Kate's smile reassured her.

With a gentle smile and tears welling up in her eyes again, Anna replied, "Thanks, Kate."

As Anna began to cry once more, Kate's expression shifted to sympathy as she watched.

Several minutes passed before the weeping stopped again. This time, Anna breathed slowly as she stopped and brushed her hand across her tear-stained cheeks.

"Are you going to be okay?"

"Okay?" scoffed Anna. "Maybe, one day. But, things have to be done. Call the drones back as soon as the shield around the pyramid is down."

"What are you going to do, Anna?"

Anna stood and climbed the ladder to the top of the ship. Looking around the clearing, her gaze fell upon the aftermath of her long, tortuous encounter with the pirates: the damaged or destroyed mining drones, the blasted security keypad next to the top hatch of the ship, a fully-functional skycycle that was low on fuel, and the remains of the turret from the cargo vessel that carried them to the moon, her moon, her Paradise.

Taking a deep breath, Anna slowly exhaled, trying to release the stress and grief within her out into the air. Pulling the hand scanner from her tool belt, she answered her holographic companion, "We're going to start by repairing the damaged drones, since it looks like you and I are going to be here a while longer."

Printed in Germany
by Amazon Distribution
GmbH, Leipzig